R. Platt

D1827162

Sinister Too

By
Writers Anonymous

www.writersanonymous.org.uk

Published 2009 by arima publishing

www.arimapublishing.com

ISBN 978 1 84549 379 0

Printed and bound in the United Kingdom

Typeset in Perpetua

Swirl is an imprint of arima publishing.

arima publishing
ASK House, Northgate Avenue
Bury St Edmunds, Suffolk IP32 6BB
t: (+44) 01284 700321

www.arimapublishing.com

Illustrated by Ralph Platt

In memory of Neil

Contents

I'm Waiting

By Nicolette Coleman

I'm hiding
I'm hiding
You'll never know
Where I'll turn up next

I'm watching
I'm waiting
I'll be there
When you least expect

And then I'll **GET** you
I'll hurt you
I'll make you
Wish that you were dead

I'll torture
I'll torment
Until you're truly
Sick in the head

But until then
I'm watching
And waiting
And hiding
Until your mind is truly vexed

The Road to NeverEver Land

By Simon Woodward

The Road

Dave Johnson had been given his annual ultimatum by his boss; use it or lose it. The way his company functioned meant that he was rewarded for working dawn 'til dusk, Monday through Friday but whenever the annual holiday request slip was put through his boss's office, invariably, his boss would come storming out shouting, "You really want a holiday during that week?" the emphasis being on the words 'really' and 'that'.

And now, as the carry-over time for his leave was ebbing towards a close, his boss uttered the quintessentially paradoxical statement: "*Use it or lose it Johnson, your choice.*"

Dave felt he'd always worked hard and never gave up his entitlement to a little R 'n' R and, though still only February, he'd been keeping his eye on the weather reports, just in case his boss would make his annual clarion call.

It seemed to Dave that the following week would be just the right time to take the winter dust covers off his classic British Racing Green Triumph Spitfire mark IV, to take it for a run down to Bournemouth on England's south coast and pay his favourite great aunt a surprise visit; an aunt who would later bemoan the fact, in her utter grief, that she hadn't seen her nephew since December last.

If he took the scenic route through Hampshire's New Forest then the two hundred mile trip would take about three and a half hours – so no need for an early start, just get up, make a snack for the journey and go.

* * *

Monday morning arrived and for a change the weathermen had been right; the sky was a spotless blue veneer and the sun was brightly crisp and low over the horizon following its winter path.

By the time Dave was ready to leave his bachelor pad he'd lost most of the morning, and the time was fast approaching one thirty in the afternoon. If he didn't leave soon there'd be no point in taking the scenic route – it would be too dark to see anything of the New Forest.

Dave packed his rucksack but, before going to his car, he quickly popped into his bathroom for a final brush up. He looked at his features in the mirror, his black haired goatee and thin moustache were pristine, but his eyes said it all – he really needed this break. Adjusting his moss green cotton drill jacket as he faced the mirror he decided he was ready to go and left the flat, looking forward to the time he could spend in one of England's unspoilt forests before arriving at his great aunt's house.

* * *

After almost three solid hours of driving he was ready to take a break, pull up somewhere, take his sandwiches out and pour himself a coffee from the stainless steel flask he'd brought with him.

He had just entered the beginnings of the road through the New Forest and kept his eyes peeled for a small sign that would indicate a track-way to one of the forest's many picnic areas. He was not disappointed; five minutes after looking, he had spotted one and indicated right to turn into the small woodland clearing; not that he'd needed to indicate, this part of the road had been almost devoid of any type of traffic since he'd been on it.

His car crunched up the small gravel entrance into the picnic area and he stopped the Triumph alongside one of the ten or so picnic benches. Turning his car's engine off, he got out and stretched, raising his arms above his head, fingers interlocked.

Although he loved his car it was a bit of a squeeze for his 6'2" stature and about three hours was all he could manage before having to find somewhere for a pit stop.

Dave walked slowly around the perimeter of the forest enclosed clearing, hoping for little glimpses of the wildlife he knew to inhabit these parts. But the forest was dense and he guessed he could only see about twenty feet into it, perhaps thirty in places, if he was lucky.

The forest was a mixture of pine trees, irregularly interspersed by the odd silver birch here and there, its white bark seemingly glinting out of the darkness as errant light from the sun caught the trees when the wind blew the forest's pine canopy to one side or another.

His stomach grumbled and Dave walked across the clearing to the rear of his car and opened up the boot removing his lunch box and flask. Sitting down on the bench he'd parked next to, he unpacked his sandwiches and filled a cup with coffee from his flask.

As he ate and drank, he started to truly unwind, glad that there'd be another six full days before he would have to return to the manically busy office, continuing his work as the logistics manager for International Global Holdings – one of the only companies left, still supposedly able to ship logged trees from the Brazilian Amazon, legally, something that was in his remit to organise.

Biting into his hastily made Cheddar cheese sandwich his gaze continually flicked across the tree line circling the picnic area, ever hopeful of at least spotting one of the Roe deer the forest was famous for.

As he wondered about the lack of deer he began to realise he could not hear any of the other wildlife that should be bringing the pristine woodland to life; there were no birds chattering and he hadn't seen any squirrels darting from tree to tree either.

Dave shivered. The sun had dipped further towards the horizon and the air had taken on the early evening chill of an oncoming winter's night. He looked at his watch, it was four forty five, and dusk had settled.

Time to get going, he thought to himself as the breeze stepped up a notch or two, making the occasional shushing in the trees a constant refrain upon the general background of silence. Dave paused for a moment marvelling at how similar the breeze in the tree tops was to the sound of waves breaking upon a pebble strewn beach.

Standing up from the bench, he put the lid back on his lunch box and screwed his cup back on to the top of his flask. It was very dark now, the trees surrounding the picnic area blocking out what remained of the vestigial sunlight. Just as he was about to slam the car's boot shut a loud clacking started up somewhere deep within the forest.

Rut-tah-tuh-tuh-tuh. It continued; a staccato sound, not quite branch upon branch as if the wind had blown bough against bough, the sound had a lower resonance than that, more-like stick against a hollow wooden bole; not as melodic as a glockenspiel but a duller, flatter tone – one without rhythm or timbre.

Dave felt the backs of his forearms prickle as the hairs stood on end. He shivered again, but not against the cold this time, it was a much deeper type of chill, one touching sensations humanity had not felt for thousands of years.

He quickly returned the remnants of his snack to the boot and closed it, then got into his car shaking his head, berating himself for the foolish reaction to the alien-but-not sound. Before starting his car he wound down his window to see if he could hear the noise again, attempting to justify his reaction. But all he could hear was the sound of the wind rustling the treetops that overshadowed the picnic area.

He breathed out slowly, suddenly aware he had been holding his breath. Dave tutted at himself.

As he reached for the handle to wind the window back up, the sound was there again; a succession of mournful clacks.

Rut-tah-tuh-tuh-tuh. His neck prickled as a sensation of icy air played upon it; the skin on his cheeks and across his forehead tightened as the unknowable sound continued its thousand year old threat.

Dave made a grab for the handle to close the window, but his hand slipped straight off – his grip unable to do anything, as his whole hand was now covered by the clammy sweat of fear.

Wiping his hand on his jeans, he reached for the handle again, this time managing to turn it. The window shut as fast as he could make it.

"Jesus Christ, you stupid shit," he said to himself as he turned his key in the ignition. "How old are you? Ten?" He continued his self admonishment.

The engine turned over under the power of the starter motor but failed to fire.

"Oh. For God's sake," he shouted aloud, hitting the car's steering wheel, frustrated by the situation and panicked by the noise in the forest.

He looked out of the Spitfire's small side window and saw the dimly lit reflection of his panic-stricken face staring back at him, eyes wide and mouth turned down.

The sun had almost finished its journey below the horizon rendering the spaces between the pine and silver birch an impenetrable black void.

"Come on you bugger," he said to his car, twisting the key once again. This time, the engine revved into life and he flicked on his headlights as dusk was no more and the early February night had arrived.

Turning the wheel in the direction of the picnic area's exit, he nudged his car to the junction with the main road. Seeing no illumination from car headlights in either direction Dave pulled out and continued on his journey.

He glanced at the clock in his car, it was still only five thirty and it would only be another half hour or so before he would be pulling up outside his aunt's house.

Dave carried on down the road that skirted the great forest and the further away from his pit stop he got, the calmer he felt. As he drove the road steepened, following a line up one of the undulating hills that defined the area of England his aunt lived in.

NeverEver Land

Occasionally he glanced to his left getting a feel for the hill that gently sloped into the shallow valley below; certain aspects being picked out by the intermittent moonlight as it shone out between the fast flowing, dark grey clouds above. Other times he looked into the forest on his right, and saw nothing but the bark of the tree line which separated the forest from the road, flickering in his headlights, as if seen through a zoetrope.

As he considered the view of the valley, being delivered by the gaps in the roadside hedgerow, when the moon was out, his attention was suddenly drawn back to the forest, when he noticed a bright light coming from somewhere within its depths.

"Those posh bastards," he thought to himself, "those posh and lucky bastards," he continued his musings, thinking about how nice it would be if he could afford such a place with so many acres, to call his own.

Luminous, nearly white chevrons, separated by black ones, interrupted his thoughts as the sign in front of him played upon his vision. He slowed the car and gently steered it to the right, the signalled bend in the road being pretty severe.

As he pulled out of the curve his Spitfire's engine coughed, misfiring, then corrected itself. Dave sighed a thanks to the engine's manufacturers. His car wouldn't have been a classic if its engine had been as temperamental when it had originally rolled off the factory line.

He looked at his milometer again and saw there were only another seven miles to go and, as he looked up, the engine failed, becoming silent.

Dave managed to guide the car into a lay-by as it gradually cruised to a halt. After trying the engine again, in the vain hope it would start and without success, he was glad he could still see the light from the obviously posh house, blinking between the wind agitated trees.

By his reckoning, the house could only be half a mile away, possibly further, but, perhaps, potentially nearer and hoped it was the latter. He could knock on the owner's door and ask to use their phone. He cursed himself for leaving his company provided mobile phone back at his flat; but it was a ritual of his – if he was going to have a holiday then there'd be no way his company could contact him during his time away. This time though, he regretted his decision. He got out of his car and locked it, then slapped it very hard.

"You stupid car. I don't even know why I keep you going. This was going to be a very simple day out and now you've ruined it," he said. The car didn't respond.

Dave opened the car's boot and pulled out his Berghaus over jacket and putting it on he zipped it up against the evening's cold, then thought about his trek through the forest to the house in the distance.

* * *

Next to the lay-by there was, what seemed to be, a path, and with no other choice for him to take, he followed it. Walking past the ferns and bracken that defined its beginnings, he entered the depths of the woodland proper; always making sure the light from the house was visible, it being his only comfort on this forced trek.

As he continued along the loamy track, deeper into the forest's unforgiving darkness, the only sound he could pick out was that of the wind in the trees' branches above, shushing them in gleeful caresses.

Dave was glad that the barely broken overcast sky of earlier had now given way to sparse patchy clouds that allowed the moon to cast its brightness upon the track more often than not. And although he was glad, it was not a light that comforted; there was something ancient and otherworldly about it – and the pitched black shadows it summoned.

To distract his growing overactive imagination, he turned his thoughts to his job and work, fighting to stop his mind drifting back to his time in the picnic area.

After what felt to him to be at least half an hour, the path finally led him into a small clearing within the depths of the forest. At its centre was a stump of three trunks, the trees having been cut down by a warder or some other kind of forest manager, he assumed.

In front of him and to his left, the light from the house could still be seen, twinkling between the trees. At the furthermost edge of the clearing the path he'd been following seemingly continued. Dave rubbed his arms attempting to thwart the coldness of the February evening, making a mental note of the clearing he'd stumbled upon. His car lay directly behind him, some distance away, and the house was almost directly in front of him; though how many more feet or yards he had to go, he had no way to ascertain, the darkness precluding any possibility of judging the distance with accuracy.

He followed the path deeper into the forest, leaving the occasionally moonlit clearing behind. And as he walked an overwhelming impression that the trees lining the path were about to take on a life of their own, somehow animated by the ancient moonlight, overcame him.

Upthrust bulks, almost arms of buried entities with a myriad of fingers pointing in consternation at the night's sky, seemed to be struggling to break free from their subterranean coffins. Each tree alive with its own individuality, moving, communicating with one another – the path he'd taken rippling with the tree-beings' struggle to attain an earth-side presence. But, perhaps, it was just an uneven track of a path not often travelled.

He quickened his pace, shaking his head, trying to rid his imagination of the cloying images that impinged on his sanity. He pushed back at the blocking branches of the undergrowth; the blocking branches that had never ever been there before, as he made his way, desperate, so very desperate, to get to the house, before something happened.

* * *

The moon slid behind another cloud and Dave had to slow. The path he'd been following wasn't particularly path-like anymore and, if he was going to avoid injuring himself, he would have to pick his footing carefully. He stared intently at the ground, trying to make sure that no twig, nor bramble, would folly him in his task.

As the cloud receded, allowing the white moon to play its light through the canopy of the forest onto Dave's path, he looked up from his feet and saw he was now way off course; the light from the house being directly to his left, instead of in front of him, where he had expected it to be.

The path through the forest was not as it had seemed. He had assumed it would cut straight through the woodland to the house, but now he was more than aware it was likely to be a run the forest animals followed. Looking to his left he now understood that he had to traipse through bush and thickets, and, in order to achieve his goal, he was going to have to make the path, following the direction the light from the house indicated. *If it is a light in a house*, his imagination taunted.

Dave pushed on, brushing aside the shrubs that blocked his path and making his way around the bushes, where they were too thick to go through. Eventually he stopped, needing a break, his journey towards the house being much harder than he had imagined. As he rested he heard the sound of his laboured breathing, then without warning his self-centred focus was abruptly interrupted. He held his breath.

Sharp snaps rang out in the forest; the sound of grounded branches shattering under the weight of unseen entities forcing them to splinter. Then more noises, noises of leaf laden shrub limbs swooshing as they were parted.

Dave mopped his brow with the cuff of his jacket, looking around, peering into the blackness of the forest's depths, listening intently, attempting to locate the direction the sounds had come from, but the noises had stopped... again – and he was alone.

Keeping his breath to a minimum he strained his ears, certain there would be something else, but the forest remained quiet. Even the wind's constant shushing had stopped: there was nothing else to be heard.

Dave pulled a hand down his face wishing that he'd never ever come across this place, this land, he now found himself in.

As the pure silence continued, Dave only just managed to overcome the paralysis his fear had wrought upon him. His heart palpitated and, with the cold and brutal fear still chilling him to his core, he staggered forward seeking the light, and hopefully an end to the nightmare he now found himself a part of.

Within a few short steps the wind came back with a force making the tree tops above him smash together, their branches clacking in unison under Nature's power. He picked up his pace, breaking into a run, accepting the slashes his face took from the unseen small branches of the bushes in his way. Blood trickled down his cheeks in many places from the vegetation inflicted cuts.

No matter how he held his arms out in front of him the twigs and branches of the undergrowth always found a way to inflict more injuries.

Without warning, a low ululating moan came from behind him, shifting his focus from the lacerating foliage. It was quickly followed by a succession of cracks as hardier ground bourn branches and ones still attached to their hosts snapped; an unknown force breaking them as if they were nothing but balsa wood.

"Oh my God, oh my God, oh my God," he heard his voice whisper above his panting and the thumping of his heart in his ears. Dave continued thrashing through the forest knowing there was something close behind, following him; ready to take him. The nape of his neck prickled as the chill of the unknown passed down his spine.

Without looking back he started waving an arm behind him, back and forth, in a futile attempt to ward off the forest's predator he believed was now very close. Occasionally his hand felt blasts of icy breath across its back, even though the noise of the breaking undergrowth was much further behind him, or so he convinced his mind to believe.

Then he saw it, it was there, in front of him in the distance, once again, glinting through the pitched darkness of the forest the light shone and he started towards it, pushing at the shrubs and bracken, struggling against the bushes and suddenly he was through; he had entered another clearing.

His initial relief immediately collapsed into despondency as he recognised the three pronged stump at the clearing's centre, and although he was back to where he'd started from he had no idea, now, as to the direction of his car. Everywhere was dark and, each way he looked, the view was the same.

Dave sat down on the stump, head in hands with fingers in ears, to apprise himself of his situation and how he could get out of it. But he could barely think as he wondered how long it would be before his tormentor broke through into the clearing to join him.

After some moments he looked up, afraid, scared for his life with still no idea of what to do, the fear he felt making rational decisions impossible. And as he looked around the light from the house twinkled in the distance between the trees, as if taunting him, *'bet you can't get me.'*

Rut-tah-tuh-tuh-tuh. The sound from many miles ago started up again, echoing, coming from no definite direction. Or was it coming from behind him? He turned his head quickly, attempting to seek its source, then turned back to see if it was *now* behind him.

"Oh shit," Dave breathed, all his nerves more on edge than they'd been before, but the clacking had stopped. Had he imagined it? He was not sure. Then there was another crack, this time to his right, he turned to look – again nothing to be seen.

Dave peered around the clearing, tenuously keeping hold of his sanity, not seeing any movement, but somehow the trees, that defined the area he sat in, seemed to be closer, a lot nearer to him, the circumference of the clearing reduced, their branches almost but not quite able to reach him. GRAB HOLD.

No, stop it, he told his mind.

He studied the circling trees again, attempting to see their movement towards him, but in the moonlight he could not tell if they really had moved any closer at all. There was only the feeling that the circle's edge was ten steps away from him rather than the twenty his mind insisted they were before.

As he watched the trees he caught a movement in the periphery of his vision, enhanced by the noise of cracking twigs. He turned to face the movement and as he did the dark gap between the pine trees, he now stared at, coalesced into a black, almost recognisable, amorphous shape. In turn, it disappeared behind one trunk of the circling trees only to appear in the gap between the trees further around the clearing's circle: Nature parodying mankind's form in the air, within her own breath.

Dave stood up on shaking legs watching the apparition's dance around the circle. All he could do was follow its movements, turning on point, as the dark thing made a complete circle, his ability to flee being sucked from him by the brutal terror of his situation. As he completed the 360 degree turn of its path around him, the entity, whatever it was, melded back into the forest's darkness and the hex that had riveted him to the spot eased its vice like grip upon him. Dave shivered, his body feeling as if iced water had replaced the blood that had once flowed through his veins.

Rut-tah-tuh-tuh-tuh, came the ancient and evil sound again. Dave felt like he was going to be sick and as he turned to throw up he saw blue and red flashing lights, flickering around and around, obviously from a patrol vehicle, piercing the forest. And as he recognised their source he saw the juddering beam of a flashlight that could only be carried by a person.

A way out, he thought. With what little commandable energy he had left, Dave started to stumble towards the blue and red light and the path back to his car and he prayed for some help.

Picking up his pace, energy coming from reserves he didn't realise he had, he made for the trail out of the clearing.

As he attempted his first step onto the path that led to the road a tree root leapt from beneath the ground's surface under its own power, throwing the path's loamy soil up, out of its way, tripping him. He fell flat on his stomach, right arm out in front of him, and left wrist under his body, snapping as his full weight landed upon its awkward angle. With his neck stretched forward, his eyes focused again on the police officer investigating his empty car. Dave took a breath to call for help, but before he could finish large red capped mushrooms smashed their way out of the earth entering his open mouth, cutting off any sound he was about to make. He breathed heavily through his nose as his lungs continued their heaving cycle.

Other roots broke free from the forest's floor encircling his ankles and his shins, retracting, pulling him back towards the clearing; taking him away from his only escape route.

He tried clawing the ground with his good arm, to halt the forest's claim upon his body, but the forest's strength was greater than his and he continued to be dragged, backwards, on his front, feet first, by the forest's living tendrils; back into the clearing's centre. *The forest's mouth*, a thought flitted through his head.

Struggling to keep conscious he saw the police car's lights stop flashing and heard a car's engine start, then gradually fade away. More chills racked his body as the February night's iciness sought to claim every part of him.

Brambles that were used to travelling the forest floor wrapped themselves around his arms turning him over, their thorns cutting through his clothing, digging deep into his upper arms.

Dave managed to cough out the Fly Garret in his mouth as bushes he hadn't noticed in the clearing before, leant over him, rustling angrily. Then the moon was obscured by a cloud for a moment and, as it appeared again, the rustling became sibilant words.

No more. The bushes rustled in quiet unison. *No more will you take us limb from limb. No more will you kill us. We are one throughout Gaia and we have started the end.*

Dave did not understand and Nature's call to arms sounded again, *rut-tah-tuh-tuh-tuh,* as if to underline the bushes' mutterings.

You can not live with us and we can not live with you. The sibilant voice of the bushes threatened.

More tree roots heaved themselves from the ground, rearing above him, and then plunged downwards through his thighs, smashing his femurs as they sought the soil beneath him. He screamed at the pain and continued screaming as the length of

the roots' uneven surface travelled through the meat of his legs, snagging tendons, nerves and arteries; but his scream was soon silenced when ivy crept out from the edge of the clearing and wrapped itself around his neck cutting him off, but only just enough to silence his voice. It was as if the forest had decided to torture him. But for what, he could not imagine.

The bushes rustled again: *Know what you do, feel what you do. You take more than you should and the gift to us, of your ones without life, put deep in our body beneath our skin, for our sustenance, is not enough. We follow you now and we take what we want, as you do to us. This is our beginning born in humankind's way.*

Rhododendrons joined the roots and brambles that had already pinned Dave to the ground, wrapping their thin branches around his arms, beginning to pull, and, as he tried to free himself, the grass of the clearing grew, sliding over his chest, weaving itself across his sternum in a mat pulling him tight to the ground, ceasing his struggles.

Dave attempted to scream again as his arms were dislocated by the plants, but he couldn't, the vines around his neck had put paid to that. He attempted to struggle once more, this time without movement and became still as his arms were finally wrenched from his body, skin tearing at the armpits, shock paralysing any further effort he could muster. The shrubs lifted his ragged, partially clothed arms into the air, flicking them around, back and forth, in noiseless triumph.

With his blood pumping into the earth from his pulverised legs and the red fluid spurting from his shoulder sockets in arcs, Dave, in his last living thoughts, almost grasped what he had been told by the plants. But before he was able to scream at the forest, that it wasn't his fault, the vines that had encircled his throat tightened, squeezing his head from his neck.

* * *

And so it began – Nature's final retaliation. Humankind had ignored her warnings; the tsunamis, the earthquakes, firestorms and floods. She had ceased to accept ignorance as an excuse for innocence. Scorned as she felt she was, the war had to start somewhere – and so it had.

Sinister

By Colin Butler

Sinister... sinister – just a Latin word,
Meaning left or left-sided,
But gradually it changed to a byword
For the dark side – resonating fear.

Left-handers were regarded with distrust,
And even today people resent them,
I'm left-handed and think it's unjust
Even tools aren't designed for us,

I'm convinced I'm normal – not different,
Although often, I believe, my right hand
Is totally ignorant of, or indifferent
To what my left hand is doing.

Whilst embracing this lovely young girl,
My left hand began to caress her neck,
Before I knew it – it happened in a whirl –
Its fingers slowly stroked her throat.

Gradually they tightened like a noose,
She tried to scream – alarm on her face
Which turned a deep shade of puce,
As she slumped, so silently, to the floor.

Sinister Too

I looked down at her lying there
So beautiful and so serene,
And slowly walked away, totally unaware
Who could've committed this monstrous deed?

Bugaboo

By Paul A. Bunn

Chapter 1: Friends Reunited

1

It had been the same for the last three years: a few old school friends getting together every summer for one evening to reminisce about old times and catch up on any news since the previous meeting.

Due to the travelling distances for everyone concerned (we now lived miles apart) we could only meet up just the once each year. The date wasn't fixed, although we tried to make it at a weekend during July or August.

We'd met again, as many old friends do, through a "school friends" web site. None of us had kept in contact since leaving school, which was more than twenty years earlier.

I had instigated "The Event of the Year" as it became known, after some months of chatting on-line, interspersed with a few phone calls. Steve, who had been my best friend at school, was the one I approached first, and he had been enthusiastic.

"Bring it on," was his reply.

The others, although not as close to me, all agreed.

We met on neutral ground at a pub called The Greyhound, which was hidden away in a small village a few miles north of London. It was an ideal location, deep in the countryside surrounded by large oak trees just off a small lane about half a mile from the village High Street. Well, it comprised of a sub post office, small corner shop and another pub so "High Street" was probably pushing it a bit.

We hired a room at the back of the pub for some privacy. I was nervous on the first face-to-face meeting, wondering if the renewed friendships would materialise as well as they had on-line. I needn't have worried; the conversation flowed, initially about our school days, before moving on to what we had been doing since.

It was Steve who came up with the idea of each of us telling a story. He was easily bored, so after a couple of hours of our bantering he raised his arm and cleared his throat. Everyone stopped their conversation mid-sentence.

He'd always had this effect; he was tall and thin, some might say lanky but his angular facial features and dark, brooding eyes commanded attention. In fact, he was the only one of us who appeared to have changed the least, a growth of stubble and long slick black hair being the only differences I could discern.

Neil, who was sitting to his left grimaced from a face that was now considerably chubbier than when we were at school.

"Oh no here we go: he speaks." The twinkle in Neil's deep blue eyes indicated the light heartedness of his comment.

I smiled, knowing that it was going to be Steve's "Big Idea." I remembered from childhood how it was Steve who came up with the plans of what to do next when we were at a loose end.

"Before I say my piece, I think we should all thank Sam for organising this…" Steve's arm swept around the room in a grand gesture, "… reunion."

There was a spontaneous round of applause from my friends making me turn away, feeling my face turn a shade of crimson.

Scott, the oldest of us pulled a bottle of champagne from behind his chair.

"Before we hear Steve talk," – there were a few muffled laughs from the others – "I would like to propose a toast to all of us." He dived back behind him and produced five champagne flutes. This was typical of the man, organised and able to spring a surprise at the drop of a hat. His hair was shaved short, (unlike the curly locks he had as a child) but it didn't hide the fact he was going bald. He seemed to have aged more than any of us, with heavy wrinkles around his droopy eyes and thin-lipped mouth. My guess was that his forty a day smoking habit wasn't helping.

"To the first of many a get together." We all raised our glass to that.

Steve placed his glass on the table and stood up, his eyes scanning all of us in turn. "As you know, when we were kids, I would sometimes come up with some suggestions of things we could do."

There were groans from the rest of us. "We've grown up now, Steve, we can make our own decisions," Scott, as he always had done, butted in. "We don't need your 'Big Idea' to entertain us for a couple of days." There were a few moments of awkward silence as our egos jostled for position within the group. We had been like it as kids and it had occasionally ended up in a fight, something I wanted to avoid here.

"Let's hear him out," I heard myself speak in an attempt to break the deadlock. "We are supposed to be friends after all and I'm sure we don't want to get thrown out of a pub on our first visit. Besides, I'm not even drunk yet."

The tension between us relaxed as the others laughed at my quip. Steve, whose eyes had bored into Scott during their exchange, gave me an appreciative nod and continued.

"To make our annual meetings more than just one big booze up, I reckon we should set ourselves a bit of a challenge."

I saw Scott about to interrupt, and shot him a warning glance, which, fortunately, he heeded. There were a few whispers from the others but Steve was on a roll now and determined to finish.

"I propose that every year, each of us in this room should have a story to tell." There were some tuts but Steve carried on. "Hear me out... please." We fell silent again.

"The best one, as judged by the group, will have all their food and drink for the weekend paid for by the rest of us."

Scott, who looked far from happy with the suggestion, pointed to Phil, who'd been the quietest of us all since our arrival.

"But he's a writer by profession, he's bound to win."

Phil wriggled uncomfortably in his chair, stroking his goatee beard nervously. "I'll sit this out, it doesn't bother me."

Steve's face lit up, showing a set of white, even teeth. "But that's the challenge for the remainder." He stood now, excited by the idea. "It doesn't have to be fiction like Phil writes. It can be based on fact, if you want."

There was further discussion about the idea into the early hours of the morning, but we all agreed, although with some misgivings, to give it a go and see how well it worked out.

2

Mostly, we were poor storytellers and so ended up telling rather long jokes, maybe with a loose connection to something that had happened to us during the preceding year. But Steve's big idea worked and it was always the highlight of the weekend.

3

This year started as normal, except I was two hours late due to heavy traffic on the M25. As the organiser I didn't like to arrive after everyone else but there was nothing I could do about it.
Steve greeted me as I stooped through the small entrance of the pub into the warm, homely glow of the main bar.

"We were wondering where you'd got to." He gripped my hand in a firm handshake. Already the tension built up by the journey was leaving my shoulders.

"Oh great," I mock groaned. "Not Abba again I hope." I could already hear the faint sound of *Mamma Mia* coming from our private room.

As we opened the door Neil, as usual, had centre stage, singing away, with the others clapping and whistling along. His white shirt had sweat stains under each arm, with his short brown hair stuck to his head as if he'd just got out of the shower. It also looked like he was losing his battle against the flab; I was certain he was bigger than the eighteen stone he'd been last year.

"I'll get you a beer," Steve shouted over the noise. "Hopefully he'll stop soon." He slipped out of the door before I could respond.

4

I was looking forward to tonight's events in particular. I didn't have a story as such to tell, but had found a book in a dusty old bookshop on the High Street in my town. I often went in there because it offered something a bit different from your normal, modern shops which had the latest best sellers at half price. This place was stuffed with good books from different eras and I loved it.

This particular book was at the bottom of a pile when I saw it and was just asking to be picked up. It was a brown colour with plenty of age cracks in it and the texture was unusual. It didn't feel like a normal cover of a book, appearing a lot thinner than I would expect.

Turning it over in my hand I read the title on the cover, which was very faint. "*Personal Forebodings.*" by Obo Bagu

I'd never heard of the author and couldn't even guess the sex but was intrigued nevertheless. Opening it carefully, I saw from the table of contents that it was a collection of short stories and/or poems with some very odd titles: *"Dark Recesses of the Mind"*, *"The Incident with Mr. Smith"*, *"The End of all Hope"*. But there was one title that stuck in my mind, as I'd never heard the word before – *"Bugaboo"*.

I turned to the relevant page number and found it was a poem so read it.

> *Tis fear that grips your heart, my love*
> *His icy blast will freeze your mind*
> *Beware the dreaded hypnotic chimes*
> *For they uncover a hidden truth.*
>
> *And should my love, this come to pass*
> *Despair will hunt its unwilling victim*
> *You must hold true and seek him out*
> *Or fade away like a morning mist*

I had no idea what the words meant, although it was seemed to be something to do with fear. Never had any writing gripped me like this and I decided there and then to buy it.

5

As usual, the evening with my friends went extremely well and by the time it came to telling stories, each of us had had quite a lot to drink. When it was my turn I felt unusually nervous as I looked at their expectant faces.

"Guys, I know that the rules are I should come up with a tale of something that has happened to me this year, but to be honest it's been pretty boring." I reached into my jacket pocket and grasped the book. "So, I am going to read something out of this."

"You can't do that, it's cheating." Neil cracked a mischievous smile as he spoke. "And it will mean you'll lose."

The others nodded agreement, except Steve who seemed fascinated by my bending of his rules. "Let's see what he says first before passing judgement," he said, winking at me. "If it's rubbish, we'll tell him and he'll definitely lose." I opened the book to the relevant page.

"This better be good," Scott interjected. I ignored him and cleared my throat. I read "Bugaboo".

I was aware of my complete focus on the reading, tuning everything else out. There was also something else, a faint ringing in my ears. On finishing, I looked at the others hoping to see in their eyes what I felt after reading it.

"Well, when are you going to start?" Scott said impatiently.

I suddenly realised that I had been so engrossed with the poem I hadn't read it out loud, just to myself. "Sorry, I erm…"

"Don't worry Sam, we've all had a lot to drink so we'll let you off." I smiled at Steve's support and started again.

The words seemed to reverberate around our private room as I spoke, and I felt cold sweat trickle down the back of my neck as if caught by a sudden chill. I thought reading it to myself had been fascinating, but out loud made the whole thing seem a lot more potent.

There were a few moments of what was obviously embarrassed silence before Phil, scratching his goatee as usual, leaned forward. "I like the poem Sam, but I don't think it's enough really to win tonight." There were general murmurs of agreement from the others.

"Oh…" I was deflated because I had been certain that the poem would have the same impact on them, as it did me.

"What have you done to your finger?" It was Neil who pointed at my right hand and the others followed his gaze.

I had put the book back into my pocket and now studied my hand in bewilderment. There was blood running down my palm from the index finger, the one I realised I had been using to follow the lines of the poem with. I must have got a paper cut whilst putting it away, although I didn't remember doing it. It was quite deep as well.

Steve came over to have a look at it, holding my hand up to the light to see it better. "Don't fuss, it's only a paper cut," I said. "I'll go and clean it up."

Steve gave a mock grimace. "If I'd known that spilling blood was going to be part of your act tonight, you would have won hands down."

We all laughed as I went to the Gents to wash the wound before applying a plaster.

By the end of the evening, or, as it was when we had finished, early morning, I had forgotten my disappointment with my reading earlier and was in a totally relaxed frame of mind.

6

The pub had had an extension built onto its side containing ten additional bedrooms to complement what had been only six in the main pub building itself. The landlord had said he'd hired three new staff including a manager to run things in the new part. This also had its own reception area with desk for checking in. We had all been placed in the new building for the weekend.

Steve put an arm around my shoulder. "You ok, mate?" I turned around and gave him a soppy wet kiss on the cheek. "You bet," I said. Steve wiped his cheek with his sleeve and Neil shouted. "Sharing tonight, boys, are we?" The others whistled and laughed as we made our way to our rooms.

7

The room was quite spacious with a double bed but I thought I could probably sleep on anything that night I was so tired. Throwing my jacket on the bed and removing my shoes, I fell onto the nice soft duvet and was almost instantly asleep.

As I was drifting into sleep I thought I heard my jacket fall to the floor, spilling its contents. I had a strange dream, filled with images of a glowing book and a strange little man appearing at the bottom of my bed. Little did I know that this dream was a portent, an indicator of the frightening night yet to come.

Chapter 2: Neil's Bugaboo

1

He shut the door of his hotel room firmly behind him, leaning back on it with his eyes closed but with a huge grin on his face.

All year he had looked forward to this weekend, just as he did every year. If he could have his way, they would meet more often, but he understood the others had families. Neil was not so fortunate.

His parents had died in a car accident when he was five years old and, being an only child, there were no brothers and sisters.

So he'd spent his younger years being brought up by grandparents who he had come to detest. Although they never said anything about it to him, he knew that for some reason they had blamed him for the accident.

He had been five years old for Christ sake!

It wasn't his fault that their precious daughter had died. A pang of guilt hit him like a sledgehammer for thinking those words and he scolded himself for it.

"Don't spoil a great night," he mumbled and pushed the thought forcibly from his mind. His stomach growled angrily at him, so he made his way to the phone by his king size bed.

"Time for a snack." He licked his lips in anticipation.

Within minutes, his food arrived: four rounds of beef and horseradish sandwiches, two bags of salt 'n' vinegar crisps, plus a huge slab of chocolate gateau.

A small part of him knew he shouldn't eat it if he was ever going to lose weight but the monster that was his appetite smothered that. In many respects, Neil hated how he was, but food was the thing that made him the happiest. He was single, having had no luck with girls, most of who looked at him as if he were something horrible on the bottom of their shoe. Even blind dating using the Internet, always ended in disaster.

He had tried every diet known to man: the issue however was that he didn't have the willpower to back it up. Eating noisily he sat on the bed, which creaked a protest as he reached for the remote and put on the TV.

As usual, there was nothing worth watching so he cast his mind back to earlier that evening, and, in particular, the story telling part. He liked this, not because he was a great teller of tales, as he always had a few jokes up his sleeve or anecdotes that got a few laughs. It was Sam's book that had intrigued him.

Even now, he remembered the texture of it, like cold flesh, that made him shudder. The poem Sam read had been weird as well, the words buzzed around his head for sometime afterwards, taking a life of their own.

"Bugaboo," he whispered. What a strange word it seemed and yet it represented something, to him anyway, so trivial.

Suddenly he began to laugh, a real fit of the giggles, which he couldn't stop, spilling remnants of his meal down his silk pyjamas.

Eventually, the laughter abated and he busily mopped up the food he'd dropped.

"Waste not, want not," he said, licking his fingers greedily. He didn't like to waste a tiny, single crumb.

Still hungry, he reached across to the phone for room service.

2

He woke with a start, and for a moment felt disorientated, not knowing where he was. As he took in the surroundings of the hotel room he soon re-focused his mind and climbed from the bed.

The TV now showed a snowstorm of white noise where he'd left it switched on all night. He didn't remember falling asleep but it wasn't unusual, especially after he had eaten. Yawning, he stretched hearing his joints crack before heading for the bathroom to freshen up.

3

He made his way down to breakfast, imagining in his mind's eye the full English he would be having in a few minutes time.

The hotel was quiet for nine o'clock in the morning, with no sound emanating from the rooms he passed along the corridor towards the lift. Still, there was nothing wrong with a lie in at the weekend. He chuckled as he thought of what some couples might be getting up to.

On reaching the ground floor he found the restaurant empty of guests, not even his friends had made it yet. Scott was normally an early riser, even after a drinking session like the previous night.

All the tables were laid in pristine white tablecloths with cutlery neatly lined up at each seating place. He hurried to a table, not bothering to wait for any of the others to arrive. Tucking a serviette down his open necked shirt he waited, and waited. Again he became aware of the silence, with no hustle and bustle coming from the kitchen. Becoming impatient, he was about to investigate when a man appeared at his side. Well, that was how it seemed, as there had been no noise of an approach from behind him.

Neil's heart jumped in surprise at his sudden arrival. Jolting in his seat, he banged his leg against the table and cursed an expletive out loud.

"Sorry, Sir, did I startle you?"

Neil gawped at the man, the strangest looking person he'd ever seen in his life.

He was only about five feet tall, with no hair on his head and very large, protruding ears. His long face was silky smooth with saucer-like large deep brown eyes, which had a fierce intensity. His lips were small and thin, which as he smiled, showed a row of regular, if unusually pointed teeth.

Shaking his head, Neil cleared his throat. "Erm yes, I didn't hear you that's all."

The man's smile broadened, showing even more wickedly sharp teeth.

"Would you like something?" He bent forward conspirationally. "A full English breakfast, perhaps?"

On hearing those three beautiful words Neil regained his composure.

"Oh yes, please, with five slices of toast."

"Tea or coffee?"

"Tea, please."

Neil's mouth began to water with anticipation.

"And when do you want this... breakfast?"

At first, Neil had to replay the question through his mind, as it didn't make sense.

"I'm sorry...?"

"I said, when do you want it?" There was a harder edge to the man's voice this time, and the smile had disappeared to be replaced by a scowl.

Neil could feel perspiration running down his neck as the sudden change in tone caught him off guard.

"Well, as soon as you can, please." He sounded sheepish, like a naughty schoolboy.

The man stared at him intently for a few seconds, before breaking into that awful smile again.

"Coming right up," he said.

As the man walked away, Neil sagged back into his chair. "What a weirdo," he thought.

It was then he heard the ringing sound, like the sound of a small dinner bell. It was coming, he thought, from the kitchen. He tried to ignore it, but after a few seconds respite, it started again. This happened a number of times before Neil felt compelled to investigate, becoming annoyed and also strangely attracted to the constant din.

He made his way to the kitchen doors and stopped just before pushing the swing door open. What was he doing? His breakfast would be ready in a minute and he was investigating a ringing bell. He'd almost made up his mind to return to his seat when the sound became more insistent, urging him on. He entered the kitchen.

4

It was empty. Not just of people but any sign of cooking: no food, frying pans on hobs or ovens whirring into life. Everything was perfectly clean with surfaces gleaming in a shiny, stainless steel, unused condition. Neil frowned in confusion; surely even with no one in the restaurant there would be some sort of preparation going on.

The bell noise seemed to be coming from the far end, which was partly hidden from view by hanging kitchen equipment. His stomach gave him a growling reminder that it needed feeding, and soon. Resting his arm gently on his belly he moved swiftly forward, wanting to solve this mystery so that he could get back to his seat in the restaurant. In the process, he almost bumped in to the man who'd taken his order.

"Are you looking for something, Sir?" He held up a small bell. "Perhaps this?"

Neil was embarrassed, unsure as to what to say for himself. It was then he noticed what the man held in his other hand – his breakfast he assumed. It looked marvellous and he couldn't stop his mouth watering at the sight of it.

The man followed his gaze. "Ahh, of course. It's this you really want isn't it?" He raised it slowly towards Neil's face. "It looks lovely doesn't it?" The man's voice became a high tuneless whine.

Neil's whole vision was now filled with this plate of food and he was mesmerised by it.

"You want it don't you? The hunger burns within, doesn't it?" His tone softened, becoming soporific.

Neil felt his head nodding the affirmative but didn't have any control over it. He just stared; and watched his breakfast suddenly become infested with maggots.

They appeared from nowhere swarming over the plate, eating everything in sight, wriggling and writhing until the plate was clean; dropping onto the floor, making light pats as they hit.

Neil's eyes widened and he heard a whimper escape from his throat. The man just laughed, a maniacal roar that went right through him.

"Still Hungry, Sir?"

Neil was rooted to the spot, unable to move.

"Not hungry, Sir? That's good, you won't find anything else to eat here either, you fat gluttonous pig." There was more laughter from the man and this time Neil ran. He got to the kitchen door but it wouldn't open, nor budge an inch. Feeling the panic rise he flew around the kitchen looking for another way out but there was none, no windows or other exits.

Running back to the original door he banged on it shouting help but no one came. Eventually, sobbing, he slipped to the floor.

The man came over to him, the smile on his lips not travelling to his eyes. "Now you will see what it is like to starve to death."

More laughter echoed around the clean, unused kitchen.

Chapter 3: Phil's Bugaboo

1

In some respects, Phil didn't like coming to these once yearly events with his old school friends. It wasn't that he didn't enjoy their company, far from it. He just didn't like to be away from home.

His mother lived with him and suffered from Alzheimer's, so needed constant care. His father had died of a heart attack six years earlier and she had gone rapidly downhill since then.

How he missed the influence his father had on the family, particularly Phil himself. His sister, Helen, had got married the year after their father's death and he rarely saw her or the two children she now had. He could tell on those rare visits that she didn't want to be there, feeling uncomfortable around a mother who didn't recognise anybody except in a very few moments of lucidity.

Shaking his head as he sat on the bed, he reached across picking up his small notebook and pen. He sometimes felt writing was the only thing that kept him sane. After putting Mum to bed, he would hide himself away in his own tiny bedroom and write, sometimes for hours on end. It was his bolthole from the misery of real life.

There had been a few articles and short story sales but nothing major as yet, however he lived in hope. The novel he was working on should be complete in a few months and he was excited about it, although he knew the hard work was getting it published. Still, he wasn't going to complain. Although his mum was hard work, he wanted to make her last years comfortable. Even though it didn't seem it most of the time, he was sure that somewhere deep down she appreciated what he was doing for her.

He put pen to paper and began to write... but was disturbed by a knock on the door.

Phil checked his watch; it was 2:15 a.m. Frowning, he wondered who it could be at this late hour. He hoped that it wasn't one of his friends; he was all talked out and didn't really want to speak to anyone now. The knocking came again, more insistently this time. Reluctantly Phil got up from his bed, throwing his pad down, and opened the door.

The man stood on the threshold smiling at Phil almost apologetically. Phil was quite taken aback by the man's lack of height and his large, deep set eyes.

The hospitality trade's bald Ronnie Corbett.

Phil almost burst out laughing when that thought crossed his mind and had to stifle it with a cough.

"Sorry to bother you, Sir," the man said, shuffling uncomfortably from foot to foot in what appeared to be embarrassment.

"That's ok. What seems to be the problem?"

The man looked up and down the corridor, as if to ensure no one could over hear him.

"We've just had a phone call from the previous occupant of your room on rather a delicate matter." He covered his mouth and cleared his throat. "It would appear the young lady concerned thinks she may have lost her wedding ring here and is desperate to recover it." Phil listened to the man's perfectly articulated voice and couldn't believe it came from such a weasel looking human being.

"Well, it is late…"

"Yes, I know Sir but the poor woman was distraught and I'm sure you wouldn't mind letting me in; just for a few minutes to have a quick look around?"

Phil was too tired to argue and opened the door fully to let the man in.

"Thank you, Sir," the man said.

2

On entering the room, he made his way to the chest of drawers first of all.

"Do you mind?" the man indicated to the drawers with his hand.

"No, go right ahead."

As Phil watched, he got the impression that the man seemed distracted. He was making no real effort to look, just going through the motions of searching for something.

Eventually, he re-closed the drawers and turned to face Phil, a quizzical look on his pasty smooth face. "I understand you are a writer of some repute, Sir."

Phil was surprised by this question out of the blue and didn't instantly respond. The man indicated with a nod of his head the notepad sitting next to Phil on the bed. "I've read one or two of your short stories; very interesting I must say."

Phil gave a weak smile, enjoying the moment.

"I'm in the presence of a fan," he thought. "Wonders will never cease." He'd never bumped in to anyone who recognised his work before, and he felt a sense of pride. Hopefully, it wouldn't be the last time he met someone who liked his work, a real fan not just those people on publications who accepted for their magazines.

"May I...?" the man indicated towards Phil's notebook.

Phil picked it up and held onto it protectively. He never showed anyone this; he had all his notes in it from the time he'd started writing. All his initial thoughts on articles and stories were born in it; it was more precious to him than the end result he produced.

Then Phil heard a ringing sound and cocked his head to one side. Where was that coming from? It held him mesmerised. As time seemed to stand still, his mind wandered back to his home and his poor mother sitting in her favourite chair staring into space. He didn't even notice the tear rolling down his face.

"Sir?"

Phil blinked and came back to the here and now. For a moment, he was disorientated before seeing the man again standing just a few feet away. "Sorry, you were saying?"

The man laughed at him, a cruel twisted laugh. "I was saying what absolute rubbish your stories are. I've seen better from five year olds."

He was showing, for the first time, a row of nasty pointed teeth. "I wonder how you would feel if you couldn't write at all. Nothing. Zilch." His terrible smile broadened. "I'll let you ponder that shall I?"

The man marched out the door, slamming it behind him.

Phil's mind was a maelstrom of confusion and fear. What had just happened? He thought back and remembered the conversation about how the man liked his stories... and then didn't. There was no sense to this. And how had he got hold of his notebook; that was one thing he wouldn't hand over willingly.

There was no doubting the menace the man portrayed but why? He'd done nothing to hurt him in any way.

But he had your notebook.

The thought was like a dagger to the heart. Had he damaged the book in any way? Snatching it off the bed he opened it to the first page – nothing. Scanning the rest of it he just found page after page of untouched and unwritten on white paper. It had all been erased! That was impossible, surely. It was in ink, so there must be some sort of trace but even on close inspection there was nothing there.

Then he remembered the penultimate words the man had said to him. "I wonder how you would feel if you couldn't write at all. Nothing. Zilch."

Feeling his world falling apart he desperately picked up his pen and held it in his hand poised over the blank paper. It remained unmoved until he fell into a restless sleep. The one thing that kept him going through the difficult times he was having had left him forever.

Chapter 4: Scott's Bugaboo

1

Scott sat with his laptop on the desk checking his e-mails. He couldn't believe how many new messages had appeared in his "inbox" since he'd logged out the night before – 106!

Scott thrived on his work and the pressure that came with it. In many respects his work was his life and there was precious little time for anything else, as two messy divorces could testify. He worked for a communications company and led a team of six sales people. With tough targets to reach every year, he drove himself and his team to the limits of their collective abilities to meet them. He prided himself that, for the six years he'd been there, he'd never failed, getting paid a huge bonus in the process.

It wasn't the money, though, that really interested him. If he was honest with himself, he was a workaholic and had no problem working 16 hours per day, even at weekends and even now in the hotel while he was away with his friends.

Steve had said to him once that he should try and slow down a bit, enjoy life at a more relaxed pace or he'd end up six feet under before his time. As usual with Steve it had ended in an argument: who was he to criticise his lifestyle when Steve himself was just a lazy bastard with no job anyway?

Although with Steve it wasn't just that he was unemployed that annoyed him, it was the way the others always looked to him for ideas, help or advice, especially Sam. It drove him mad sometimes when they met up, after all, wasn't he the one who'd made a success of his life?

Scott drove the thoughts from his mind as they only wound him up and he couldn't concentrate on his e-mails. Besides, he knew part of the problem was his own failing in not coming up with the so-called "big idea" which was Steve's claim to fame. Scott begrudgingly felt that generally speaking they were great ideas, particularly this story telling lark, which he had to admit, was great fun.

There were so many things that went on around his office environment he had no problem in coming up with some great yarns to tell. This year had been especially juicy as he told of the torrid affair going on with his manager and a woman who worked on his team, both of whom were married already – it had been the talk of the department!

He didn't notice the man standing next to him until he reached across for his glass of water, catching a glimpse of him out of the corner of his eye.

"What the f…" Scott jerked back in surprise, almost dropping his laptop onto the floor.

"Sorry to surprise you like this, Sir," the man quickly said by way of an apology.

Scott was stunned, unable to think why he'd not heard the man approach or, for that matter, how he'd got into his room.

As if reading his mind, the man continued. "I let myself in, Sir, using the hotel's own universal key. We use it only in emergencies, I assure you." The man flashed a smile at Scott that only managed to give him the creeps.

"Well, you could have knocked and I would have answered just as quickly you know." Scott's composure was returning and he began to feel irritated by this interruption. "What do you want?"

The man mumbled to himself as he fished through his jacket pocket before producing a wallet.

"I believe this is yours, Sir." He held it out towards Scott, indicating for him to take it and check.

From its worn, cracked leather exterior, Scott was reasonably certain it was his, but checked anyway by unclipping it to show all his credit cards and £100 of cash that he knew he'd drawn out earlier that day.

"Where did you get this?" Scott couldn't believe he'd misplaced it, as he was always so careful with his wallet. He could have sworn he'd locked it in the room safe before joining his friends earlier.

"I'm afraid we apprehended a thief who was just about to leave the premises. He was not a guest here, and was acting rather suspiciously." The man shook his head with disapproval. "This is the first time I remember it happening here since my arrival, Sir."

Scott was still confused; he walked over to check the safe, pulling at the handle. "My safe doesn't look broken into; how did he know the combination? I changed it as soon as I got here."

As Scott turned he found the man staring intently at his laptop. Moving swiftly, Scott slammed the lid shut. "Excuse me, but that is private and confidential."

The man stepped back, making a grunting sound of surprise as he did so. "I'm ever so sorry, Sir, I didn't mean to pry." Scott's eyes blazed furiously at the man who began wringing his hands together in embarrassment.

It was then Scott heard the ringing sound, making him stop and cock his head to one side. It was such a sweet noise that he felt drawn to it, forgetting everything else that was going on around him. A soppy grin crossed his lips as its hypnotic chimes took hold.

The man's face had changed from embarrassment to contempt. "Another little fish has taken the bait," he cackled gleefully. He again picked up the laptop and closed his eyes. A new chime, this one indicating a new e-mail message escaped from the laptop.

Putting it back on the bed the man left the room, tittering away to himself.

The ringing stopped and Scott blinked as if moving from a dark room into bright sunlight. What had just happened?

It all came back like a flood into his memory and Scott scanned his room for the man. He was gone, but the laptop and his wallet were sitting side by side on the bed.

Double-checking his wallet, everything was there and his laptop appeared untouched as well. It was then he noticed the new e-mail in his "inbox" above what had been the most recent mail from one of his team colleagues. It was from his boss. Thinking it very late to be sending any mail messages and very unusual (his boss was a strict 9 till 5 person) he opened it. It was titled: "*Urgent – Resource Management.*"

He read it with growing disbelief.

> *Scott,*
> *You've done a great job for us over the years and we wouldn't be where we are today without you.*
> *However, as you know the business has to reduce headcount due to the poor overall performance of the company, indicatively shown by the poor share price.*
> *It is therefore with great regret that I am going to have to let you go at the end of the month.*
> *I would like to take this opportunity to thank you for all your efforts since you have been with the company. Please come and see me Monday and I'll run through the compensation package that we will be offering you, which I believe generous.*
>
> *Regards,*
> *Mike.*

Scott had to re-read the e-mail three times before the impact of what was being said sunk in. He didn't know what to feel; anger – certainly, but the overriding thought was that he was being sucked into a black hole with no way out. No job; and with the current climate as it was, no guarantee of a quick return to work.

Roaring his rage he threw the laptop against the wall, the crunch as it broke into two giving him some satisfaction. "Six fucking years," he screamed, needing to fuel his fury further as he knew the alternative was a long dark road to depression.

Remembering the strange conversation with the man earlier he knew he had something to focus his anger on: the thief and the man himself. Flinging his door open Scott strode purposefully towards the lift and reception.

He didn't notice the man watching him from another room, a mocking glint in his eyes and with a row of sharp, even teeth glinting in the half light.

Chapter 5: Steve's Bugaboo

1

Steve went to the mini bar to grab another drink and found a bottle of ice-cold beer. Pulling the cap off with a bottle opener he drank deeply before placing it on the table next to his bed.

He stared at the photo again; it was of his wife, Suzie and his two children, Clare and Ben, his eight year old twins. The picture had been taken a few months earlier, when they had been on holiday in Majorca. He remembered it well because they had gone on a boat trip and Ben had been seasick for virtually the whole two hours they had been out on it. That day had been enjoyable, though, along with the rest of their break, spending days on the beach and evenings in the colourful local restaurants.

Running his finger over the frame he wished Suzie was here now so he could fall into her arms and inhale her intoxicating fragrance. They had been married for ten years next month and it was what you might call a modern marriage. Suzie was the breadwinner in the family and he spent his time bringing up the children, what is called nowadays a househusband. It didn't bother him in the slightest, as to Suzie and him it was a logical step. When they had both been at work she had earned more than him; considerably more as a director of a pharmaceutical company whereas he was a postman. So, when the twins were born they had made the joint decision that his being at home was best.

Although initially wary of taking the step into house husbandry, he loved it. Watching his children grow and seeing their personalities develop was the most rewarding thing he'd ever done; worries about Suzie not being around all the time as the mother proved unfounded as they were growing up happy and contented.

He didn't understand Scott's attitude towards him, calling him "unemployed" seemed infantile and stupid. Then again, there was always friction between them in some form or another, but Steve didn't hold a grudge, and admired Scott for how well he'd done in his chosen profession.

He turned the photo slightly, so that he could see it better when he got into bed before kissing his fingers and blowing towards it.

"'Night love, see you tomorrow," he whispered.

A sound from behind him caused him to turn towards the doorway. Something was being pushed under it from the corridor, which Steve couldn't make out at first.

Climbing from the bed he walked over to investigate and picked up a folded piece of paper. On it was a note from the hotel reception.

> *Sir.*
> *Could you please call your wife, she left a message for you to ring her.*

Steve opened the door to see who had left it but found the hallway empty of life. Puzzled, he re-read the note and checked his watch: 2:15 a.m. Why hadn't she called him earlier on his mobile? Taking it from his pocket he was surprised to find it switched off and hit the "power" button – nothing happened.

"Shit," he swore under his breath.

Worried now that it could be something urgent Steve picked up the hotel room phone and punched out his home number with shaking hands. At first, there was a strange chiming sound on the line and he pulled the phone away from his ear, looking at it like some strange foreign object. He decided to re-dial and was relieved when Suzie picked up the phone on the second ring.

2

When the call finished he put the phone back slowly into its cradle trying to stop the tears from falling down his face. Just a few hours earlier, when he'd left home, she had kissed him passionately as he stood on the doorstep, not really wanting him to go but understanding his desire to meet with his old school friends... and now this.

As soon as he spoke to her he sensed something wrong, the warmness in her voice was replaced by a business like, almost cold tone.

"What's wrong Suz, I got this message?"

"Oh, so you finally found time to ring me then."

"I'm sorry love, my mobile battery has gone flat otherwise..."

"I'm leaving you Steve and taking Clare and Ben with me."

"You're what?"

"You heard me."

"But I don't understand, that's ridiculous."

"The only thing ridiculous is you. I don't know how I've put up with you this long."

"But..."

"No buts, Steve. We'll be gone when you get back and a solicitor will be in touch. Goodbye."

The phone went dead.

He must have dreamt it; this conversation couldn't have happened surely? It was as if someone had sucked the life out of him so utterly lost did he feel at this terrible turn of events.

It took him sometime to realise there was a gentle knocking on the door. Reluctantly, he stood up and opened it, seeing this strange little man staring at him with hands clasped in front as if in prayer.

"Sorry to disturb you Sir, I just wanted to make sure you got the note I put under your door earlier."

At first, Steve couldn't grasp what he was talking about before remembering how the conversation with Suzie came about.

Swallowing hard he replied, trying to keep his voice from wavering with emotion. "Yes, thank you."

"Nothing serious I hope, Sir." Steve didn't notice the insincerity in his voice or the mocking eyes. He just wanted the man to leave him alone.

"No, nothing serious."

The man bowed extravagantly. "I'll bid you good night then, Sir."

Steve sat on his bed, allowing the tears to fall freely down his face. The same question repeatedly passed through his mind: how can I live without my family?

Chapter 6: My Bugaboo

1

I held the book in my hands deep in thought; still disturbed by the dream I'd had earlier. Its images were crystal clear, not fading with my waking up as they usually did.

My friends and I were sitting having dinner, laughing and joking as we always have done. Then, one by one they disappeared; first Phil, disappearing like a drawing being rubbed out then Scott, followed by Neil and finally Steve. None of them noticed each other going, just carrying on their conversations as normal until I was on my own.

That wasn't the worst of it though; a terrifying laugh then filled the air, so loud I had to cover my ears.

I was still clasping them, a silent scream caught in my throat as I woke, with sweat covering my body.

I knew it was only a dream but it unsettled me, pushing any vestiges of sleep away. Maybe I had drunk too much this evening.

Trying to forget my nightmare, I opened the book to the poem I'd read out earlier as my input to the weekend story. The pages were old, with a light brown tinge to them and a slick, greasy texture. None of the others, when they looked and touched the book, liked it very much.

"It feels like dead skin," was the odd analogy that Neil came up with, recoiling away immediately after touching it.

I noticed suddenly that my finger had started to bleed again.

"Shit." I placed the book on the bed and heading for the bathroom.

It took some time before it stopped. I had some plasters in my bag and hastily placed one around my finger before the bleeding could re-start. Steve always laughed at me, saying I had everything in my bag except the kitchen sink, but I did like to be organised and prepared for any eventuality when I went away.

"Are you ok, Sir?"

I spun around at the sound of the voice coming from my bedroom, heart leaping into my mouth.

"Who is it?" I called back nervously, hurriedly drying my hands and reaching for the door.

"The hotel manager, Sir," came the immediate response.

I sighed in relief and then felt some annoyance. He shouldn't just barge into a hotel room unannounced, even if he was the hotel manager.

Opening the door I became even angrier as I found this strange little man, sitting on the bed reading my book.

He looked up as I entered, a weird lop-sided grin on his face. "I like your book Sir; but then again I should, seeing as I wrote it."

I stared at him for a moment, taken completely by surprise by what he had just said. The man closed the book gently and placed it on the bed next to him. "You look shocked, Sir," he said, clasping his hands on his lap in front of him.

My thoughts were jumbled as I tried to work out what to say. "You wrote it?"

"Exactly right. Well done, Sir." I didn't detect the sarcasm in his voice.

A frown crossed his impossibly smooth face and he patted the bed next to him indicating for me to sit down.

"What do you want?" Although intrigued by the fact that this man said he had written *that* poem, I was unnerved by his sudden appearance in my room unannounced. "And how do I know you are who you say you are?"

The man stood and bowed stiffly from the waist. "Oh, I have forgotten my manners, I do apologise, Sir." He stretched out his arm, offering to shake hands. "Allow me to introduce myself, I am Mr. Obo Bagu, Hotel Manager and some time writer."

I looked at the proffered hand for a few moments; my first reaction was to draw away from it. There seemed something not quite right with this situation, which I couldn't put my finger on. Reluctantly however, I did reach across and gripped a small, but decidedly strong hand. He shook it enthusiastically. "And you are Sam Morrow. I am *so* pleased to meet you."

On releasing it, my first instinct was to wipe my hand on a towel or cloth of some sort, but I stopped the compulsion to do so.

"It's late and I'm tired, what do you want?" My initial confusion was clearing and now I just wanted to get rid of him as quickly as possible, even though part of me still wanted to ask him about his work.

The man's demeanour changed, taken aback by my blunt question. His back stiffened, and his dark eyes held me with a glare that had me fixated. "Believe me, Sir, you won't be so discourteous once I've told you about your friends."

My heart quickened: what had my friends got to do with anything? They were all safely tucked up in bed sleeping off hangovers after a heavy night out. Still, a sliver of fear touched my stomach at their mention. We had had some great times over the past few years and it was something I wanted to continue with for as long as everyone was willing and able. There had been a distinct threat in the tone of Bagu's voice, which didn't sound like an empty boast.

"What about my friends?" I felt my body tense, ready to grab him by the throat if he didn't explain himself.

Bagu raised his hand as if realising my intent and smiled, showing a set of unusually pointed teeth. "They are fine, Sir, do not worry; all off in their own little world," he laughed, as if enjoying a private joke. "Let me show you something." He picked up the book and opened it, indicating for me to have a look.

I saw but I didn't believe…

2

On the left hand page of the book, next to the poem on the right, the page was split into four distinct frames. There was a faint white glow coming from around the edges, but it was what each frame contained that made me gasp, my mouth turning dry. Each one was like watching a miniature movie – with my friends as the stars of the show. Impossibly, I watched as they moved around within their respective frames. No sound came from them but I could tell that each of them, in their own way, was distressed about something.

I wrenched my eyes from the scene and saw the look of quiet satisfaction on Bagu's face. "What is this?" I almost screamed, not daring to focus back on the book. At first he didn't respond, he was so fixated on my friends' images. Then he glanced towards me, flicking his tongue hungrily across his lips.

"You see, Sir, they are all suffering in their own way, and fear has taken hold of them." He then brought the book to his face and inhaled deeply, his eyes closing in blissful contemplation. "They don't know it but they are trapped within these pages for as long as I want them, to feed off what they are frightened of." He turned his head slowly, his face now in a state of rapturous excitement. "Their Bugaboo if you prefer, Sir."

I wanted to run, but found my feet rooted to the floor. It was then that I heard the chimes; softly I heard them, from which direction I couldn't tell. I heard Bagu's voice, but it seemed to come from far away. "What are you afraid of, Sir?"

I felt suddenly tired, wanting to close my eyes and sleep. The chimes were such a soothing sound that I could feel my eyelids begin to droop. "Perhaps it's the thought of not seeing your friends again." At the mention of my friends I wanted to force myself back towards consciousness, shaking my head I tried to rid myself of those hypnotic chimes and open my eyes. I was losing the battle, falling ever deeper into a black hole that would never set me free. Then, as I struggled, there was a release and I felt myself falling before, eyes snapping open, I found myself lying on the hotel bed.

I sat up, breathing heavily, staring wildly around the room. Letting my heart slow it's thundering in my chest, I looked for Bagu, but there was no sign of him.

I tried to make sense of what had just happened; had it just been a bad dream? Nothing appeared out of place; the room seemed as it was when I came in earlier. Then I remembered what he had said about my friends and not seeing them again; uncertainty stirred within me. I had to check on them. Part of me thought this irrational; they would be fine I was sure, but…

Grabbing my jacket I rushed out of the door, making my way to Scott's room first.

3

Everything was quiet, as you would expect at that time of night, just the sound of my footsteps along the corridor could be heard. Reaching Scott's door I raised my fist to knock but hesitated; this was stupid. What was I going to say if he answered? Sorry to disturb you Scott, but I thought you'd disappeared into someone's book. I'd have the mickey taken out of me mercilessly with that one. The problem was I still needed to know. What had happened earlier had seemed so real that there would be no way I could sleep without being sure. I'd think of something to say, even if it is to just ask if he wanted a nightcap. Making up my mind, I knocked and waited for a response.

Five minutes later I was running back to my room, panic rising in waves. No one had answered. After Scott, I'd tried each of my friends door in turn, finishing with Steve. By that time I was pounding on them so hard it should have woken the whole hotel up, but there was nothing. I'd tried other doors but again there was no response. With my breathing coming in gasps and terror coursing through my veins like ice, I reached my room, flying through the door and slamming it behind me.

"Enjoying your stay, Sir."

Bagu's voice seemed to be coming from all around me and he gave a harsh, humourless laugh that sent shivers up and down my spine. I looked around wildly but saw no sign of the man himself. I wanted to be out of this nightmare but felt myself teetering on the brink of an abyss I knew I would never escape from if I entered.

"Ahh, the fear, Sir. It tastes so good, making me feel so strong, and your friends are such willing victims."

The laugh came again and I closed my eyes and covered my ears trying to shut it out.

An image came to my mind of my friends: Neil as a child in his "slimmer" days with his sense of humour having us in stitches even then; thoughtful Phil the shy one now developing into a superb writer; Scott the serious one who had a head for business and a brain to match, and finally Steve, my best friend who was always loyal and would do anything for me.

I focused on these images, knowing I didn't want to lose them forever but unsure what to do. Then, I opened my eyes.

The book was sitting at the bottom of the bed and I reached across, my hand trembling from the memory of what I had seen (or what I thought I'd seen) in it earlier. Picking it up gingerly it felt warm to the touch. I shuddered, not wanting to open it, but felt compelled to do so any way. I knew the page number off by heart.

They were still trapped as I knew they would be, each image of them showing misery and pain etched onto their faces as they wandered, seemingly lost in their own private worlds. And then I saw myself staring out from the last frame on the page and my heart leapt, making me almost drop the book. I was gripped by a sense of despair when I realised I had been caught as well.

Chapter 7: End Game

1

I was startled by a knock on the door. "Can I come in, Sir?" It was Bagu. He didn't wait for an answer, sweeping in to the room with a smug grin creasing the smooth skin of his face. He was different from before; a good deal taller; I guessed almost six feet and much broader, muscle rather than fat.

He was a more imposing figure and any resolve I did have melted away in his presence. He glanced down at the book, his smile broadening. "You now see your predicament?"

I nodded; even the effort of doing this seemed great.

"Where are we all?" I mumbled, wanting more than ever to see my friends in "real life" again. I returned my gaze to the book, touching each of the images on the page feeling a hint of static, similar to when you place your finger on a recently used TV screen.

"A good question, Sir," his voice warmed to the subject. "I have simply used a little magic that I have learned over the many years of my existence to trap each of you."

My mind was groggy, as if stumbling through deep fog, but I needed to know everything. If I was going to get us out of this, I needed some weapon with which to fight back. "I don't understand..."

Bagu snorted, staring at me like a teacher about to scold a schoolboy. "The book, Sir, the book," he tutted.

"Your terror sustains me, Sir," his eyes bore into mine like a drill, "and my book is the conduit for that fear."

I shrank back, feeling the menace flow from him as he leaned over me. I saw the satisfaction on his face as the icy grip of dread latched hold of me once more.

"But, I couldn't have done any of this without you." I looked up at him, startled at what he had just said.

"What do you mean?"

"It is you who released my energy, when you, oh so kindly, recounted my poem, Sir." His face softened for a moment. "I owe you so much." Then he laughed again, mimicking on his face the surprise that I must have shown.

My stomach churned as the realisation of what I'd done hit me. I had released this monster, allowing him to wreak havoc. It had been my fault.

Rage grew within me, firstly at my inadvertent folly, then at Bagu for wrecking our lives.

"There is no hope, Sir."

His arrogant voice stirred me from my thoughts. I stared at him defiantly, and for the first time I saw uncertainty in his eyes.

"Something wrong, Sir."

I didn't answer, knowing my reaction wasn't as he'd expected, but unsure how to press home the advantage.

"Perhaps you should worry about your friends rather than trying to disorient me with your glare." His index finger tapped at the pages in front of me. Was that a hint of concern as well as disapproval I saw from his expression?

I knew my friends were suffering and didn't want to look any more, knowing my new found resolve would disappear just as quickly as it had come. Then I remembered what Bagu had said about how it was the poem that had brought him here; that was the key, I was sure.

Frantically I read through the poem, but nothing came to me. Then, slowly, things began to change...

I was suddenly calm; everything around me seemed to slip out of focus as I watched the page that the poem was written on alter. My finger started to bleed and as it swirled around the paper below the two verses of the poem, to my surprise a third verse appeared. The letters took shape and the new prose had the same pull over me as the first two verses, but I could see the answer was here. I smiled as I began to read.

Tis hope that grips your heart my love
To lighten up and free your mind
And now that you have faced down your fears
The spell is broken: Bugaboo out!

Nothing happened at first, Bagu was staring at me perplexed; then he began to scream. It was a high-pitched sound, so loud I had to cover my ears, for fear my eardrums would split.

"What have you done?" He was furious and tried to make a grab at me, I had to throw myself backwards to try and avoid him. He was quick though and seized my wrist in an iron like grip. For the first time, I noticed terror in his eyes and felt a vicious sense of satisfaction.

"Let me go," I shouted. This time he flinched, dropping my hand instantly. There was a moment more when our eyes met before there was a blinding flash and I felt pulled back at great speed before falling into unconsciousness.

Chapter 8: Return

1

We now sat at the breakfast table in silence. We had each relayed our stories in every detail earlier in hushed tones, not wanting to be overheard by anyone else. We were all still confused, looking around the hotel not quite believing we were back from whatever alternative universe we had been sent to.

I thought that when I had woken up that morning, drenched in sweat, it had all been some horrible nightmare, to be forgotten about as soon as it was possible. Then I had sat up and seen the book at the bottom of my bed and knew instinctively it hadn't.

Reaching across I gingerly picked it up and opened it; all the pages were blank. Turning back to the cover the lettering was still there, but now much fainter.

Remembering my friends, I'd then thrown the book down and knocked on each door in turn and was greeted by familiar faces which were now haunted with doubt and uncertainty.

Talking about it had helped, but there had been no humour or laughter from anyone.

"I just don't get it, Sam, it seemed so real." Steve was absentmindedly stirring his coffee whilst making his comment.

"That's because it bloody well was," Scott said angrily, as he stood up knocking over his chair and storming out of the room.

Neil got up to get him and I held his arm. "Leave him for now, he'll cool down." Reluctantly, he sat back down.

"I don't know about you lot but I just want to go home."

Phil, who looked decidedly pale got up and made to leave.

I was losing them. My friends had been changed by the experience and we now seemed like strangers. Bagu was going to have the last laugh after all.

"Wait," I raised my voice just enough to grab everyone's attention. "Neil, go and get Scott."

As he hurried off I thought about what I was going to say. It was clear now that each of them had had their worst fears realised, their bugaboo if you like and it had scarred them deeply. This is what Bagu had fed from: people's fears. Now it had to stop.

As they all sat down again I looked at them all individually, my friends were still there but frightened.

"Firstly, I want to apologise for bringing that book here." I almost spat the words out. My friends just mumbled and nodded, like automatons obeying a command.

"I can see it affected you deeply, but we got out of it and do you know how?" Blank faces looked back at me. This was going to be difficult.

"Hope." There was no change in their expressions. "When I faced Bagu for the final time he became frightened of me."

Steve was the first one I saw a stirring of understanding.

"If you don't have any hope then fear will wash through and claim you." I needed to hammer the point home. "My greatest fear was to lose you and I nearly did." I was surprised to have tears suddenly spring up in my eyes. "But I had to have hope and that's what brought me, and the rest of you, back from the brink."

There was silence for what seemed an age. Then Neil stood up, that twinkle in his eyes now returning. "That was a very fine speech, now can we eat breakfast – I'm starving." Everyone laughed at that.

2

The maid found the book when she was cleaning the room, stuffed under one of the pillows. At first, she was disappointed that it wasn't money but then turned over a few of the pages. It had a repulsive, dead skin feel to it and was ancient looking. One particular poem caught her eye; it was called "Bugaboo." It held her spellbound as she began to read it out loud.

Gossamer Ghost

By Jessie Hobson

On fragile faery wings it flew
The dainty woodland moth
So blithe and carefree spirited
No thought of pending wrath.

It skittered to and fro at ease
A light and dancing sight
In sunshine, then through shaded trees
Which trapped fragmented light.

Perchance the moth would featly pass
All danger in its flight
But dappled dusk deceived the eye
And hid the deadly fright.

Along a gnarled and knobbled branch
A silent figure lay
With eyes of jet, its muscles tensed
To spring upon its prey.

The filaments of woven gold
That earlier were spun
Invisibly would terrorise
The creature of the sun.

An awesome movement of the mesh
Sent shock-waves through the air.
The scurry of the enemy
Arachnid now aware.

The lissome insect on the wing
Was coming near its fate
Too close for comfort by the net
No rescue now, too late.

No sense of danger as it swooped
In deeper gloom enclosed
The silken threads ensnared the sylph
The snapping web exposed.

At last the victor could advance
Towards the struggling wraith
Embracing with a venom shot
Encompassing its death.

The time so brief twixt life and death
Too numb to even feel
The spider parcel-wrap the corpse
And then commence her meal.

What Justice?

By David Shaer

Chapter 1

My wife is mad.

I am not being derogatory because she really is mentally unstable.

When we got married, nearly sixteen years ago, she was a sweet eccentric whom I found vivacious, fun and actually quite pretty. We shared everything and loved each other dearly. Sure, there were little things, which each of us found niggling in the other but that, I am assured, was perfectly normal.

She found my inability to put away my suit, albeit neatly hung on a clothes hanger, into the wardrobe until the following morning untidy and irritating. I always maintained it was my way of letting my suit breathe, after I had worn it for a day in the City, before closing it away in a concealed place.

By comparison, I found her insistence that tea cup handles pointed to the left in cupboards, whereas coffee cup handles pointed to the right, was petty and illogical but if those were the only things that wound us up, life was easy and stress free.

Money was another issue, but isn't it with everybody? We never had enough but one day our years of training for better jobs would pay off and we would be able to look back on the years of very mild financial stress as part of growing up.

We had holidays, never extravagant, but always relaxing and enjoyable. Getting home afterwards with barely enough money to be able to get through the Dartford Tunnel was always a challenge, to the extent where it actually became a fun target. I never actually told my wife, Sally, that, one year, I had left a pound coin in the car at the airport, just in case, and possibly that marked the beginning of deceit, the source of our downfall.

Our problems started a mere two years after we got married. I was studying hard to qualify and sometimes found it easier to do so at my office desk, rather than in our small flat, where Sally liked to relax with her television. I know that I was often late but rarely more than an hour or two.

One night I got home early, nursing a stonking headache, and the flat was empty. Sally came in about twenty minutes after me, agitated and short tempered but I couldn't find out about what. To be honest, I really wanted simply to lie down and shake off my headache. Sally's attitude was strange in that she didn't want to eat, drink or talk – she just wanted to watch some fairly inane television program that I had never seen her watch before. Whatever was upsetting her was going to be held close to her chest.

I tried for about ten minutes to understand and help but eventually her mood was beginning to rub off on me, so I gave up and retreated to bed, alone.

Next morning, when I woke up, Sally's side of the bed was empty and had not been used. My headache had eased, so I leapt out of bed to make coffee and find Sally. Nothing. No explanation, no sign, no note.

As I could feel my headache coming back with a vengeance, I decided to retreat to bed again and rang the office. It was far too early and nobody was in. I would try again later.

Three hours later, I woke up with what I subsequently discovered was my first migraine. Zig-zagging flashes struck havoc in my eyes, the outside light was harsh and the ticking of the grandfather clock by the "front" door (we didn't have a back door) was deafening. Its chime on the hour was enough to break me but I held on, clutching my temples and screwing my eyes up.

There were, of course, no drugs or pills anywhere, since I had never experienced anything like this before and still there was no Sally. The phone rang and with relief, I snatched it up, thinking that Sally had sorted herself out and was ringing to let me know where she was. I must have called out my greeting too loudly because the phone went dead instantly. The caller had withheld the telephone number.

I spent the day with the curtains drawn, sipping at water and feeling sick, a sensation that was to last for two more days. By day three, at last the clouds in my head lifted and I could open my piggy red eyes sufficiently to make myself breakfast, well, a slice of dry toast, and a cup of tea. If that's what migraines are about, I needed to find a cure urgently.

Suddenly, I remembered the office and worked out that I hadn't contacted them at all. I rang and got straight through to my Boss who seemed pleased to hear me.

"How's your head now, Ben?" he asked. "Nasty things, real migraines," he said.

"What?" How did he know?

"Sally rang and let me know." I wasn't aware that she knew his name, let alone his telephone number. And if she had been home and found me asleep with a migraine, why hadn't she woken me or, at least, brought me some pills or something?

"Yes, I'm sorry, Jon. I've never had one before and I certainly don't want one again. With a bit of luck, I should be back tomorrow. Sorry."

"Listen, mate. It's Friday tomorrow. Don't worry – just make sure you shake it off properly and hold back until Monday. Hope it sorts itself out quickly and we'll see you Monday. Have a good weekend," and he was gone.

Chapter 2

I sat down, confused. At least I didn't have to worry about the job or the office for a few days but where was Sally and how come she had rung the office and from where? How did she know that I had a migraine if she had not been home? And since when had I become Jon's "mate?"

And then, as suddenly as it had gone wrong, there she was, letting herself in through the "front" door. I didn't know what to expect of her but I was seriously relieved to see her.

"Christ, you look dreadful," she said, really boosting my ego. I rubbed my chin, which gave me the first clue to what she meant. A quick hand to my head told me that I hadn't washed or brushed anything and my teeth itched. She was probably right. In fact, I was still wearing the suit I had gone to work in on whatever day it was. It looked as though I had slept in it. Come to think of it, I had.

"Where have you been?" I asked. As I was about to lay into her verbally, she raised a finger to her lips and implored me to stay silent.

"Ben. I need to tell you something," she started. I could feel the room heat up instantly and I thought I had better sit down before I fell down. I sat on the arm of our sofa and waited.

"Ben. We're pregnant."

Wow. Well that certainly wasn't what I had expected. I felt the floor surging up to meet me, and the lights went out.

I don't have a clue how long I was on the floor but when I came to, I seemed to be surrounded by people, one of whom was trying to trickle a beaker of cold water into my mouth. I didn't have a clue who he was but he seemed to know what he was doing. It seemed to be working and, within minutes, I felt strong enough to sit up, stand up and talk, something that I probably hadn't done for three days or so.

I thanked the stranger for what he had done and he indicated, without talking, that it was a pleasure, that he was an off-duty paramedic and he lived in the flat next door. At that moment he suddenly stood and jumped, in one bound, across the room to where Sally was sitting on the floor, throwing up into a plastic bucket that I didn't recognise. This guy was good. He was actually quite old, which is when I realised that Sally must have dragged the poor guy round from next door so quickly that he hadn't had the chance to wake up properly and put his false teeth in. How embarrassing for him that must have been. But he didn't seem to care. Unlike Sally and I, who were in no state to criticise anybody else.

Sean, for that was his name, I found out later, commented, when he had put his teeth back in, that normally I should expect to wait for about another 9 months before I would pass out like that again but then he looked more closely at me and decided that perhaps I needed to go and lie down again. He was an alright guy and he and I would become quite close friends over the months to come.

Chapter 3

After he left, I sat down quietly, uncertain how to handle Sally. In fact, I decided that I needed to stay silent and let her do the talking, the explaining, and the grovelling.

I waited for about ten minutes, just staring at my feet. This was obviously going nowhere and my only options were either to start conversation myself or get up and leave. I had no intention of leaving so I was surprised that Sally jumped when I said, "So what's been going on? Where have you been?"

She glared at me and said nothing. The only sound was the ticking of that damned clock.

"Come on, Sally, when did you find out about the baby?"

Nothing and another long, pregnant pause. And then, suddenly, Sally stood and walked over to the kitchen. I assumed she was going to be sick again and decided to follow her.

By the time I reached the kitchen, she was coming back out towards me, brandishing in her right hand a vicious carving knife, with a menacingly long and sharp blade. My instinctive reaction was to grab her hand but I was far too slow and the knife slashed the back of my wrist. Blood spurted everywhere and I stood there, mouth open, wondering why I hadn't hit out. I clutched the back of my bleeding wrist and backed off, muttering under my breath.

Suddenly, I saw the knife being raised as Sally brought her hand up to strike again. With absolutely no hesitation, I got in before Sally's arm started to come back down and punched her in the face, jumping to my right to avoid the knife, but not quickly enough. The blade ripped into my left shoulder, tearing through my suit jacket and spraying more blood in an arc over Sally's head. I aimed my right fist back at Sally's chin but managed to hold off as I saw her knees suddenly fold and she collapsed onto the floor, sticking the knife into the floor as she fell. As she went down, her eyes rolled up and back into her head. I have never hit a woman ever before in my life but, for that instant, I was prepared to make an exception. I had done so and there, on the floor in front of me, covered in blood was my dearly beloved wife, unconscious and pregnant. What on earth had happened?

Then the lights went out again in my head.

Chapter 4

As I came to, I could hear a dull thumping in the background that was getting louder and closer. And then a voice, again in the distance but getting closer. I gradually opened my eyes and saw the "front door" on the receiving end of a good punching, accompanied by someone calling out on the other side.

Sally was still unconscious and I suppose I should have been concerned but at that precise moment my thought process was to get up and crawl my way to the door and, rather than have it smashed to pieces, open it. In what seemed to take for ever, I struggled across the floor, aware that I was leaving a trail of blood and somewhere behind me was a mad woman who wanted to kill me. I reached the door and tried to stand to reach the lock.

Behind me, I could hear movement and turned just in time to see Sally roll over on the floor. Somehow my body strength reappeared for the first time for a week and I was up on my feet and pulling at the "front door." It flew open, still being thumped and shoved from the outside. As it opened, my legs gave way again and I felt myself dropping. But I didn't reach the ground as Sean, my newfound friend and neighbour, and an unfit uniformed policeman caught me as I started to fall.

"I heard a scream and lots of thumping going on, so decided to call the police. What the hell happened?" Sean was my hero again.

"I really don't know," I started. "She lost it and just came at me with a knife. I think I need your urgent help – I've been stabbed. I think you need to be careful, though. My wife is dangerous and probably still armed." I was trying to turn round to see where she was but the two guys were blocking my view.

Sean spoke first, saying that he and the policemen would disarm her and take her to hospital immediately. The policeman disagreed, wanting to arrest us both, an idea that I found singularly attractive. That would involve waiting for back-up before anybody could move. I knew that whatever was going to happen next, it was not normal. After all, how many men discover that their wife is pregnant and trying to kill them? I thought that this was supposed to be a happy moment in one's life.

As though in direct response to my thoughts, there was another knocking at the door and Sean opened it to admit four equally unfit looking members of the local police squad. I failed to realise that they were wearing bullet-proof vests and were expecting to be under siege. Their obvious relief to see me bleeding profusely, the weapon still stuck in the floor and the perpetrator, my wife, under arrest, as was I, sort of put the whole thing in perspective, but the whole issue was far from over. One of the policemen held the door open and let in a couple of paramedics, both of whom addressed Sean as though he were their superior.

Sean, however, kept talking to me and offering his support, a sentiment that I found somewhat confusing. By the time he had mentioned it about four times, I assumed that the guy was somewhat simple and was using the expression because he had heard it used on Holby City or perhaps some other television hospital soap. However, it turned out very soon that I was the simple one and he was far more perceptive.

When Sally and I were taken in separate cars to separate places, Sally to a police station, and I, with a police guard to a hospital that was not my local, I just assumed that it was an administrative thing. But, by the following morning, I was still under police guard in a single hospital bedroom and had faced some very strange questioning. Knowing very little about the protocols of investigations, I just assumed that things were taking a long time because we were an insignificant domestic row. The treatment to both of my wounds had been efficient and quick, so why was I still in hospital being treated regally and with police protection?

You can imagine my horror when by mid-morning, I was read my rights and offered access to legal representation and then arrested, charged with a potential common assault and grievous bodily harm, pending further investigation into attempted murder and a conspiracy to commit murder. At first I assumed it was just a formality because I had punched Sally as she tried to stab me a second time. It wasn't until much later that I discovered that Sally had accused me of starting an unprovoked brutal attack on her and she had tried to fight me off as I dragged her into the kitchen still punching her and that is where she found the knife to defend herself from assault.

This was so unreal and just wasn't happening to me.

Chapter 5

My hospital treatment was over, save for the subsequent removal of thirty eight stitches, something I felt that I should note for my defence. I was led away in plastic hand restraints, with an instruction not to wriggle because they would automatically tighten. Led was not strictly true; it was more like pushed and shoved, then finally thrown into the back of a police patrol car, driven by an angry soul who had been interrupted in the middle of his lunch, a burger that was still lying on the front passenger seat half eaten and smelling repulsive. My escort was an older version of the driver and it was obvious that both of them resented my recovery from the stabbing.

By the time we reached the police station, an ugly grey building out of the 1960s that was overdue for demolition, I was pleased to think that I would be thrown in an empty cell. However, my thoughts were rapidly dispelled when I was shoved into an interview room that was a small windowless box with a tubular table and three chairs. The older angry soul and I were then left glaring at each other for about twenty minutes before the door flew open and an even angrier soul stormed in carrying various bits and plonked himself in the remaining chair.

"Thanks, Nathan," he grunted and my guardian got up and left, shutting the door behind him with as much of a bang as he could achieve with a door that had a closing mechanism. I think his day was going marginally better than mine. At least my Boss had given me the day off.

I just didn't see it coming. I was totally unprepared. Having expected the new arrival to turn on a recording machine and introduce himself, I was thinking about interviews I had seen on television as being the normal standard. The very last thing I expected was for the guy to turn round and punch me in the eye. He came at me out of nowhere and just thumped me so hard that my chair flew backwards and I was looking at the ceiling just long enough to notice that it now had a blood splattering on it – a very new one – mine. And then the back of my head hit the floor.

I think my attacker could see the stars coming out of my head because suddenly he was picking me up and dusting me down. "I think he slipped and fell against the door 'andle, Guv – p'r'aps he was passing out," he said, realising that my original guardian had re-appeared to retrieve his helmet that he had left behind.

I already knew that my guardian angel didn't like me much either, as he shrugged and walked away. My world was closing in on me.

For the next couple of hours, or so it seemed, the war of attrition started. Not a word was said. My attacker and I just sat and looked at each other. Occasionally he thought about breaking into a smile, then controlled himself. And then he suddenly rose, collected his things and walked out through the unlocked door. As he shut it, however, he locked it and left me sitting inside, unsure of what to do, what to expect.

After what seemed an eternity, but was probably only about ten minutes, I became incredibly tired and just wanted to go to sleep, which was not easy with only a chair or two and a table. I stood and shuffled around, in an attempt to stay awake and occupy my mind. Then I lay on the floor, on my back. With my knees and feet together, I raised my knees and rolled them from side to side, like I had seen cricketers doing, when waiting for an incoming batsman or the return of a lost ball. I had assumed it was through boredom but discovered rapidly that it helped one's spine and back muscles. After just a few minutes, I could feel my back muscles pulling and straining and decided that I needed to move onto the next stage, which was to stand and then touch my toes.

Any weak vertebrae would simply click back into position and leave me in screaming pain again. Which was, of course, the moment the police re-appeared.

"Right, Mr. Janson, you can go. All charges have been dropped and you can collect your things from the Desk Sergeant as you leave."

"What? How did that happen? How do I get home? Who dropped the charges? What happens next?" I was more than confused now – I was angry, very angry.

"Just go now. You can call me in the morning when even I might know some more. Here's my card. Now just go before anybody changes their mind." And with that, the brutal policeman, DC James Turnbull, according to his card, turned smartly on his heels and was gone, leaving the door of the interview room open.

Chapter 6

I was standing outside a strange police station and it was already dark and drizzling. I felt elated but still confused. I needed fresh air and I needed to walk: which was just as well because I had no money on me. I had left the flat in a bit of a hurry and had only my "front" door keys. The cold, damp night air helped blow away the cobwebs and, by the time I had walked home, which took over an hour, mainly because I was initially lost, my mind was beginning to clear. I was soaked through, but my mind was much clearer. The bruising around my eye was incredibly sore and it had already started to turn black.

Something evil and sinister was happening to me and I had no control over it. What really concerned me now was how my bitter experience had suddenly "gone away". How come suddenly all charges had been dropped without any explanation? I felt sure that any phone call I might make to DC Turnbull in the police station in the morning would reveal nothing but I wasn't going to let my battering be glossed over. I had been systematically stabbed and thumped and for someone whose most violent moment before was having my bottom slapped at birth, this was all a bit of a shock to the system.

As I let myself into the flat, I sensed immediately that something else was wrong. The debris I had left, trails of blood and a few items of upturned furniture, for example, had been cleaned up and tidied. Somebody had been in and removed all traces of the incident a day or so earlier. As I reviewed my estate, the flat looked to be pristine. Even the hole in the floor, where the knife had been stuck, had been filled and sanded over. I reckoned that whoever had dropped all charges had realised how seriously wrong they had been and were now trying to make amends.

And then, as if to prove the point, the bedroom door opened slowly and a beautifully manicured hand slid slowly around the door and beckoned me. The long, slim arm behind it was lightly tanned and very persuasive. As I approached the beckoning hand, I could smell expensive perfume, not one that I knew, and my intrigue grew higher. A silky sleeve slid down the tanned arm and still the hand implored me to advance.

Typically, for a man, my thoughts were controlling my body and I approached the door, probably more slowly than I would have expected, so perhaps I had my sensible head on after all.

The hand stopped and I recognised one of the rings on the fourth finger. It was the one I had bought Sally on our last holiday in Florida and she had lost it almost as soon as we had arrived home. The perfume smell and the nail varnish were alien to me, but the ring was definitely Sally's. I stood still, not knowing how to react. I didn't have very long to wait as a second beautifully manicured hand rounded the door but this one was offering a glass of slowly sparkling champagne. At least both hands were visible and there were no armaments on display. I stepped forward around the door and there, standing scantily clad in a very revealing and short silky dark brown nightdress was, not Sally, but her younger sister, Penny.

"What on earth?" I exclaimed. "What are you doing here? And why the seduction kit?" I asked Penny, totally confused.

"Ben," she smiled. God how I loved that smile, and she knew it. "Sally told me everything and now that she's moved in with me, I just knew that you would need some company and help."

"Help? Yes, of course I need help but what are you doing? What's the idea? You know Sally would kill me if she could see me now. She probably wouldn't thank you too much either. What are you trying to do? I'm your brother-in-law!"

"And when has that ever stopped me?" she asked. "Look, Sally's packed her bags and has gone. Her last words were that she was going to visit Aunt Noreen in Dublin until the dust settles. Then she'll think about what she does next. In the meantime, I couldn't stop thinking about you and what she had done to you. Or what she said she had done to you and I just had to come and see for myself. I can't believe that she's been such a bitch. Come here and let me look at you."

Even as she said it, she pulled me towards her and started to unbutton me. First my jacket, then she started to pull off my tie and then she began to unbutton my shirt. I realised that she was becoming frenzied and suddenly I was lying on the bed, totally naked, apart from my socks and shoes and a stupid grin.

"Oh, Penny," I groaned. "This is all wrong. Sally could walk through the door any second and we'd both be dead."

"Yes, I know," she said, undoing my laces and slipping off my last trace of clothing, giggling as she did so. Her hands slithered up my legs and she came and stood over me, letting the edge of her nightdress glide across my body. It was all too much for me and I simply slid my hand under the dark brown silk.

Suddenly we were groaning, moaning, wrestling and dragging each other all over the bed. For years I had noticed Penny's invading beauty and often wondered about her single, independent status but, now, tonight this was totally different. The rest of the world didn't matter anymore and we crushed each other with lust, passion and uncontrollable drive.

For more than twenty-five minutes, we fought, penetrated, conceded to each other with complete heartfelt and physical devotion. Nothing could separate us until, finally, totally exhausted and ultimately satisfied, we separated and rolled apart, completely spent. We rolled back into each other's arms and entwined limbs in total calm comfort.

Speech did not come easy as we both knew that we had done something seriously wrong but how could something so beautiful be so wrong? After struggling with my thoughts and thinking back to the frenzied attacks with which both sisters had surprised me, I eventually struggled to sit up and turn towards Penny.

"Penny," I started, "That was the most beautiful experience of my life but..." She put her forefinger on my lips and stopped me in mid-flow.

"That, Ben, was something just between us. A present from me. Ever since I first saw you, I have always wanted to do that and now I am so glad that my wish has come true. But it is something that must stay just between us. It was so good that we must never try it again because anything less would be such a disappointment. For the rest of our lives, we can always savour that moment and know that nothing else will ever match it." And with that she got up and started to walk towards the bedroom door.

Just before she reached it to walk out on an experience that I had never even contemplated – she had always been my wife's celibate, sweet, little sister – a sound outside stopped her in her tracks. A key was being inserted into the front door lock.

Penny gently shut the bedroom door and turned instantly and walked past me, scooping up her clothes from the chair by the side of the bed – I hadn't even noticed them before, so occupied had I been with our activities – and swept into the bathroom, locking the door as if it came second nature to her. There was no trace of her visible anywhere, she had even taken her half drunk glass of champagne with her. But the lingering odour of her invasive perfume was everywhere. Not even I could miss that.

With strength that I didn't know I could muster up, I leapt out of bed and jumped into my boxers and suit trousers as I slid across to the dressing table and started to rummage through drawers in the hope of finding something that I could counter the intoxicating smell of perfume. Nothing. Most of the drawers had been emptied and I was just about ready to throw up with fear when I heard the bathroom door unlock, open at the same moment as a can of something was rolled out on the floor and then the door shut and clicked again instantly.

I looked down at a can of fly spray rolling across the bedroom floor towards me and realised how naïve my view of Penny had been. She was good, very, very good and had probably done this sort of thing before, often. Sweet little sister, my Aunt Mary!

I grabbed the can, ripped the lid off and had started to spray randomly as the bedroom door started to open slowly. Standing there, silhouetted in the lights from the lounge, stood Sally.

"God, this room smells like a Chinese brothel," she said, without hesitation, and turned away. "Go and have a bloody shower. You stink."

"Ah, she's feeling better," I thought, "usual terms of endearment." I stepped out of the bedroom, shutting the door behind me, something I rarely did before and wondered if Sally would notice. She was already sitting in one of the armchairs, looking at me with disgust written all over her face.

"You're still wearing that bloody suit," she proffered, maintaining her level of charm.

"The birthday suit with the bloody and ripped arm where you stabbed me," I thought but said nothing.

"Look, Sally," I started.

"Shut up and listen," she snapped back at me. "I have decided that I'm going to forgive and forget and we are going to have this baby and become a normal couple. Now there will be some dramatic changes and you will have to toe the line considerably more than you have done, but I'm prepared to give us another chance. Don't speak, just listen." She had noticed that my jaw had dropped open in complete amazement.

"I am staying at Penny's but don't try to contact me there because I won't be there until you've tidied and cleaned up this place and then I might consider moving back in with you. But there will be some changes, the first of which is that I shall use the bed and you can sleep somewhere else. Do I make myself clear?"

She stood up and was already opening that bloody "front" door before I had even shut my mouth, let alone thought of anything to say.

"Two weeks and I'll be back to inspect," she finished as she walked out and slammed the door.

"Yessir!" I saluted at the back of the door, and stood there with enraged silence. What the hell was she talking about? Forgive and forget? She'd tried to kill me and very nearly succeeded. She'd had me charged, banged up in a police station and beaten. And *she* was prepared to forgive and forget *me*. I was steaming but suddenly felt drained and useless. I sunk to my knees and would probably have burst into tears, had not a pair of strong hands grasped my shoulders from behind and started to massage.

"What a total bitch," said Penny. I had almost forgotten she was still there but only for a second. She slid her arms around my waist and somehow we stood up and hugged. I so wanted to cry but, from somewhere, this sweet little sister had generated strength and determination.

"You won't believe this," I said, "but staying away from you is going to be much harder than living with Sally. Whatever happens to me from hereon in, I shall never, ever forget today and what we just shared."

Penny laughed and said, "I doubt it very much. You'll just look back on it in years to come as a moment of unbelievable madness with that insane little sister-in-law and you'll be so ashamed that you won't even want to tell your mates in a pub."

I turned her towards me and approached her sweet lips.

"Whatever I do for the rest of my days, I most certainly will never view that moment as anything other than total perfection, total beauty and the ultimate ecstasy. I shall never think anything less about either that experience or you and would certainly never talk about it to anyone. It is our sacred secret and I just hope that one day we can not only talk about it with love and affection but we could do it all over again, albeit under different circumstances." And I kissed her. Tentatively at first, but eventually with deep and genuine passion. We finally forced ourselves apart and gazed at each other with total understanding. Of course, she was right, but secretly I think we both hoped that one day we would prove her wrong.

The comment about the shower seemed good but my invitation to join me received Penny's determined refusal because she knew that she needed to go home and try to handle her sister, unless, of course, she really had gone to Dublin and her return was just to check up on me and issue her ultimatum.

Penny then glided towards the door before I could even thank her for everything, including cleaning up the flat. As she walked out she turned back, winked at me and touched the side of her nose with her forefinger. Our secret.

Chapter 7

My life had virtually ended at that point and I started the existence of an alien.

I passed my exams and we sold the flat and bought a much more appropriate semi-detached three bedroomed house with a small garden. It was still close to where we had been but Sally had now moved into her own bedroom and we rarely touched, and certainly never slept together again.

Penny had found a new job and had moved away but still sent me the odd text message, always during the day when I had my phone on me, never when it might be within the grasp of Sally. She never, of course, mentioned directly our secret but, occasionally, I lapsed into a moment of devious complexity and tried to reintroduce the thought in my responses.

Sally began to grow larger and we even started to plan life around three of us, Sally, me and the baby. My job took on new responsibilities, some of which involved my being away from home. Sally didn't mind about those trips and, in fact, seemed to encourage them in the early months of her pregnancy. But as the day of the arrival grew nearer, she became far more removed, tetchy and aggressive, traits which I sort of understood, I thought.

Jon, my boss, always asked how we were and asked to be remembered to Sally, on almost a daily basis as the day drew close.

I planned to take off the week of the expected birth but, at the very last moment, Jon called me into his office just before I was about to clear my desk and started a strange conversation.

"I know that this appears to be totally out of order and I wouldn't normally dream of doing this but that project you've been working on for the last five months has suddenly changed. Our client has been approached by one of their biggest competitors in a takeover bid, which normally would be something I might handle myself. But it appears that both companies have been tendering for the same enormous contract and this could be a complete con-trick to ensure that we don't get the contract and lose out on the takeover too. I offered but they have specifically asked that you go there, Aberdeen, next week and try to dig up some dirt to prove it. It all sounds as though the timing is far too coincidental and you know both the market and our side of the business more than anybody else."

I had to admit that this pharmaceutical contract was critical for the survival of our client, being worth roughly half of their existing turnover if they won the contract at only a small proportion of cost through pure synergy that they were already geared up to handle. Not winning the contract would involve having considerable excess capacity and would probably have to involve a material downsize in operations, costs and, inevitably, staff. Jon was right, I knew the market better than anybody, including the management of our client. I had been involved in most of the negotiations to date and knew that there was some competition but none that really lived up to our ability to produce the required goods. This was indeed a crisis and nobody was better suited to go there than I. Jon said that he was more than grateful for my understanding and thought I should take the rest of the afternoon off to prepare for the trip and also to talk to Sally.

Expecting to be screamed and shouted at for such a weak, thoughtless and inconsiderate response to his suggestion, I went home, fearing the worst. However, as I explained it all to Sally, she surprised me totally, agreeing that my input was vital and that the arrival of the first baby was rarely on time so the week would not really be a problem. Besides which, she was fully ready and her parents were already on standby if the baby started early. I was stunned but relieved and started to pack. I had nearly finished when my mobile phone buzzed and I grabbed it, half hoping it might be Penny. There were two text messages and the first one said *"Need to speak urgently next week – ring"* with the suffix of *"From JP"*, Jenny's ID. The second message simply said *"Done xx"* and I deleted both before I realised that the second message could not have been from Penny because we never put 'x's and there was no *"From JP"*; obviously just message to a wrong number, which would never reach its intended destination.

Penny and I hadn't talked in months and I felt a sudden movement of thrill at her level of urgency. Packing seemed to take far less time than normal and within quarter of an hour, I was on my way to the station to start my journey. The only flight available was from London Cityport, which to me was brilliant because it was still like a personal service, rather than the cattletruck treatment at any other London Airport.

As soon as I reached the station I rang Penny's mobile and she answered immediately.

"I can't talk right now," she said, "I'm in a meeting but I'll call you tomorrow and we must meet. I'll find somewhere special," she said and was gone. Something was obviously wrong but any further attempts to call her were thwarted as she had obviously set her phone onto 'divert.' The best I could do was to text her with "In Aberdeen."

"I know," came her surprising response.

By the time I had landed and started to look for a car to hire, the Managing Director of our client came striding across the airport arrivals floor to greet me.

"Ben, laddie. It's great to see you," he said, almost shaking my arm off with his fierce handshake. "You will na need a car — you can take mine," and he tossed me a set of keys. "But first we need to talk. We're away to the Silver Darling Restaurant. I trust you love the best seafood. You can drive though, I need to talk and I think it could be safer if you were just listening." Graeme Patterson was a big man, a presence who filled a doorway as he passed through it. Nobody ever really argued with him, although he had never met Sally. He was the epitome of the gentle giant and still in his late thirties. It turned out that he and I had been born on the same day but we were two totally different characters. He knew what he wanted and got it. I eventually worked out what I wanted, just after it had sold out. On that basis alone, he got everything roughly right whilst I got it precisely wrong. And yet we got on so well because of that very combination.

But this turn of events was not going according to plan. The deal of his life seemed to be doomed and neither of us liked that.

The car was immediately outside the terminal building and came as another shock. It was an old Volvo Estate with battered wings and not very clean. It was not his usual Mercedes Convertible, which came as something of a disappointment.

"Look, laddie," Graeme offered immediately. "We are taking this car for a reason. All I can say is that it will be safer than the Mercedes."

Suddenly, my thoughts wandered to an earlier text message and I wondered if this was connected in any way to Penny's urgency. "Just give me a couple of minutes first, Graeme," I said. I need to make an urgent phone call."

"Nae problem," he said, "although there is a car phone in the Volvo."

"That's very kind," I said, "but this is just a bit private. I should talk to my wife, please."

"Of course. Jon told me. I hope everything is fine."

I wondered what Jon had told him? I suppose all he needed to say was that Sally was very pregnant but somehow, I felt he may have said more. I slipped back into the terminal and rang Penny.

She answered immediately, obviously waiting for me to call.

"Oh, good, you made it safely."

"Did you think I wouldn't?" I asked.

"Let's just say that you need to watch Jon. I think he's up to something and I wouldn't trust him. I spoke to Sally yesterday for about ten minutes on the phone and she mentioned his name more often than she mentioned yours. I know that you're in Aberdeen and that Jon insisted you went there. What Sally also said was that Jon also had some different business up there and she was surprised that Jon hadn't gone himself. She seemed to know a great deal about Jon and I thought I should tell you. It seemed strange."

"Yes, thanks, you're right. Jon has been doing something else recently I didn't know about and he has had a lot of whispered phone calls. It's certainly not like him to be so secretive but I have wondered recently. I'll certainly watch my back and thanks. Hey, Penny, I want to see you. I miss you and I need to talk to you."

"Now just listen here, Ben. Rules is rules. One day we'll meet again somewhere but we agreed that that was our moment. We both know that it will never happen again in this life. So please don't even think about it. Now change the subject before I do. Please."

The use of the word "please" gave me a warm glow. Twice.

"OK, Penny. But just keep that thought, forever. Right, change – any news on your sister? No, OK. How are you and where are you?"

"I'm actually at Heathrow and about to board a flight to Edinburgh so I won't be too far away but I don't like not being close to Sally. She is acting strange and keeps calling me. I know it's nearly her time but she's never been this close before and I get the impression it's not because it's her first birth. I think that she is having doubts about what happened recently – I mean your being charged and all that. I get the feeling she is not telling either of us the whole truth about that episode. What's she been like at home?"

"I'm probably the last person to ask. She sleeps alone and rarely tells me anything," I said. "She's aloof and treats me like shit. No matter what I do, it's always wrong and, quite frankly, if she is up to something, the sooner she does something about it, the better. There – I've said it now. It's been getting at me for months now. I can't do anything right. My God, I've done everything possible to help prepare for this baby from changing houses to decorating throughout, working my socks off and generally doing absolutely everything required of me. The whole episode has turned sour from the day she announced she was pregnant and I sometimes think it would have been better if her knife attack had been successful. She could have sorted it all out on her own then and it would have been perfect.

"Penny, I'm sorry. I didn't mean to sound off like that but sometimes it just gets to me and being up here has brought it all to a head. Please forgive me."

A long silence followed and then Penny almost whispered, "Ben, we'll sort it. You and I will somehow, together, sort it. Just hang on in there, Big Boy, and we'll sort it." And then she hung up, leaving me staring at my mobile as though it was about to talk to me itself.

I wandered back outside and found Graeme having words with a couple of aggressive meter wardens. "It's alright, she's not dead but it was touch and go. I've spoken to the paramedics directly and they think she'll pull through," I said, putting my arm round his shoulders. "Just hang on in there, Big Boy, and we'll sort it. We'll get there as quickly as we can. There'll be a police escort joining us at the motorway. Sorry, gents, is there a problem?"

The two wardens muttered something embarrassed and waved us off. I opened the driver's door and leant across to let Graeme in. As I kangaroo hopped across the forecourt, Graeme turned to me and winked.

"That was a bit over the top, laddie. But thanks anyway. I dinna have a clue where you're gonna find a motorway here but let's go east. The restaurant overlooks the harbour and the bay. Pocra Quay, North Pier, here we come," and off we went, with Graeme giving directions and me pushing the pedals.

I had to admit that not only did the view live up to expectations, the restaurant being right bang on the Aberdeen Harbour entrance but the food was exquisite. Afterwards, we went up on the conservatory level and watched the twinkling lights on the beach and the coastline. If it weren't for the importance of the occasion, we could have stayed there for all of the night but the matter in hand had to be paramount.

As we sat back and sampled some of the best malts I have ever tried, Graeme began to outline the issue and the more he revealed, the more I became troubled. The competitor for the contract, who was also the potential buyer of Graeme's company, was not a name I knew well. They were Swedish and appeared to be private. The structure was peculiar and it looked as though about ten wealthy entrepreneurs were funding the attack. One of them was an English property guru, whom I knew by only reputation. He was an untrustworthy man who had made his money as an estate agent, probably by ripping off clients by buying their properties below market rate and then selling them on to third parties who were already dealing in the first place, an old, unpleasant trick of the trade.

I listened to all of the details, the parties, the individual names, the deals and suddenly fell upon a name I knew. The Finance Director of the company, with whom the contract was due to be signed, was an Alan Kordowski, an old friend of mine from my auditing days more than ten years earlier. He had gone to a large fisheries group when we last knew each other. The group had been based in Immingham but had outgrown its facilities and moved to Aberdeen. It was about then that I had lost touch with Kordowski but that was about to change. I had assumed that he had not moved and had probably headed back down south. First thing in the morning, I would find out.

Suddenly the lights of Aberdeen mattered no more and I persuaded Graeme to pack up our evening session and we headed for his home and my hotel.

Chapter 8

By 6:30 in the morning, I was ready to face the world and was on my way over to Graeme's house when my mobile phone rang. Sally. I had forgotten about Sally and not even spoken to her the night before. As I pulled over to answer my phone, I saw that it was Penny.

"What's wrong?" I asked.

"Good morning to you too," she giggled. "How are you, Penny? I'm alright, thanks, Ben and thanks for asking. What about you?"

"Oh, Penny, I'm sorry again. I'm not very good at this, am I?"

"It's just a good job that we're *not* having an affair – you would be useless!"

"At what?" I responded, trying to get back into the mode.

"Well, we'll have to find out, won't we?" she goaded. "But before we do anything, I may have something of use to you. I know you won't believe this but guess who was on my flight to Edinburgh last night? It may not be relevant at all but you never know. Jon bloody Walters, your boss, that's who. Now wasn't he unable to go to sort out your problem? Seems strange that he could be less than an hour or so away from Aberdeen, though!"

I let that pass because that wasn't quite the way Jon had explained things but what he had said had certainly seemed odd, particularly if he was just around the corner.

"Thanks, Pen, that's brill!"

"Penny to you," she replied, "before I make you call me Penelope."

"Ooh – I could like that, Lady Penelope," I said, mockingly.

"Bugger off, Perv," she retorted, but still with a little giggle.

"Look, Lady P, I've got some serious business to attend to shortly but I'll get back to you as soon as I can. Are you going to be ultra busy today?"

"Always am, darling," she replied, "but always find time to talk to you, Lover Boy."

I dropped my phone and struggled around on the floor of the car trying to find it. By the time I had battled my way through the apple cores and mountains of mislaid car park pass tickets, Penny had either rung off or dropped her phone too.

Graeme had given me Alan Kordowski's office telephone number and since it was nearly 7:00 a.m., what better than to surprise him with a mysterious voicemail message? I was slightly miffed though when he picked up on the first ring.

"Kordowski," came his charismatic response.

"Still as friendly as bollocks then," I answered.

"Ben Bloody Janson! Where the hell have you been?"

"Oh, everywhere and nowhere. Up and down. In and out – although more of the latter recently. Got time for a cuppa, old buddy?"

"We're not in the City now, Ben. I'm up in Aberdeen."

"Funny that, so am I. Perhaps that is how I got your telephone number. Now have you got time for a cuppa?"

"Of course, but it may have to be a bit quick – I'm a bit busy at the moment. When can you get here?"

"About three minutes? Or have you got a woman in there? Should I make it five?"

"Sod off, Janson. You know that was all ugly rumour. I've never had a cleaning lady in my life and that includes two wives."

"What? You've had two wives since we last met? Was either of them yours? That would have been a first!"

Alan was a very old buddy and we went back an amazingly long way. We were both surprised that we managed to stay employed as long as we had done, particularly when we had worked on audits away from home. We had both been serial adulterers but only when we were between wives, sometimes our own.

As I walked into his office block, I glanced at myself in the mirror in reception and realised that I had gone completely grey since I had last seen Alan. The doors to the first lift opened and out stepped this completely bald man whom I had not seen since his hair was long, wavy and blond. He had wisely shed a few pounds but I was eating for two, or so it seemed. We clasped hands, shook and finally hugged. We had a lot in common but would never have enough time to talk about it. We had done some amazing things together over a life long period, in particular between the ages of eighteen and twenty eight which had been the years when everybody else had been studying hard. For us, these were very important years, far too important to be spent studying. They were more reserved for gaining experience.

We sat down and both looked at our watches. "Thirty minutes?" asked Alan.

"Forty?" I asked.

"Thirty five it is then," we both agreed and shook hands again.

"One question each to start and one to finish then?" Same old rules as every other time we had met.

"You first," said Alan, ever the gentleman.

"What happened to that red-head who was the oldest daughter of the guy who owned the last B&B in Stratford-upon-Avon? Pippa, I think." I thought he would probably end up with her.

"Her old man died after we finished our audit and she took over. Bitch wouldn't let us stay there the following year, especially when she found out that I was in charge of the audit!" Alan had never been lucky with red-heads.

"Ah! So there is a God after all!"

"My turn now. What happened to that Caroline girl you were seeing then? You were due to get married at the end of the audit and she was getting miffed because you were going home to get married." Alan had an amazing memory.

"Now she was something else. She became a professional stalker and would have come on honeymoon with us, had the marriage gone ahead. Fortunately, my wife to be woke up on the morning of the wedding and bottled out. It seems she had been seeing somebody else while I was working in Stratford and decided that he was much more of a man than I. So I missed out on both of them."

"Which sort of proves that not only is there a God but she's a woman!"

"OK," I said. "First round, seconds out!"

Alan started. "So what have you been up to since we last met?"

"Eventually qualified and moved around in the profession to gain experience. I now specialise in Corporate Restructures, which is sort of where I am at now. Nothing else wildly exciting, except that I did eventually get married and any minute now I am going to become a dad for the first time. What about you?"

"Well, as you know," started Alan, "I left the profession and got a proper job. None of this recommending until you are blue in the face, I decided to go into commerce and the last time we met I was FD of that fisheries conglomerate based in Immingham. But then we moved up here and I decided not to stay. Moved into Pharmaceuticals up here and have never looked back, until now. I've got an ethical problem here and might need to run something past you to ask your view, if you wouldn't mind."

Ah! Now that was interesting. A trade off? "Go on," I said.

"Well I'm not sure yet but there's a very big contract out there and two companies are trying to win it. The first is our regular supplier but the second is a new boy on the block. In fact they're from Sweden and, as far as I can see, know nothing about the business at all. But they have put together a package and some of our guys seem to think it is good. There is a complication. They have made a bid for the other competitor and if that other competitor fails to get the contract, their share price will collapse. I have already heard that the Swedes will drop out very soon from the takeover bid which will obviously cause our current supplier's share price to collapse. Some of our guys here will then recommend that the new supplier, the Swedes, get the deal and at that point, the new suppliers will be able to rebid at a very low price for the British firm. The Swedes will then have the new contract and all of the old contractor's business for a song and the current contractors will not only lose out but we will have lost our genuine supplier.

"My trouble is that I don't trust the Financial Advisers to the Swedes. Something odd is going on and I get the impression that something underhand is being done here and they are trying to force our current suppliers out of business. Have you got any ideas?"

I sat there in silence trying to work out if I could crack this for Alan, without landing me, my firm or Alan in the pooh. I came to the conclusion that I couldn't and somebody was going to suffer.

"It might help if I knew some of the players in the Swedes team because I might be able to cut them off at worst or shop them at best. The whole deal sounds appalling to me." I couldn't let Alan know that I was "related to" the current suppliers, although I was disappointed that he didn't already know. Perhaps he did and was testing me.

"The current suppliers are represented by a London firm called Pierson Walters but the strange thing is that the Swedes are also using a London firm, but one I don't know, called SalMarg Jensen. I can't seem to find anything on them. Do you know them? The strange thing is that the guy who has been representing SalMarg Jensen has the name Walters – Jon Walters. The trouble is that no-one has ever seen him. I wonder if you have heard of him."

My heart bounced and, for a moment I thought I was going to be sick.

"Shit," I said. "Shit."

"What on earth is the matter?" said Alan. "You look like you've seen a ghost."

"That's because I probably have. I have a real problem here and I need to discuss this with someone before you and I get any older. The Procurate Fiscal would be good but I think this will tread on other toes too." I sat there in silence again.

"Ben, I need your help on this. The whole thing sucks and my gut feel says I should recommend that we go for status quo and avoid all the rest of the shit. But that is going to piss off some of the powers that be. Help me here, old buddy, I don't know how to get out of this."

Conflict of interest hit me between the eyes. Whatever I said next was going to incriminate somebody and even any experience I may have gained throughout my life was not going to help here.

So, in the turmoil that was already bubbling through my head from matters personal, I decided to try the low key approach.

"Alan. We have known each other a very long time. We have been through all sorts of crap, most of it good crap. But this is different. I realise that you have a mega dilemma here but, actually, so do I. The next five minutes in our lives is going to be awesome and outrageous. But, before it starts, I need to ask you something that will require a totally honest answer. Ready?"

"Shit, man. Now you're really scaring me. Go on then, hit me."

"Alan. Can we have the next five minutes totally off the record? It is critical."

"Before I answer, I get the feeling that you mean this, and it's not a joke – you know, one of our old wind up gags that we used to play against each other. I'm right, aren't I? This is no joke?"

"Alan, I have never been more serious in my entire life. Off the record or nothing."

"OK, then. Off the record. Nobody is in the office yet and there is no technical wizardry anywhere. Come on then."

"I think we have come across a major fraud issue here. I think there is something so suspicious going on that you and I have to stop. But the moment we try to do so, I think we are both in seriously deep shit. So before I start, now do you see what I mean about off the record? From what I have experienced so far, lives could be at risk – almost certainly yours and mine when we go on the record. We have got to be totally straight with each other – and I mean totally."

"Alright – you've scared the shit out of me so go for it. Off the record." Alan looked really worried and I had not seen that face since we discovered an audit fraud together once as juniors and we struggled with our consciences for days before we had the confidence to tell somebody else.

"I think that Jon Walters is pulling a seriously fast one here. He is playing on both sides and it looks to me as though he is setting this all up to destroy your current supplier. He is my boss at Pierson Walters and I have to confess that he has seen most of the papers throughout the whole deal. I've worked with him for years now but something strange is going on. He has been softening me up for something but I hardly think that losing my job along with a few colleagues is what this is about. It sort of fits in because he virtually ordered me to be here this week because he had something big on at home and now I have found out that he arrived in Edinburgh last night. So he is closing in for the kill. I'm sorry, old buddy, but you are in the middle of this and I now think that I am too. The trouble is that nobody else will pick this up until it's too late and contracts have been signed – and I bet his signature won't be on either of them."

I paused for breath, trying to collect my mind, in case I had missed anything out.

"Hang on," said Alan getting out of his chair. He paced up and down for a few seconds then came back and took a key out of his pocket. He used it to unlock a drawer in his desk and retrieved a thin unmarked file. "We used to call this the '*Not to be shown to the Auditors*' file in our days, remember?"

He opened it and showed me a few transcripts of telephone calls, all in his own illegible hand written notes.

> *"I had a feeling Walters knew more than he should. We have spoken several times on the phone and on a couple of occasions he said things that I thought he should not have known about. Some of the drugs we currently get come not from China, as would normally be expected but specifically from the Philippines, Manila. He knew about that but I couldn't see how. I think he also had details of the last shipment, as though he was reading from the ship's manifest. He even knew the order of loading, which was odd because our supplier had to break a container for customs clearance and we needed part of the consignment urgently – so it had been shipped separately by*

*air for the last leg to the UK. He knew all about that because
he was talking about it as though it was routine and this was
the only time it had ever happened."*

Alan began to open up to me. "I had always thought that, for a
Financial Consultant, he knew far too much about the operating
detail and he certainly couldn't have got that from his Swedish
colleagues.

"Look, I have done a lot of work on this Swedish outfit but it
has been bloody nigh on impossible. They have no track record. It
is virtually impossible to trace where their funding comes from.
The individuals funding them all seem to have gaps in their
history. I reckon that a lot of it doesn't exist; it isn't there; it's
wishful thinking. They have no street cred, no record, no 'audit
trail', to put it bluntly. I have been totally against it from the start
but one or two big names here have been pushing for the Swedish
deal and I think you've hit it. There must be some serious back-
handing going on somewhere. I reckon they're a load of rogues,
but I couldn't prove it though it looks like you've come up with
the link – Jon Walters."

He then closed his file slowly and leant back in his chair,
stretching with both his hands behind his head.

"Shit. Now what?" we both said, just like the old team.

I sat there even more confused now. If we were right, and I
was sure we were, the deal had to be stopped. We had to go for
outside help quickly and appropriately. We needed access to top
quality professionals without any red-tape delays. We needed
back door entrances to fly open for us.

"I can stop the deal briefly," said Alan. "Our lawyers have
already expressed doubts over the wording of the contract
because the Swedes have asked for it to be changed slightly so that
one of their guarantors is happier. It would be easy to say that that
might be critical and show-stopping because it actually could be.
Contractual issues are always a good way of holding things up. But

what we need is much more difficult – someone seriously high in the Fraud Office or Government. Got any contacts, Ben?"

"No," I said, "but suppose somebody critical to whole deal disappeared – you know, got kidnapped or something?"

"Oh great! A bloody comedian! That's all I need. I thought that this was serious. When are you going to grow up, Ben? That's so bloody...... brilliant! It has to be someone critical. I've just thought of the perfect person. Someone whose absence would seriously jeopardise the whole deal. Who better than you, Janson? If you disappeared, the only person who could fill your gap would be......?"

"God, you're right! Jon bloody Walters – and there it is – out in the open. Hey – a masterpiece! High Five!" and we raised our arms and slapped hands like the ten year old kids we always wanted to be.

I thought for no more than a few seconds then started to babble. "If I take my car back to my hotel and leave it there, I can disappear from there and nobody would know for several hours. It's still early enough and nobody is expecting to see me until about 10:00 – come on, let's go."

"Oh, no. I can't help. Too many people will see me, recognise my car. You have to do this alone."

"Crap. Come in my car – we can leave the hotel in a cab. No-one need see you."

"Except the cab driver – get out of here, Janson. You started this – you finish it. But don't ring me to tell me where you are – make it genuine. Now go. Go! Go! Go! Good to see you again, mate. Bye!" and he walked across the room and opened his office door.

Of course, he was right. I hadn't thought it through at all. Actually this could be quite fun, particularly if it worked.

As I got to the lift, Kordowski opened his office door again and called out, "Hey, Janson. Last question. Whatever happened to that stunning girl with the magnificent body in the legal firm we were auditing? Jenny?"

"Penny," I replied. "I married her ugly bitch of a sister," and stepped into the lift, allowing the doors to close behind me. Enough had been said.

Chapter 9

I drove back to my hotel and put the car back where it had been overnight. Fortunately, I had brought a fair amount of cash with me from London so didn't need to use any plastic give-away-my-location cards. There was a crowded bus stop just outside the hotel so I got onto a bus and set off to wherever "All the way" would take me. Of course, I got off before there because I have watched too much Inspector Frost. Needless to say, I hadn't got a clue what to do and drifted aimlessly for hours. Eventually I caught a train having bought a ScotRail Rover ticket, which I thought was quite a smart move. By lunchtime, it wasn't such a good idea, because I was hungry and lost.

I discovered that my train ticket also covered buses and decided that if I was lost, then being seriously lost would be even better. So I took a country route and eventually saw a small country pub that sat in the middle of nowhere. So I got off the bus. That was my first and second mistake combined. The pub didn't do food and the next bus was in about two hours. There are only so many packets of crisps one can eat without drawing attention – like two, if you are on your own. My third mistake was answering my phone when it rang. It was Penny.

"Where the hell are you?" she asked.

"Can't tell you," came my truthful response.

"I've had a call from Sally who says you've been kidnapped."

"That was quick."

"What do you mean, quick? Have you been kidnapped? What's going on?" She seemed more angry than concerned. "Jon has been arrested."

"Now that really was quick!" I replied.

"Ben. Stop pissing around. What the hell is going on?"

"I'm sorry, Penny. I can't tell you anything yet, in fact I've probably already said too much."

"Oh, don't be a tosser, Ben, you've said nothing at all yet. Are you alright? Where are you?" She was getting miffed.

"Look, Penny. Yes, I am perfectly alright. No I can't tell you where I am, because I don't know. All I can say is that something very serious has happened and Jon is not to be trusted at all. If he really has been arrested, I am amazed and very pleased. I can't tell you more because it wouldn't be safe for you. All I can say is that I am so pleased to hear from you but please don't try to get hold of me again unless it is seriously urgent. I must go now, sorry. And, by the way, I think I love you."

"Ben, pack it in. Oh and yes. By the way, you are a dad now. You had a son about an hour ago." The phone went dead.

Chapter 10

By the time the bus arrived, I was slightly the worse for wear. Everybody in the pub (all three of them, including mine host) was aware that I was now a first time dad and had joined me in wetting the baby's head. My first attempt at disappearing off the face of the Earth had been an unmitigated disaster because my picture was on the television news in the pub now, as was Jon's and a group of Swedish and English "wide-boys" whose attempt to take over a business had now been broadcast as an immense fraud.

Everybody in the pub shook hands with me, had my autograph and demanded that I went back there for a real drink when all of the dust had settled. The bus driver wanted to take me to the nearest town, where he had a cousin who was the local newspaper editor, and then promised to put me on a train back to civilisation, after I had given his cousin the scoop of his life.

The lift to the nearest town sounded like a good idea but I hoped that the guy's cousin would realise that I couldn't say anything until certain things had happened, *sub judice* and all that.

Ironically the bus driver understood that better than his cousin who had been out for a liquid lunch and was "off his trolley". After a lot of repetition and falling asleep, the editor finally gave up and went off for a sleep. The driver, however, was more pushy and said he would keep in touch for his cousin's scoop. I regret that he meant it.

The first phone call on the case came, surprisingly not from Kordowski, but from Graeme Patterson, who, I assumed, would be looking for his car. But no, he wasn't interested in that at all. He had already spent a great deal of time onto the Pierson part of Pierson Walters, a sleeping ex-senior partner of the firm, who still had a share of the action, and had arranged for me to be collected by his chauffeur and brought back to Aberdeen for a high-level discussion with several banks, lawyers and Government Officials, mainly from the Fraud Squad. It appeared that both Kordowski and I were in trouble with the Fraud Squad but the matter was no longer in our hands. We would be arrested and charged with intent, and conspiracy to pervert the course of justice but would be released on police bail.

Graeme didn't understand my question about "Would there be any door handles involved?" but I would explain it to him later. I would have plenty of time because the interrogation by the Fraud Squad lasted nearly two full days, which, as I explained to them, was considerably longer than the half an hour that Alan Kordowski and I had had to work out what was going on in the first place before we reacted. I could tell they were not impressed with that comment, so I thought I would save it for my bus driver's cousin.

In the meantime, Graeme and his Board of Directors had
taken over my life. Everything had been upgraded and the red
carpet treatment implied that they were somewhat pleased about
the turnout of events. They knew, however, that this was only for
a short time as I now had responsibilities back home to attend to.
Initially, I turned down their very generous offer of an executive
jet to take me back to London when all affairs were in order but
the use of that made me change my mind and I tried to contact
Penny, by text, of course.

Eventually, I was able to glean that she would be leaving
Edinburgh on the last flight to Heathrow on the Friday and I
boasted that I would come and pick her up in my executive jet.
Her initial reaction was as expected.

"Bog off, Ben. Who d'you think you are kidding?"

"No, this is serious, Penny. Friday is good for me too, say
name your time and I'll be there. Honest!"

"Well I'm supposed to be on the 18.45 but I hear that it is
going via Manchester, which is a real pain in the bum. It'll be too
late to eat when I get home and I have a non-stop day here all
Friday with no chance to eat at all."

"Penny. I'll pick you up for dinner at 18:00 and we'll be back
in Heathrow before 21:30 – promise. How about it?"

"What about your wife, my sister?"

"She is staying in hospital until Saturday morning, when I shall
pick her up. Your parents are going to visit on Friday night and
they still don't like me, so I am not allowed to be there anyway."

"You sure?"

"Never surer – I'll pick you up at six o'clock Friday."

Chapter 11

Kordowski and I duly got our wrists slapped and told never to do
it again but, next time, could we warn the police first, please?

Jon Walters was in deep trouble, suddenly deserted by all of his entrepreneurs but, eventually, the copies of legal documents would shoot some of them down. In the meantime, each of them was being monitored closely, awaiting the moment when they slipped up.

Dinner with Penny was enjoyable but tense. She was still Sally's sister, as she pointed out all too frequently and I duly kept my hands to myself.

Her spell in Edinburgh had been very hard work and she received several phone calls, one of which caused her to leave the table and she was obviously under pressure when she returned. Consequently, our 20:45 slot at the airport was easily attained and, in fact, we took off long before that.

As we began our approach into London City, Penny's car was waiting there for her, she turned to me and began the moment I had been dreading. She took my right hand in both of hers and said, "Ben. I'm afraid that there is something I need to say."

I knew exactly what was coming and had, all along, been expecting her to terminate any possibility of ever seeing her again. Of course, she was right and whatever had happened on that one occasion had to be considered to be a very big mistake.

"Ben. Listen to me and please don't react, there is nothing you can do right now. Sally discharged herself from the hospital yesterday afternoon and walked out – without the baby. She rang me while we were eating and made me promise not to tell you about it. She assumed that I would ring you immediately but I told her that I was away from home and couldn't contact you until tomorrow. She was very blunt and very cruel and I don't know how to say this. To sum it up, she doesn't want the baby, she doesn't want you. She is absolutely mortified because all she wants is Jon – Jon Walters – and you have destroyed him."

"What?" I was absolutely flabbergasted. I hadn't got a clue. I sat there with the bottom having fallen out of my world. I was totally speechless. I was left with my mouth open and my head spinning. When had all this happened? Why didn't I know? What signs had I missed? I tried to think back – just a few weeks; then a few months. There must have been some tell-tale signs but I just hadn't seen them.

Penny squeezed my hand and brought me back to my senses. She put an arm around my shoulders and kissed me gently on the cheek. "Don't worry, Ben. We'll sort something out. My car is at the airport and we'll go straight to the hospital. That's probably not the best thing to do but I think you ought to see your son first."

"First? Before what? I wouldn't have a clue what comes next. How could she do this? Who else knows about it?"

"Ben, shush. There's no point in blamestorming right now. Let's speak to somebody at the hospital. They must have experience of this. Imagine if a mother dies in childbirth, that would be similar. They must know what we can do."

"Penny. This is me. Not we. It's very kind of you but I've got to do this."

"Stop it, Ben. She's my bloody sister too, so you're not on your own here. Whatever happens now, we're going to do this together. Just let me help you to get through the first few days, weeks, months. No ties or commitments – but let's just sort this mess out. Please."

She sat there holding my hand until we landed and then we found her car and drove straight to the hospital.

Chapter 12 – Twelve years later

"Daniel, are you ready? It's time we were on our way. You know your mother gets uptight if we're not in court on time. Come on, there's a good chap."

Once every fortnight for the last three years, Sally has, at last, assumed some responsibility for our son. Prior to that, he has had a hard life, having to deal with me, and occasional visits, as often as she could, from his Auntie Penny. We have struggled together to retain a proper father/son relationship but actually we are best mates. I have employed a good nanny from the week Daniel was born and Daniel and I have grown up very, very close to each other. We have played football together, have learned to play cricket together and have fallen off two wheeled bikes together. Holidays have been such fun. We have been to all sorts of places and are both studying French as a consequence. We are as close as any father and son can be and now this. What on earth is she playing at?

I have been arrested. I have been charged with beating the son I love and have brought up without any help from his mother. I have never laid a finger on him. I have managed to keep him with me because his mother doesn't even know him.

But today the Social Carers, who have not even visited us once, have listened to his mad mother and are taking me to court for the third time to have him removed from me. I have fought this from end to end but with no evidence whatsoever, these stupid, stupid people are going to deprive my son of his life. They are going to recommend that he be handed to the mother who deserted both him and me the very week he was born. Why? Because she didn't want me. She wanted my greedy, corrupt, wicked boss who was filling her with evil. And that is what she is. Evil, bitter and twisted. And now she wants to get back at me for taking that bad man away from her. She has never been a mother or a parent. She knows nothing. She is mad. Daniel has bruises. She has lied. For all I know, maybe she has hit him. Maybe he is just a young man growing up and has, as did we all, fallen over, played sport, anything that inflicts bruises. But the law listens to her.

Today my solicitor tells me she will win. Not only shall I lose but, much more important than that, so will Daniel. I probably won't even get access to my own dear son, whom I have brought up all of his life. This mad woman is going to take him away from me. I shall have to pay her but I shan't be able to see him.

She doesn't love him. She doesn't even know him. We have a whole Government Department that is more dangerous even than my mad wife. They can produce absolutely no evidence whatsoever but, because his mad mother wants to get at me, Daniel's life is over. My life is over. Even Penny can't help me now.

Call that justice? There is no justice.

Aldeburgh Apparitions

By Colin Butler

Glowering, lowering, slate-grey clouds
Foreshadowing the imminent storm.
Easterly winds impelling the waves
To smash on the shifting, shingle shore.

The warning bell tolls out the alarm,
And the sound of splintering timbers
Echoing eerily in the stormy night
Heralds the fate of the hapless vessel.

The sea fret clings like a second skin
As it slinks, silently along the misty shore.
From out of the fog, figures lurching
Up the beach, towards the sleeping town.

I watch with horror the gruesome sight
Rotting flesh on dry, bleached bones
Covered by scraps of sailors garb,
As the macabre crew march slowly by.

Fleeting figures in the swirling mist,
Spectres of fishermen from years gone by,
Drowned in these treacherous, icy seas,
Their cries resonating down the years.

Their recurring ghostly visitations
To wreak vengeance for their sad demise,
Seeking those responsible for their fate
Rich ship-owners long since deceased.

Let Us Prey

By Nicolette Coleman

The church service ended with Amazing Grace and a prayer and we all began to gather our bags and coats in readiness for going home, or into the hall for coffee if we were feeling sociable. I looked at Dave and he smiled back.

"Shall we stay for coffee?" I asked. He nodded, so we joined the queue in the hall. Some weeks Dave didn't want to bother with others, he seemed in too much of a hurry to get home and shut the door behind him. He could be very gregarious, but he had a private side too. I found myself queuing behind Sally and John, and we struck up a conversation about their wedding plans. Both had been married before, so I would have expected them to be planning a quiet affair, but it seemed I was wrong.

"I've ordered my dress," Sally told me. "Obviously I can't tell you about it in front of John, but it's big, flouncy and cream. We're having my two girls as bridesmaids and John's Bobby as page boy." I smiled, wondering how eleven year old Bobby felt about that. I hoped they wouldn't dress him in some terrible Little Lord Fauntleroy outfit.

* * *

Back at home I started dinner, while Dave rounded up our three teenagers, encouraging them to get washed and dressed before dinner. Long gone were the times when they had happily accompanied us to church – we were lucky if they came along at

Christmas these days. It made me sad, as I'd enjoyed the days when we filled half a pew with our family, but I also accepted that trying to force them along to church was the worst thing I could do.

After the dishes were cleared away Dave went out and bought the Sunday papers, and we settled down to read them. After a while he lifted his head and asked: "Do you think John and Sally are happy together?"

"What a strange question!" I said, "I never really thought about it. Sally certainly seems happy enough, and I assume John wouldn't have asked her to marry him if he didn't love her. Why do you ask?"

"It's their body language. I was watching you talk to them after church, and John seemed irritated by Sally, he seemed more interested in you."

"Well, I do think Sally witters on a bit. Perhaps John was just embarrassed by all the talk of wedding dresses and such."

"Possibly. I've sometimes wondered if he is just marrying her to provide a mother for Bobby. After all, the poor lad never seems to see his mother any more, does he?"

* * *

It was very sad. John and Diane had divorced five years previously and at first Bobby had lived with Diane, visiting John every weekend But within a year he had moved in with John, and it seemed he'd seen less and less of Diane. I couldn't understand it, as I couldn't imagine not seeing my children, even now that they were galumphing great teenagers who barely muttered "alrite?" when they passed me on the stairs. I did worry about Bobby sometimes, but John certainly loved his son, and Sally would make a kind, if over-fussy, step-mother to the boy.

* * *

Two days later I had a day off and was busy catching up with the housework when the doorbell rang. I answered it, only to find a delivery man standing on the front step, holding a large basket of oranges in his arms. "Mrs. Landers?" he asked, I nodded in response and he handed me the basket and began walking back down the path. I stood where I was, looking at the basket of oranges, puzzled. I certainly hadn't ordered them, and if I had done, would have preferred a basket of mixed fruit, rather than this embarrassment of vitamin C. I noticed there was a card on the top of the basket, with my name on, so, closing the door behind me, I took the gift into the kitchen to read the card. Inside the card read: *Julie. A present for you, just because we are so in love. John.* John? John from church? It did look like his writing, which I had seen on Christmas and birthday cards. I wanted to think it was a mistake, and that the gift was meant for Sally, but why then would he have written my name, and sent it to this address? I felt confused, and slightly nervous.

When Dave returned from work I showed him the card and gift, and he was as puzzled as I. At length he decided to telephone John and try to clear things up. I left him to it and went and folded the day's washing. When Dave returned he didn't look very happy. I raised my eyebrows at him and he said; "John said it's a matter between him and you and I have no right to interfere." I began to laugh – it was all so ridiculous, and eventually Dave laughed too.

"If I was having an affair with John I imagine I'd hide it from you, not let you ring him and ask him," I said, and we resolved to forget about it. We laughed, but unease fluttered around my insides for the rest of the week.

* * *

The following Sunday John sought me out after church. My stomach lurched as I saw him approaching, and I wished Dave was with me, but he was on the other side of the hall chatting to Jim and Rupert. I tried willing Dave to turn in my direction, but as always my mental powers were non-existent. John reached me, a smile plastered on his face. He looked smug.

"Julie! Lovely to see you. I like you in that red dress. Did you get my present?" I nodded, not trusting myself to speak. "What did you think?" John continued.

I took a deep breath. "The oranges were very nice thank you. Dave's been taking them with him for his lunch all week. But John, I was a bit upset by the odd message on the card. And I'm not sure why you needed to send me a present." My heart was hammering. I'm unused to being direct or confrontational, but I felt that if this wasn't dealt with straight away I would worry at it for weeks.

John looked surprised, but then his face cleared. "Oh! Right! Sorry Julie, I should have thought not to put a message like that where Dave might see it. Oh dear, I bet you had some explaining to do!" He seemed delighted.

I was stunned. I was at a loss for how to respond, so I simply walked away, over to Dave, where I slipped my hand through his arm for comfort. He looked at me and smiled, and I began to feel safer.

When we got home that afternoon I told Dave what John had said and he was angry. He wanted to go and see him, to 'have words' as he put it, and this scared me. I wasn't sure why, but I felt ignoring it would make it go away quicker.

"OK, if it makes you happier we will ignore it for now, but any more of his nonsense and I will have to do something about it," Dave said. I wasn't used to seeing him this angry. Dave was usually a peaceful man, keen to keep on the right side of people, but I could see he was as rattled by this as I was.

For the next few days things settled down, and I began to feel happier. I no longer thought of John whenever the phone or doorbell rang. Life began to seem normal again. The next Sunday I was relieved to see neither John nor Sally were in church, and

Dave and I stayed for coffee, free to chat to friends without the need to look over our shoulders all the time.

* * *

The following day I left my office on the dot of five. Autumn was drawing in and I wanted to be home before dark. It was chilly and the wind pulled at my coat as I wrapped it round me on the way to the car park. I had made a casserole that morning, and when I got home all I would have to do was to put it in the oven so that we could eat when Dave got home. The children were big now, but I still liked to be there to make dinner for them and for Dave when he returned from London at seven. It would leave me time to sit and read the paper over a cup of tea. The little things in life were often the nicest. I hurried to my car before I got too cold, but stopped dead when I reached it. Under the windscreen wipers was a bunch of red roses and a note. My hands shook as I open the note; "*I knew you felt the same. You must have missed me yesterday. Ring me. John xxx.*" I felt sick, and the keys rattled in my hand as I struggled to get into the car. I threw the roses onto the car park floor. I didn't want them anywhere near me. I slipped the note into my pocket so I could show it to Dave later. I locked the car doors and accelerated out into the rush hour traffic.

It seemed an age before Dave got home. The children were all busy with their own pursuits, so I was left to my own devices until I heard Dave's key in the lock. I wanted to rush to him and tell him about the flowers, but the children had heard him arrive and all appeared downstairs wanting their dinner. I would have to wait before revealing what John had done. Over dinner Dave commented on my quietness and Danny, my seventeen-year-old son laughed; "She's been quiet ever since she got home. Must have something on her mind." Emma and Jason laughed too, and Danny ruffled my hair, something he'd begun to do once he'd overtaken me in height. I tried to smile, but felt as though my face was stretching to breaking point.

Once everything had been cleared away the kids had gone back to their rooms, Dave put his arms around me. "What is it love? I know you, there's something bothering you." Through the lump in my throat I told him about the flowers and the note. I went to my coat pocket to fetch the note, but it was no longer there. I even went out to the car and searched the floor and seats, but there was no sign of it. I could only assume that it had fallen out of my pocket, but where? It was a mystery, made worse by the fact that I was sure that I saw a moment's hesitation in Dave's eyes – almost as though he was unsure whether to believe me. But the moment passed, and Dave hugged me and talked about how we should deal with the situation.

"You know, I really think the best thing would be to ignore him," he said. "That way he gets no reaction from you, or me, so hopefully he'll give up this silliness. Try not to talk to him unless you absolutely can't avoid it." Sensible stuff, I thought, but easier said than done, as when John wanted to talk to me it was hard to ignore him. But I was determined to try my best.

* * *

The next few days passed uneventfully, something for which I was extremely grateful. The next Monday was a Bank Holiday, and in the morning Danny went off to his supermarket job, Emma disappeared to town with her friends, and Dave and Jason decided to go to the park to play football, leaving me alone to get on with the housework. Ten minutes after Dave and Jason had left there was a knock on the door. I sighed as I went to answer it, wondering what they had forgotten. To my surprise, John stood on the doorstep. I stood there for a moment, unsure what to say, and then I looked behind me as though someone was there.

"It's OK," John said, "I know Dave and the children are out. Dave and Jason have gone to play football, so we'll be alone for a while." I was so shocked I slammed the door in his face and ran into the kitchen. I had no idea what to do, especially when John kept knocking on the door. I was just plucking up the courage to ring the police when the knocking stopped, and after a few minutes I peaked round the curtains to see that John had at last left.

Dave came home to find me a shivering wreck. I had managed to make some dinner, but was too upset to eat any, and he and the children soon noticed that I wasn't eating.

"What's the matter, Mum?" Emma asked me, aware that I always encouraged her to eat.

"Oh, just a bit of a sick headache," I lied, "I think I'll just have a cup of tea and lie down for a while – see if I feel any better."

I hid myself in my bedroom, hoping they would all leave me alone, but soon Dave was there, filling the doorway with his comforting bulk. I looked up at him and burst into tears. What was I to do? I was afraid that if we involved the police the whole matter would get blown out of proportion, or worse, ignored. I also had fears that Dave would confront John, and I wasn't sure what that would achieve. I told Dave what had happened after he'd gone out, and he sat for a few minutes, looking at me.

"What shall we do? Do you want to call the police?" I said, shaking my head. Dave nodded. "I don't know if it would do any good," he agreed. "They would probably say there was nothing to be done without proof. I think I'll go and have a word with John." I tried to stop him, but was shaking too much to do more than just protest weakly. After the front door had slammed and the car had gone up the road I found myself relaxing a little. Perhaps this really would do some good? It would show John that we weren't afraid of him, and that Dave and I were a team, that we talked to each other and told each other everything without secrets.

It was a long time before Dave came back, and I had worked myself into a frenzy by then. I had visions of John beating Dave to a pulp. I had no idea who would be the stronger of the two, and I really didn't want to find out just now. At long last I heard Dave's key in the door and rushed into the hall to meet him. There were no signs of damage to his dear face, and I threw my arms around him. To my consternation he did not return the hug but moved away from me.

"Dave?" I asked. "What happened?"

"Perhaps you'd like to tell me?" his face was grim, and I felt fear lacing my insides.

"I told you what happened here. You were going to go and talk to John. What's the matter? What did he say?"

Dave looked at me, his face inscrutable. I wasn't used to my husband looking at me like this, and my heart felt heavy in my chest.

"John told me he came round this afternoon because you rang him to let him know the coast was clear. He also said that the two of you had been seeing each other for three months now, and that you were trying to pluck up the courage to tell me about it. The oranges were a present because of a 'private joke'. Oh, and the flowers and note in the car the other day? John tells me that you were frightened that you'd left the note where I'd find it. Which was why you told me about it."

I was dumbstruck, my mouth opening and closing like a goldfish as I listened to Dave. "You believed him? Dave?" but the coldness was still there in his eyes. "Why would you believe him rather than me? Why on earth would I have an affair with him anyway? I'm not the kind of woman who would cheat on you, and I thought you knew me well enough to know that. But if I *did* I certainly wouldn't choose John."

Dave still looked at me, then sighed, scratched his chin and replied; "He had dates of when the two of you had seen each other. And, surprise, surprise, they all matched up with dates when I was out for the evening or away on business. Quite frankly Julie, I feel as though you've been making a fool of me." There were tears in his eyes, and I stepped forward to hold him, but he stepped smartly out of my way.

"I think John has been stalking us. That's how he knew you were out this afternoon, and how he obviously knows about dates and times when you've been away. I would have hoped you'd believe me rather than that rat-bag."

Dave looked at me. "I don't know what to believe right now Julie," he said, and walked out of the room, his back a defeated question mark.

I sat down heavily on the nearest armchair. Tears were blocking my nose and eyes and my hands wouldn't stop shaking. John must have made up a really believable story if Dave would believe him rather than me. I was tempted to ring him to find out why he was doing this to us, but I couldn't bear the thought of speaking to him, and was afraid that any contact I might have with him would only 'prove' our involvement. I had no idea what to do or who to turn to.

That night Dave slept in the spare room, leaving me to wallow about in our bed, alone and scared. In our fifteen years of marriage we had never slept apart before, even after an argument. I slept badly, my dreams full of tears and shouts, and awoke feeling heavy and sad at heart.

Dave had obviously slept no better than me from the looks of him, but he refused to speak to me before he left for work and my heart bled into a puddle at my feet, which I hoped the children wouldn't see. I smiled for them as they all left for the day, and was sure they hadn't seen through my disguise.

* * *

I spent the morning sluggishly churning my way through the housework, although my heart wasn't in it. What was the point of keeping the house nice if Dave didn't want me any more? As I desultorily swished cleaning fluid around the bath I came to a decision – I would speak to our church minister, Paul. He would be sure to have some wise words to help me, and perhaps would be able to find a way to make Dave listen to him. I picked up the phone and dialled the Manse. Paul answered on the second ring, surprising me, as the phone usually seemed to go through to answer phone.

"Ah, Julie," he said when I announced myself, "I was hoping to speak to you. Would it be convenient for me to pop round this afternoon?" I was so surprised I found myself agreeing, and hurried to tidy the kitchen and put the kettle on.

Paul arrived less than half an hour later, to find me wringing my hands. He smiled at me, telling me not to worry. As I finished making coffee and set it on the coffee table he began to talk, not giving me the chance to tell him why I'd wanted to see him.

"I had a phone call from Dave this morning," he started, "I expect you know why? And then I rang John and had a chat with him. Now the thing is Julie, I didn't think you were the kind to have an affair, and Dave is quite distraught about it. John, on the other hand, seems quite happy with the situation, and seems to feel that Dave will soon be out of the picture, leaving you free to be with him. Now, do you want to tell me your side of the story?"

Tears filled my eyes and ran down my face, making the side of my nose itch. "Where do I begin Paul? For starters, none of it is true. I have never cheated on Dave, I just wouldn't, I love him and respect him too much. John has been, well, stalking me or something, for a while now. I just don't know what to do. I can't believe that Dave is even considering the fact that what John says could be true." I stopped. There was nothing more to say. I looked up at Paul, but didn't see the reassurance I expected in his face. "Paul? Please don't tell me that you believe John too? I can't believe this is happening."

Paul looked at me for a few moments before answering. I could almost hear his mind whirring, trying to decide who to believe, what to say. "I feel very confused Julie. I want so much to believe you. I've always thought you were an honest, moral woman. But on the other hand, I've known John for ten years now and have never had reason to doubt him. I've never known him lie before."

"But you do think he's an adulterer? Me too? You are more inclined to believe we would have an affair than that John would lie to you?" I was almost shouting now, my voice breaking. I had never felt so let down and confused in my life. I was losing the trust of the people I admired most in my life – Dave, and now Paul. The next thing I knew people would be telling the children. A sob caught in my throat and I covered my face with my hands.

When I looked up Paul had stood up and was putting his jacket on. "I have a meeting to go to now. If you want to talk some more you know where I am." He paused. "It would be a lot simpler if you all told the same story. John seems to think the pair of you will be together soon, so I'm confused as to why you're denying it. Can I ask you to please think of your children before you do anything rash?" He patted my shoulder and left.

I sat for a while, too stunned to move. Paul believed John rather than me. Even Dave believed him. Dave, who ought to know me better than anyone. At length I decided to ring my friend, Nora. She was wise and funny, and we had been friends for longer than I could remember. I should have thought to call her first, rather than Paul.

Nora answered the phone on the second ring. "Julie! I was just about to ring you! Are you OK? There are *rumours* doing the rounds about you – I expect you know about them? Do you want me to come round?" I snuffled into the phone, managing to squeak out a "yes," before breaking into sobs. At last I would have someone to talk to, someone who would understand and believe me.

Nora arrived soon after, and I let her in, wiping my face on a piece of kitchen towel. She hugged me, and I dissolved onto her shoulder. Like the good friend that she was she stood and patted my shoulder as I wept on her smart blue jumper. When I finally pulled myself together we sat down in the kitchen with a cup of coffee and I told Nora what had been happening. She listened, her mouth a round 'O' as I explained about John sending the oranges and roses and turning up on my doorstep. She looked even more flabbergasted when I told her what Dave and Paul had said. By then my tears seemed to have dried up, and I felt dehydrated and exhausted. "What do I do now Nora?" I asked hopelessly.

"I really don't know," she replied, as honest as always. "I can't believe that Dave believes that toe-rag rather than his own wife, and Paul! You'd think he'd know you better than that! I know he's known John a long time, but to believe him over you is terrible." We sat there in sad but companionable silence for a while. My heart was warmed by Nora's faith in me. She would stand by me, and perhaps could persuade Dave and Paul to see sense.

After Nora had gone home I washed my face, determined to appear as normal as possible when everybody came home after work and school. Once the kids were home they did their usual disappearing act into their bedrooms, leaving me free to mooch around the kitchen trying to throw a reasonable dinner together. At seven o'clock Jason came downstairs insisting that he was starving to death and where was dad? I told him that Dave must have been caught up in traffic and we would wait a while to see if he appeared. Jason sighed theatrically and clumped his way back upstairs. At seven thirty I gave in and served the children their dinner, telling them I would wait for Dave. And I waited my heart a slow painful throb in my chest as the minutes and hours ticked away.

Finally, at nine thirty the phone rang and I pounced on it, gasping out a breathless "Hello?" I was relieved to hear Dave's voice on the line, but saddened by the dead, reserved tone in his voice.

"I think it would be best if I stayed with my Mum for the moment. It'll give us time to decide what to do," he said, killing me with the arrows of his words. He couldn't see or hear how I was dying at my end of the line.

"Dave? Dave, there's nothing to decide about. I've told you the truth. I would never be unfaithful to you. I love you and......"
I slowly became aware of the dialling tone in my ear. Dave had hung up on me. I curled up into a ball on the floor, my arms clutched around my stomach, trying to keep myself intact. After a time I became aware of Danny, Emma and Jason standing over me, matching distress on their faces. There was a strange, high, keening sound in the house, and as I lifted my head to listen to it I realised the sound was coming from me. Slowly I sat up, like an old, old woman. Danny knelt down next to me, putting his arms round my shoulders.

"What is it Mum?" he asked "What's happened?"

"Your Dad," I managed, before the tears stopped me. As the latest surge of grief passed I looked at my beautiful children and realised that they were imagining a worse horror – that something had happened to Dave. "No! No, Dad's OK. Oh God, it's a long story. I don't know where to begin, or what to say to you."

Danny hauled me up by my elbows and led me into the lounge where he sat me on the sofa while Emma put the kettle on in the kitchen. Jason sat down next to me, his face looking far younger than his thirteen years. I reached a hand out to him and squeezed his wrist. Emma appeared in the doorway, a cup of tea trembling in her hand. She put it down on the side table and sat on the floor at my feet. I struggled to know how to begin, but seeing the children's worried faces looking at me I knew I had to find a way. I began with the basket of oranges, which they all remembered, and finished up with today's events, including my conversations with Nora and Paul. The children sat stunned when I had finished. I knew how they felt.

"I promise you all that there is *no* truth at all in what John is suggesting. I really hope you believe me. I have never been unfaithful to your Dad and I never would."

"But if that's true, why does he believe John and not you?" Emma sounded plaintive and my heart went out to her.

"I wish I knew Emma, really I do. John seems to have given Dad dates when he says we were together, and something about that has made Dad have doubts, because they are apparently all dates when Dad was working late or away. But I know that John has been, well, stalking me. He appears to know when Dad and all of you are out, like yesterday. I know it's horrible, but I think he must be watching the house or something."

Emma shuddered, and I put my arms around her, taking as well as giving comfort. We all sat together for a while longer, then I encouraged the children to get ready for bed as they all had school or college the next morning.

"Will you be all right?" Jason asked, hugging me.

"Yes, knowing I have all of you here with me is a great help. And let's hope and pray that Dad realises the truth soon and comes back home where he belongs."

I sat listening to the sounds of three teenagers getting ready for bed; the opening and shutting of doors and the gurgle of water in the pipes, until eventually the house was quiet. I thanked God for the children – without them I would be completely lost. At least I had their company tonight and I had to keep going for their sakes. That was something. I stood up, deciding I ought to go to bed, although I was sure sleep would elude me. I turned out the lights in the lounge and kitchen and made my way to the foot of the stairs. As my hand brushed the light switch preparatory to turning it off there was a tap on the glass of the front door. I nearly jumped out of my skin, but immediately I thought 'Dave!' He must have decided to come home after all! A delighted sob caught in my throat and I flung the front door open, only to be confronted with – John. My heart sank and I was aware of a trembling in my hands and legs. I tried to shut the door in his face, but he held his hand up, stopping me.

"What do you want?" I whispered.

"To see you of course!" he too whispered, although his voice was full of glee, rather than the fear and trepidation which I was sure my voice held. "I know Dave's finally got the message and left, so I knew you'd want me to come round. I thought I'd wait until your kids went to bed. Can I come in?"

"Of course not!" I spluttered. "What is the matter with you? Can't you just leave me alone? Go on home to Bobby. And think of Sally."

John looked baffled. "Leave you alone? Why would I do that? You know I love you, and I know you love me." He looked beyond me, and then light dawned on his face. "Oh! Are you afraid to let the kids know about us? I suppose you need a bit of time to get them used to the idea. OK, I'll call back tomorrow." He leant forward and I realised he meant to kiss me. I reared back and managed to slam the door shut, only just missing his nose. Before I knew what I was doing I shouted out "Just fuck off and leave me alone you creep!" I stood in the hall, my breath coming in ragged sobs, my arms protectively tight around my middle. I had never used such language out loud before and had shocked myself. At last I felt able to move, and I crept into the kitchen, filling the kettle to make hot chocolate. I didn't dare put the light on, afraid that even now John would be outside watching my movements. I felt my way around the familiar kitchen in the dark, and managed to make my drink, which I then carried carefully up to the bedroom. The bedroom seemed huge and empty without Dave. He ought to be here now, emptying his pockets into the saucer on the dresser and hanging his good trousers on the outside of the wardrobe.

I sat in bed and slowly drank my drink. The house was quiet and I felt lonely, despite the presence of my three teenagers, asleep in their bedrooms down the hall.

The night seemed endless, the dark pressing in around me, and sleep was elusive. The morning finally came and I was glad of the chance to get out of bed and begin another day. I hoped this day would be better than the last. Well, it could hardly be worse I told myself.

I rang work and made my excuses not to come in, feigning sickness. But once the children had all left for the day I wished I had gone to work. I would have been too tired and distressed to work well, but at least I would have been busy. I had no idea what to do with myself to fill the next eight hours. I would ring Nora, but I had to give her time to get all her chores done before ringing – Nora liked to do all her housework and errands first thing, and I knew better than to ring her before eleven. I flitted around, not settling to any one task for more than a few minutes. I kept spying the telephone out of the corner of my eye, and knew that I was desperate to ring Dave. He was sometimes able to talk at work, if he was alone in the office. Would it be a good idea to call him? Dave was my best friend as well as my husband, and there was no one else I wanted to talk to more.

Eventually I gave in and rang his office. Dave answered on the second ring and my heart swelled to hear his dear voice. "Hi Dave, it's me," I said hesitantly. There was a long pause, far too long for my liking, before he replied;

"What do you want Julie? I thought I explained that I need time to think about things."

I tried not to cry, although my heart was breaking. "I miss you Dave. I can't begin to tell you how unhappy we all are without you. I need to talk to you. You're my best friend and I need you."

"Perhaps you should have thought about that before taking up with John."

"I haven't taken up with John! How can I make you believe me? I have *never* been unfaithful to you and I never will." I was trying so hard not to shout, not to sound unreasonable, but the anger and frustration were blocking my throat until I felt that I might burst.

"Perhaps we can talk tonight if I come round after work?" Dave's voice was very soft in my ear, turning my legs to jelly.

"That would be lovely," I managed, "What time do you want to come round? Will you come for dinner?"

"Thank you, I'll come straight from work."

I practically raced through the afternoon, so excited at the thought of Dave coming home. Perhaps by tonight all would be OK again? I spent a long time in the kitchen, making Dave's favourite dinner – shepherd's pie. He loved it when I made it with baked beans in and lots of cheese melted on top. I was happily mashing the potatoes when there was a ring on the bell. I went to the door and was pleased to see Nora there, although the look on her face warned me that all wasn't well. I led her into the kitchen and switched the kettle on, finishing the potatoes before making tea.

"You OK, Nora?" I asked, setting a steaming cup of tea before her.

"Not really, no." Nora looked down at the table, moving a place mat back and forth in front of her rather than looking at me.

"What's happened?" I asked, the now familiar feeling of dread stirring in my stomach.

"John came to see me earlier. He was in a bit of a state Julie." Nora now looked at me, and I didn't like the look on her face. I opened my mouth to speak, but she held her hand up to stop me. "Let me finish please. John was in a terrible way when he came round. He told me all about your affair and how you had suddenly ended it last night. But what he is most upset about is that he'd just come back from the doctor and it seems you've given him a sexually transmitted disease. He just doesn't know what to do and he says now you won't talk to him. Julie, why didn't you tell me all this before?"

I was stunned. I opened and closed my mouth foolishly. Nora too. "I don't know what to say, Nora. Last week you believed me, and now you don't. What is it that John does that makes people believe him rather than me? People like you, who have been my best friend for years?"

Nora looked at me. "Perhaps it's that he tells people the truth? Hmmm?" And with that she got up and walked out, leaving me sitting in a puddle of despair. I'd lost my earlier excitement and felt drained and really quite distraught. It was unbelievable that Nora would believe John over me. I couldn't imagine what he could have said to make her stop trusting me so completely.

I went back to my cooking, although my heart was no longer in it. By the time the children had arrived home I was back to my earlier nervous state, and my hands shook as I laid the table. I was reminded of how I had felt on my first date with Dave, when I had been so anxious that I'd been unable to eat more than a few mouthfuls of my dinner when he took me to a restaurant. At long last I heard Dave's car pull into the driveway, and Emma and Jason raced to let him in. I was glad of that as I had been afraid that he would ring the doorbell like a visitor in his own home, and that would have broken my heart. As Dave came into the kitchen I smiled at him and raised my face for a kiss. He hesitated before chastely kissing my cheek, which flamed with disappointment and shame.

Dinner went fairly well, with the children competing for Dave's attention, leaving me to watch his reactions. Dave was tense and acting like a stranger in our home, letting the children get his drinks and take his plate to the kitchen. I began to feel worried about our forthcoming chat. Finally the meal was over and Danny herded Emma and Jason off upstairs, having realised that Dave and I needed to be alone. I made coffee, stalling for time before joining him in the lounge. I wanted to sit next to him on the sofa as I usually did, but felt constrained by the awkwardness of the situation, and sat opposite him instead. Then I worried that he would think I didn't want to be near him. Oh, this was so difficult – I really shouldn't feel so uncomfortable around my own husband. John had a lot to answer for. I smiled at Dave, uncertain how to begin, but managed; "How are you doing?"

"As well as can be expected I suppose," was his reply.

"I don't know what to say to you Dave. I know I've said it over and over, but there is not, and never has been, anything between me and John. I don't even like him particularly! And I have never been unfaithful to you."

"I want to believe you, I really do. But the things John told me – it's hard to disbelieve him. I know, I know, I ought to believe you first as my wife, but I just don't know. I'm so confused." And Dave's eyes filled with tears. I walked over to him and put my arm around his shoulder. To my relief he let me, but I could feel his uncertainty about hugging me back. We sat there for a few minutes until Dave pulled away and wiped his eyes.

"What do we do now?" I asked, drying my own face.

"I wish I knew. I would so love to just come home and be with you all again. It's so hard Julie. I was talking to my brother last night and he was telling me about when Lesley left him for that fat bloke from Tesco's, and it rang a lot of bells about things with you." Dave's brother, Pete, had been married to Lesley for seven years when she had left him for someone else. But I was nothing like Lesley – she had always seemed discontented with her marriage and life in general, whereas I had never hidden my love for Dave and my happiness with our family life.

"Dave, I'm nothing like Lesley! How can you even say that?" The tears were back again, and despair filled me. If Dave thought there was any correlation between Pete's marriage and ours there was no hope for us. I put my head in my hands and cried. Hot tears dripped through my fingers and ran down my arms. Eventually Dave put his hand on my shoulder.

"I'm sorry, Julie. So sorry. I just wanted you to understand how hard this is for me. If you could try and put yourself in my place?"

"I'd like to think I would trust you more than you trust me right now. Don't you know me at all? Don't you know how much I love you and how much our marriage means to me?" I noticed that at last Dave's face had softened slightly. Had I finally got through to him? He pulled me closer and kissed the top of my head, setting off a fresh bout of tears.

We sat like that for some time, until Dave eventually pulled himself away from me.

"I have to go now. I know! I know I ought to be here with you, but I still need a little more time to think. Don't worry. Please. I think everything will probably be OK eventually. Just give me a bit more time; this has all been a huge shock for me." And with that he kissed me gently and left. I wanted to shout after him and tell him what a shock it all was for me too. So shocking that someone would tell people lies about me, and even more shocking that my husband and best friend would even think of believing him! But it was too late. The door had shut behind Dave and I was left alone. Again.

* * *

The following few days were horrible. Dave didn't come to see me again. We talked often on the phone, and he was kind and loving and no longer accusing, but he still kept his distance. My heart ached so badly that I began to worry that I was having a heart attack. I would awake in the night with my heart thudding so hard that I was afraid, and would have to sit upright and breathe deeply until I was calm again.

Almost every time I left the house I would see John drive past very slowly, looking at me. It seemed that wherever I went John would appear. One day I went for a check up at the dentist, and when I came out of the surgery there was John, sitting in the waiting room as though he had every right to be there. I ignored him and left quickly, without making a follow up appointment.

It began to seem as though John would appear whenever I thought about him. I wished it was like that with Dave, whom I missed with every part of my being. I thought about Dave all the time, but he never appeared. Whereas John – well, I didn't want to think about him, and I certainly didn't want to see him, but he would pop into my head, and soon after was bound to appear in my line of vision. The day after the dentist, I went to Sainsbury's, even though the thought of being amongst so many people filled me with horror. I pushed the trolley around the aisles, trying to keep my mind on what I was doing. If I thought about Dave I would probably cry, and this really wasn't the place to do that. But oh, the memories! There was the cheese he liked but the children called 'stinky cheese' and refused to eat. There was the deodorant he used. I tried to shut these thoughts out of my head and get on with the job in hand. At long last I had managed to fill the trolley and made my way to the checkout. As I was paying I found myself coming over all panicky. My breath quickened and my heart raced. I almost ran to the supermarket doors, desperate to reach my car and then home. With fumbling fingers I found my car keys in my bag, and touched the button to unlock the doors. I rushed round to the boot, and as I opened it I heard a noise behind me. I turned around, and there was John, sitting in his car watching me. He had a small smile on his face, which I itched to slap off. I wanted to go over and ask him just what he thought he was up to, and why he was tormenting me this way, but my legs were shaking so much that I knew I would make a fool of myself. When I'm upset I find it very hard to get my words out, and I was sure that I would stutter and stumble, which would hardly lend gravitas to what I wanted to say. I practically threw my shopping into the boot, then jumped into the car. My hands were shaking, making it hard to start the engine, but I managed, and pulled out jerkily, refusing to look into the rear view mirror until I was safely on the main road. To my relief there was no sign of John's car, and I found myself sobbing as I drove the few miles back to my house.

That evening I rang Dave and asked him to come home. "I need you," I sobbed, "I just can't do this on my own. I miss you and I want you here to protect me. I'm so frightened of John, and

I think that he thinks I'm fair game as you're not here. Please Dave!" I hated myself for begging, but I was so lonely and afraid, and I missed Dave so dreadfully. I felt that I had finally reached my lowest ebb and it frightened me. There was a long, painful, pause while Dave thought about what I'd asked. Finally he answered;

"OK, Julie. I miss you too, and the children, and actually, after all that's happened and all that's been said, I realise that I do believe you. And I'm so very sorry for doubting you." I was unable to speak, reduced to sobbing incoherently into the phone. I had never felt such relief in my life. Dave was coming home to me! I wanted to run and shout and skip, but all I could do was cry, and cry.

I told the children that Dave was coming home and they, of course, were thrilled. We dashed about the house, straightening and tidying, and making sure there was a hot dinner ready for him. And we laughed as Danny reminded us that Dad would hardly notice if we tidied or not. We were all giddy with happiness and relief, and the house felt joyful for the first time in weeks.

Dave eventually arrived just after nine o'clock, and we all fell on him with whoops of delight. He grinned at me over the heads of the children who were surrounding him, and I moved forward to be enveloped in a huge family hug. I felt warmth spreading through me. With my family surrounding me I could cope with anything.

That night Dave held me tight as we lay in bed and talked through all that had happened. I told him how frightened I had been feeling, and how John seemed to be following me. Dave told me he would go and talk to John at the weekend, and promised not to get sucked into his lies. That night I slept through the night for the first time in weeks, and woke in the morning to find Dave lying next to me, smiling at me.

After everybody had left for work and school I plucked up courage and rang Nora. When I introduced myself there was a moment when I was sure she would put the phone down.

"Nora, please don't shut me out. I promise you that there never has been anything between me and John – I just never would behave that way. I'm sorry that he lied to you, but that *is* what he did."

"I don't know," Nora replied after a moment. "I do want to believe you, Julie. It's hard to imagine you cheating on Dave, let alone with John of all people. Sometimes I feel as though I was hypnotised when I spoke to him that day! I can't remember now what it was that made me believe him rather than you."

"You said it was because he cried," I reminded her.

"Well, there was that I suppose. Oh gosh, Julie, I just don't know! I feel as though the world's going mad. My best friend needed me and I turned my back. I must be the most horrible person in the world." Nora's voice was wobbly with emotion and I loved her for it.

"Not you, Nora. I think John's the most horrible person. He's a creep and he scares me. I do find myself feeling a bit sorry for Sally. I thought they were getting married? I wonder what she thinks about all this carry-on?"

Nora cleared her throat. "Actually, Julie, I did speak to her last week after I'd seen John. She said that John had told her that you fancied him and were trying to cause trouble because you were jealous of the two of them getting married. To tell the truth I think that was when I began to realise that John was lying."

I found myself wanting to laugh, although the situation was anything but funny. "Poor Sally. I suppose that's why she's been avoiding church for the last few weeks. She must think I'm crazy."

"But hey! Look on the bright side – you've got Dave back home where he belongs and I've finally seen sense, so hopefully the rest of the world will soon follow suit."

I felt that life could only get better from now on. I had those I loved on my side, and would learn not to listen to those who had turned against me. The sun was shining, a beautiful, fresh autumn day. I decided to treat myself to a walk around the park before thinking about housework and cooking. Humming to myself, I collected my walking boots from the hall cupboard and was about to put them on when the doorbell rang. I opened the door, and was unsurprised to see John on the doorstep. Although my stomach lurched at the sight of him, I didn't feel as nervous as before. It didn't matter what he said, I had Dave back with me and that was all that mattered. I raised an eyebrow, not bothering to speak.

"Hello, Julie," John began, pausing, but when I didn't respond he cleared his throat and went on; "I see Dave's come back to stay with you. I must say, he must be a very forgiving man."

I felt my jaw tighten, but was determined not to give him the satisfaction of replying.

"I'm hurt but I think I can forgive you because I love you. I just wanted to let you know that this is the last time you'll see me." He paused, waiting.

"Whatever," I replied, and shut the door in his face with a sense of satisfaction.

I waited a while before venturing out to the park, but I enjoyed my walk and was happy to see no sign of John along the way. In fact I didn't see him again that day, or the next.

* * *

Two days later I had a phone call from Nora.

"Julie? Have you heard the news?"

"No. What's happened?"

"I just heard from Paul. Apparently John is dead. He hung himself in his garage yesterday. He left a note for Sally, apparently apologising for all the trouble he's caused. Although it didn't explain what the trouble was. Julie? Are you OK, love?"

I was having trouble breathing, and I had to sit down suddenly on the stairs.

"He spoke to me two days ago. I think I told you? He said I'd never see him again. Oh God! Nora! I had no idea he'd do something like that."

"It's OK, it's hardly your fault. How do you feel?"

I trawled through my emotions. What did I really feel? "I mainly feel relief," I said quietly, "Which is terrible. But also very, very sorry for John. He must have been mentally unwell or something. And for Bobby, who's lost a Dad, and of course for poor Sally, who must be hurt and confused."

"I know, it's terrible. But at least you will be able to put this behind you now."

* * *

On a cold, grey day the following week Dave and I stood at John's graveside as his coffin was lowered into the ground. Sally stood the other side of the grave, still refusing to even look at me. As the coffin descended into the grave I offered up a silent prayer, thanking God that John was out of his misery, but also thanking God that I had the love of my husband, who stood beside me, his arm around my back. As the ceremony finished we turned away and didn't look back.

A Night Crawler Called Ween

By Simon Woodward

Drifting under a moon-bright sky
with shadows shivering as I pass by.
Along the beach I leave my trail.
And in my wake even banshees wail.

For I'm the one of whom no-one speaks.
A nameless entity that raises shrieks;

from all those;
– that come across me.

From the dunes, I am born.
The gaps between grains from which I'm torn
creates the mist from which I'm made.
It's oil-slick black, cold, and made of shade.

But some know the name who no-one speaks;
still leaving me as nameless freak.

In their world
– some don't know me.

There are the foolish who use my name.

Who summon me and think it's game,
to raise me from my sleep so deep,
but never hang around to make a peep.

Then there's the idiots who stay to look
when I seep out from my little crook.

Then try and hide themselves,
 – from me.

When I am summoned they know I'll act.
I don't flit mindlessly like a large winged bat.
I seek my caller to take their breath.
And, with satisfaction, I'll watch their death.

They know not to use my name in vain.
But for some it's still a game.

They say "Hallo Ween!" when I appear.
 – Then DIE before me.

Journey to Regression

By Colin Butler

Chapter 1

The man gradually regained consciousness and looked warily about him. Where was he? He felt sure he'd been drifting in and out of consciousness for sometime. Could it be hours? He didn't know.

His head was throbbing and he ached all over. Trying to raise himself from the bed, he fell back, his head hurt too much. Lying there he tried to gather his thoughts, until the darkness reclaimed him again.

Eventually his eyes flickered open and he attempted to collect his thoughts, but everything was a blank. He couldn't remember how he got to this room and more worryingly, he couldn't remember who he was. What had happened? Nothing came to mind. It was as if a black cloud had settled in his brain and inside it, everything he needed to know was trapped.

He had vague recollections of walking down a street but nothing more. He opened his eyes again, turned his head and flinched, pain forcing him to stop. Slowly he reached up and gingerly touched a large, egg-like lump on the back of his head. He looked at his fingers and saw they were covered in blood. Raising himself on his elbows, he glanced at the pillow and saw that it was also stained with blood. What had happened to him?

Slowly, he looked around the dimly lit, medium-sized room with gaudy wallpaper. Some light filtered through the closed curtains, but not enough to tell him whether it was early morning, early evening, or just overcast. He sank back on the pillow and consciousness left him once again.

He didn't know whether it was a noise from outside, or just something in his head, but he was awake again and the room was now somewhat brighter, so he reasoned that it must be early morning. The only sound he heard was a car starting up somewhere nearby.

Grimacing with the pain, he made a big effort and gradually raised himself into a sitting position and looked at his surroundings. The wallpaper was peeling in places and the room was very sparsely furnished, just the single bed, he was sitting on and a small bedside unit with a lamp – he tested it, but it wasn't working. On the wall opposite was a dirty and cracked mirror; he peered into it and was shocked by the image that confronted him. A haggard and unshaven man stared back at him, with one eye blackened and several bruises on his face.

He gingerly lifted his somewhat bulky frame off the bed and made his way over to the window. Having drawn the curtains, he looked out on a tiny backyard filled with old bricks and other rubbish. Opposite the window was the plain wall of another house and as he looked, rain began to fall adding to the bleakness he felt.

He was thirsty, his lips were cracked and he had this bad, sour taste in his mouth. He tried speaking, but no sound came, his throat was too dry. His thoughts continually drifted back to his predicament, who was he? He checked his trouser pockets; in the left was a dirty handkerchief, whilst the right one only produced a wrapper from a bar of chocolate and the back pocket was completely empty. Where was his wallet and where were his keys? He wondered. He also had a feeling that he'd been wearing a jacket of some sort, but that was nowhere to be seen. He'd lost everything, his diary, his credit cards, even his library card, if he ever had one. There was nothing to identify him. Who was he, and where did he live?

He slumped back on the bed trying to concentrate, trying to recall who he was. Was he married or single? He checked his ring finger, nothing. Was he a working man and if so what sort of job? Everything was blank, as if a thick fog had descended on his mind. He had lost his life and didn't know why.

He struggled to his feet and staggered around the room. Reaching the door, he turned the handle, which was unlocked, and stepped out to a dilapidated landing. To the left was a scruffy bathroom, decorated in a horrible lilac colour. The toilet and sink were filthy, but of necessity, he relieved himself in the toilet before washing his face and hands under the tap. Feeling somewhat refreshed, he ventured to explore the other rooms on the first floor. The next bedroom he presumed, had been the main bedroom, but was now bare – not even a bed and again the wallpaper was a ghastly colour – a sickly green. Whoever had lived there had certainly lacked taste. The final room on that floor was a box-room, full of old junk – a broken pram, an old ironing board and a table with three legs.

Feeling the need to continue discovering where he was, he slowly descended the stairs, gripping the banister tightly, fearing his legs would give way. His head felt woozy and everything began to spin. Reaching the bottom, he noticed that the hallway had a phone socket – but no phone. After a few moments for the hall to stop spinning and to recover his strength, he entered the front room, which was empty apart from a pile of rubbish left in the corner – old boxes and newspapers. He sat down and took the opportunity to thumb through the newspapers. The first was dated 15th November 2007. Was this a recent date or some time ago? He couldn't tell. He read some of the headlines – war in Iraq, wherever that was, the price of petrol up. All the news seemed bad, but none of the items rang any bells in his mind.

The back room was also empty so he continued into the kitchen, which only contained an old table, some greasy saucepans and a frying pan. He desperately wanted a drink to relieve his parched mouth and also craved some food, as he felt it must have been ages since he last ate and his stomach was making very strange gurgling noises in protest. Sadly, like Mother Hubbard, the cupboards were bare. He pondered, how did he know about Mother Hubbard – most probably a childhood memory? At least, he could pour some water from the tap to slake his thirst. As the cool refreshing liquid slid down his throat, he concluded that the house must have been unoccupied for some considerable time.

It was time to get out, so he tried the front door but it was locked, as was the back door. He tried the windows – again locked and realised, with annoyance, that he was a prisoner in this house. What could he do? After a few moments deliberation, he decided to break a window and from somewhere deep in his brain, recalled that you should wrap some cloth around your hand for protection. A search of the kitchen produced a dirty old piece of cloth. Wrapping it around his hand, he hit the window hard, but nothing happened. After several more attempts, however, the window smashed with a loud noise, leaving a jagged hole, which he managed, with difficulty, to make large enough to crawl through. He jumped down into an overgrown garden, bereft of flowers or plants, but it had cultivated a rusty bicycle, with one wheel, several tin cans and some bottles of drink, sadly empty, while in the corner a very ancient stone gnome appeared to be smiling triumphantly at him.

Looking around, he discovered that the house, numbered thirty-six, was situated in the middle of a row of ordinary terraced houses, so he went next door and rang the bell at number thirty-eight, but there was no answer. He decided to try number thirty-four, which had a well-kept garden, complete with more gnomes, one of whom was fishing in a tiny pond. He rang and after a short delay, the door was opened by a well-upholstered middle-aged lady, with blond frizzy hair and dressed in jogging bottoms, trainers and a blue, woolly top. She stared at him with a quizzical smile on her face.

"Yes, can I help you," she said with a certain caution in her voice.

"Well, you may think this very strange, but where are we?" he replied.

She stared back in amazement and not a little fear.

"Well, this is Sebastopol Street," she said, hesitantly.

"And what town are we in?" he asked.

She stared blankly at him, probably thinking he was some sort of madman or foreigner.

"Why, this is Camberwell," she spluttered.

"Perhaps I should explain. I woke up this morning in the house next door and I have lost my wallet and all my possessions. In addition, I have lost my memory – I don't know who I am! I just don't know what to do," he told her.

"But that's impossible; the house has been empty for several months. I'm very sorry to hear about your predicament, but I'm afraid I can't help you," she said and quickly slammed the door shut.

The man was left standing in the drive, not knowing what to do. He walked or rather staggered down the street, his legs still feeling like jelly, and looked at all the houses as he passed, hoping to see a friendly face.

The woozy feeling returned, as he walked, his legs getting more and more unsteady, as he went. Eventually he had to lean on a gate to stop himself from falling.

At the end of the road, he turned the corner and to his left was a road consisting of a row of shops and a church with a spire at the end. The spire resonated with some vague memory which stirred him. Next door to the church, was a plate affixed to the wall, stating it was St. John's Vicarage and, rather nervously, he walked up the path and rang the bell. After a short delay, the door was opened by a slender middle-aged lady with mid-brown hair and rather owlish spectacles and dressed in a beige jumper and skirt and flat sensible shoes.

"I, I, wonder whether you c-c-could help me," he stammered.

"In what way?" she asked. "I must warn you that we do not give money or food, we've had too many bad experiences in the past."

As he stood there, he recounted his story and she was obviously moved and interested.

"I think you had better come in and I'll get my husband," she said, as she led the way into the study and immediately called her husband.

Her husband, the vicar, entered and shook hands. He was a tall thin man, balding and wearing spectacles, which covered eyes that had a friendly twinkle.

"Well, sit down, and we'll see if we can help," he said reassuringly.

The man sat in a comfortable chair and was given a cup of coffee and a biscuit by the vicar's wife, who also offered him a cheese sandwich, which he accepted gratefully. He then proceeded to tell his story and at the end the vicar questioned him.

"So you can't remember anything at all?"

"No, I've a vague feeling of walking down a long street and then nothing," he said.

At this point, the vicar's wife brought his cheese sandwich, which he consumed hungrily and noisily.

"I think we should get the police involved and you need to be seen by the hospital. I'll get my car out and take you to the A & E," said the vicar, his voice having a friendly reassuring tone.

They soon reached the hospital and, on arrival, the vicar, Reverend John Staples, dropped him at the entrance and assured him that he was available to help in the future, if needed.

Chapter 2

In the A & E department, nurses cleaned the head wound and a doctor asked various questions, to ascertain whether there was concussion and to investigate the memory loss. It was eventually decided that the victim should be kept in hospital for a few days, at least, for observation.

"As we don't know your name, we'll call you John Camberwell, for our record purposes, till we can ascertain your real name," said the doctor, with a twinkle in his eye.

John was soon taken up to the observation ward, undressed and put in the bed. They took various tests, his temperature, blood pressure and checked his heart. The Indian doctor was very young, probably only recently qualified, and seemed distinctly puzzled. He went away quickly and soon returned with another doctor, who was older and obviously more senior, with a definite air of authority. He was thick-set with thinning grey hair and glasses that strayed down his nose, as if going to meet the patient. Carefully, he re-took John's temperature, shook the thermometer briskly and took it yet again.

"That's very strange," he said in a voice both grave and disbelieving. "Your temperature is very low – how do you feel?"

John replied, "Well I feel a bit faint, but then I haven't eaten for some time, apart from a sandwich at the vicarage."

The senior doctor then re-checked the blood pressure, and again stared at the dial in disbelief, before going over to talk to the young doctor. John overheard the words. "He should be dead, with such a low blood pressure and low temperature. His blood pressure is only 80 over 35 and his temperature is only 93.3 that's 35.4 in Celsius – they are abnormally low figures. Urgent treatment is required. Arrange for a bed in the Intensive Care Unit, straightaway,"

Once John was installed in the Intensive Care Unit, the doctor instructed the nurse to make the patient comfortable and arranged for him to be drip fed and given a blood transfusion.

John had just settled himself in bed, when a police officer appeared at his bedside, but was quickly ushered away by the nurse and told to return the next day. Various tubes with drips were fixed to his arms. John relaxed and gradually began to feel better. The room was silent apart from the rhythmic bleeping of the monitor and the occasional hissing as colourless fluid dripped into his arm.

John soon drifted back into unconsciousness; probably they had given him some drugs to make him sleep. Eventually, he awoke to see sunlight streaming in the window through pretty, yellow floral curtains. Nurses were dashing about with drugs and John, thought that one in particular was very pretty. His mind again tried to recollect whether he was married, engaged or single, but it remained blank. In any event, he gave her a smile, which she returned and this really lit up his whole life.

He lay quietly until the policeman re-appeared by the bed and began to question him about his experiences. The policeman was tall, slim and rather serious and it seemed to John that he was too young to be a policeman. He introduced himself as Detective-Sergeant Jonathon Wilson and after listening intently to John's story and writing various notes in his notebook, he said

"We must set about finding your identity and that of your attacker, so I'll visit the property, to see if we can find any clues."

"In the meantime, I must now take your fingerprints and a DNA sample, as this may help to identify you," DS Wilson said gravely, producing a sheet of white paper and a pad inked with black ink. "Nothing to worry about," he said reassuringly.

DS Wilson carefully placed each finger and thumb on the black pad and then on the paper. There was silence for a while, before he asked John if he could repeat the exercise. Again he placed each finger of John's left hand on the inked pad followed by each finger of his right hand. He then stared at the paper with a look of total bewilderment on his face. Finally he took a DNA swab.

"I will also have to take your clothes for forensic tests."

As the policeman left, John Camberwell settled down to sleep, he was so tired and his head still ached. After about an hour he awoke and his mind began again to attempt to remember any facts about his life. Again he could only recall walking down that dark street – nothing before and nothing after until he woke up in that room.

The following day, two policemen arrived to talk to him, DS Wilson joined by another older officer, who introduced himself as Detective Inspector Grant.

"We would like to talk to you about your experiences," DI Grant said, in a voice that was superficially friendly, but had an air of suspicion and hostility lurking in the background.

"We've got the forensic results back and the good news is that you're not a known criminal," he said with a hollow laugh.

"Also you're not on our database for fingerprints, but then as you appear to have no fingerprints at all, that is hardly surprising! But, of course, the down side is that it doesn't help us to identify you."

The two policemen continued to question John, about his movements, his memory, and his lack of fingerprints, but John could only reply that he did not remember anything.

Back at the station, DI Grant discussed the matter with his sergeant and another detective. They were all puzzled by the lack of fingerprints. Had they been burned off, because John was a well-known criminal? They'd sent the photos of John to the Criminal Records Office to ascertain if they matched photos of known criminals and circulated the photos to other forces. In addition, they were still puzzled by the hospital reports of his blood pressure and temperature.

John spent five days in hospital, during which time the doctors tried to spark some memories, but to no avail. His mind was like a blank canvas, awaiting an artist to paint a picture. Nevertheless his head wound was gradually healing and he felt physically better.

The doctors agreed that he was probably suffering from Retrograde Amnesia, caused by the head injury and aggravated by the trauma. They thought his memory might return soon or, alternatively, it might never return.

On the fifth day, John was visited by a Salvation Army officer who specialised in finding missing persons. Usually, though, they were seeking a person who was missing, but this time it was the person's identity that was missing.

In the afternoon, Detective Sergeant Wilson returned and reported the forensic results.

"The house contained a few clues, but we are in touch with the estate agents, to ascertain who has keys. It was owned by a Mrs. Owen, who has now been re-located to an old people's home," he explained.

"I'm afraid, your clothes were of little help- the shoes are a common make, as are the shirt and trousers. We did, however, find fingerprints and some other blood stains in the room where you were lying and we hope these may prove helpful."

So John was discharged from hospital with no money, no possessions and no identity. However, a Salvation Army officer, Captain Norman Hargreaves, came to collect him and take him to their local hostel. There he was fed, and provided with some fresh clothes, whilst they tried to assist him in recovering his life. Captain Hargreaves was a rather squat individual, who was friendly, loquacious with a definite twinkle in his pale-blue eyes.

In the hostel, John began to relax and, at last, had one or two glimmers of memory, mainly of his childhood. Each night he avidly watched the television and read at least one of the national papers which were delivered to the hostel. He showed great interest in history programmes and always sat with unwavering concentration during documentaries. Captain Hargreaves passed this information to the police, but they did not consider this to be relevant.

Day followed day and John, the police and the Salvation Army seemed to have reached stalemate. John was becoming bored just sitting around watching television. He felt he should be working, doing something useful. His frustration began to build; surely someone could find out who he was. John's memory had not returned and no-one had come forward with any information, despite the fact that his picture had been circulated on Crime Watch and in the national press. He was proving to be a real mystery man.

After about two weeks, DS Wilson received a phone call from a lady in Romford, saying that she thought she recognised the man in the photo, and immediately travelled to meet her there. Her name was Doris Williams, a shop assistant, in a local chemist, and she said that she was sure the man in question was a regular client at the chemists. Recently he had come in with another man, who had purchased a large supply of hydrogen peroxide.

Meanwhile in the hostel, John avidly watched all the news programmes and documentaries showing great excitement when items about the Islamic extremists came on the television. One evening, they showed a film about the events of 9/11, the Twin Towers disaster and the plane where the passengers had fought back causing the plane to crash-land in a field. When the planes were shown striking the towers, John became very agitated, whilst he showed deep concern at the sight of the passengers resisting the terrorists, on the other flight.

DS Wilson immediately reported this to his superiors, who informed the Anti-Terrorist authorities. That evening, John was resting in his room, when the door flew open and he was grabbed by two men who showed him a badge identifying them as anti-terrorist officers. John was completely bewildered but before he could gather his thoughts, he was bundled into a large black car.

"Where are you taking me?" he asked

"You're being taken in for questioning," the first officer, a burly, man with crew-cut hair, replied brusquely.

"But what for, it was me who was attacked and abducted," John replied angrily.

"You're under suspicion in connection with terrorist activities," answered the burly man, in a non-committal tone.

There was no further conversation, just an uneasy silence, as the car sped through the streets of London, where the street lights were just coming on. At last it drew up outside a plain-looking brick building. John was bundled inside for questioning, but again he protested that he could not remember anything.

"I have told you time after time, I cannot remember anything!" John shouted.

Nevertheless, he was subjected to various techniques, but the police failed to obtain any information from him. The medical officer warned that he still had low blood pressure and a low temperature, which would limit the courses of action the police could take.

John sat in his cell, contemplating the injustice of it all. He had been attacked, lost his memory and all his possessions and here he was, accused of terrorism, locked up in a cell and subjected to pressurised interrogation. He could not believe it.

As a last resort, it was decided to employ hypnosis and so an eminent hypnotist and psychiatrist were called in.

Chapter 3

"Please sit down, John," said the psychiatrist with a friendly smile and hand shake.

"My name is Dr. Quenby, I'm a psychiatrist and this is Dr. Fitzgerald, who is a well-known hypnotist."

"We are here to try to ascertain your identity and to help you remember- so don't be alarmed, just relax," said Dr. Fitzgerald in a quiet soothing voice.

"I just want you to relax and concentrate on this glass paperweight, O.K?"

"I'll do my best," replied John.

Dr. Quenby closed the curtains on the grey afternoon outside, so that the only light came from a shaded desk lamp.

"Now just relax and concentrate on the paperweight, alright?" Dr. Fitzgerald's voice was slow and gentle.

"Your eyelids are heavy, you are getting sleepy." The hypnotist's voice took him deeper and deeper. The hypnotist began to count very quietly and slowly, using a repeated mantra, all delivered in a very quiet, soporific voice,

John concentrated on the glass and listened to the words of the hypnotist, until his eyelids felt heavy; the paperweight became fuzzy and disappeared.

When Dr. Fitzgerald was satisfied that John was hypnotised, he asked him.

"What is your name?"

"My name is Mustapha Bakri," replied John

The hypnotist and psychiatrist exchanged puzzled glances.

"Was that your name as a child?"

"No, my name was Paul Williams."

"When and where were you born?"

"It was 1971 – on June the 15th in Tottenham, North London."

"Tell me about your childhood."

"I went to school in Hackney. I was happy at school and did quite well, in several subjects. After passing my AQ Levels, I went to college. "

"Why did you change your name?"

"After college, I began to work in a bank and when I was twenty-four, I met some friends who were Moslems and they persuaded me to convert to Islam. I should explain that my parents were Church of England and, as a child, I'd been to Sunday school, but as I got older, I gave up going to church. It seemed irrelevant and I was more concerned with playing football, girls and getting a career. The friends repeatedly told me that I had led a selfish and useless life and that I should now serve Allah, the one true God," he replied.

Suddenly John/Mustapha got off his chair, knelt down facing east and intoned, "I bear witness that there is no God but Allah and Muhammad is his Prophet."As he said this he raised his head, before lowering it to the floor.

Slowly he got up, bowed to the doctors and resumed his seat. As he talked, the psychiatrist began to notice a change in him. His speech began to have a slight middle-eastern accent and even his posture changed. He became very serious, making his points with extravagant arm gestures.

"What happened after you became a Moslem, Mustapha?"

"I went to classes to learn the Qur'an, I found this difficult, but felt it important to persevere. I regularly had homework to learn sections of the Holy Book and had to give up football training to fit this in. I visited the Mosque regularly and prayed five times a day. I soon became aware that the faith of Islam was the one true religion. My friends invited me to attend various rallies, especially at the mosque near Finsbury Park, in North London, near the Arsenal stadium."

Mohammed's voice was now raised and he became vehement in his statements. The two doctors sat transfixed by the revelations, Dr. Quenby making copious notes.

"When the Imam talked about the world of politics, I began to realise that American policy in Iraq and in other countries was wrong – it was evil and against the will of Allah." Mustapha was now talking even more belligerently and began to stand up to express his views more forcibly.

"Gradually, however, I became aware that some of the group were advocating violence, which disturbed me, as I am not a violent person. I was torn between my new faith, my friends and my dislike of violence."

"One day about a month ago, they began to plan a suicide bombing in London. I was appalled and argued against it. I had already had some disagreements with the views of the extremists and I opposed quite forcibly the group who wanted to set off bombs in London. I argued vehemently that the majority of the victims would be innocent people, going about their business and would include women and children! They argued, however, that it was part of the Jihad and was the wish of Allah. If they succeeded, but were killed, they would become martyrs. In the end I told them that I could not agree to participate in their plan."

"At the next meeting, they said, threatening me, '*You know about our plan and you know our identities. We must ask you to co-operate with us or face the consequences.*'!"

"So what happened on the night before you woke up in the strange room," asked the psychiatrist.

"I had been to the mosque for a prayer meeting and afterwards, there was a discussion in the adjoining room. Yet again I stated that I was prepared to protest about the war in Iraq, but that I disapproved of violence. Again they threatened me. When I left, I was walking along a quiet road, near the Mosque, when I heard footsteps behind me. I turned around quickly and saw three men hurrying towards me, but before I could do anything, I was seized, my arms trapped by my side by one of the men, whilst another man began to hit me with some sort of wooden club."

At this point, Mohammed stood up and waved his arms about in an effort to defend himself and there was a look of pure terror on his face.

"I quickly lost consciousness and the next thing I remembered was waking up in that strange house. The attackers must have taken all my possessions and, of course, I had lost my memory."

"Thank you, Mustapha, I think we will leave it there for today," said the hypnotist.

"I will now count slowly up to ten and when I snap my fingers, you will wake up."

So the hypnotist counted, snapped his fingers and Mustapha slowly came to, shook his head and relaxed in the chair. He was sweating profusely and still had the look of a hunted animal on his face.

The hypnosis sessions continued and they gradually got to know more and more about the life of Paul Williams/ Mustapha Bakri. Strangely they failed to find out much about his early childhood – all their questions seemed to hit a brick wall. The Psychiatrist felt that this was important. As a consequence, at the next session, they concentrated on his early life.

"Did you have a happy childhood, Mustapha?" asked Dr. Fitzgerald.

There was a long silence. At last, Mustapha began to speak, but after saying "It is difficult," he hesitated and after a further delay in which he seemed to be struggling with his sub-conscious, he finally blurted out.

"No, I was unhappy as a child, in fact, I was abused by my father. He abused me both physically and sexually. I have no idea why he abused me. He just seemed to take a delight in hurting me," he sobbed. Mustapha was clearly distressed and went silent for a while. After a pause, he went on to give further graphic details of the abuse.

Chapter 4

At the next session, Paul/Mustapha was again hypnotised by using the same mantra and they began by asking him…

"Can you give some more details of your early life, your first memories?"

"I was born in Dusseldorf in 1920 – 15th September. My earliest memory was being taken by meine Mutter zu Der Tiergarden."

The hypnotist and psychiatrist looked at each other in amazement.

"What is your name, then?"

"Ich heisse, Helmut Schmidt."

"Do you speak English?" they enquired.

"Ja, enschuldigen sie, bitte, yes, excuse me, I will speak English.

"My name is Helmut Schmidt and my earliest memory, was being taken by my mother to the Zoo. My father was a factory worker in Dusseldorf."

"Tell us about your childhood and early life?"

"Life was very difficult; my father had been severely wounded in the 1914 to 1918 war. When he left the army, he got a job in a local factory, but it was not well-paid and when the hyper-inflation began, we became very poor. They were incredible times, with the price of food doubling every day. Bank notes became worthless and you had to take a big wad of notes to the bakery, just to buy a loaf of bread. There was never enough to eat and I only ever wore second-hand clothes. My father deeply resented the way Germany had to pay for their part in the war and the retribution exacted by Britain and France."

"I was lucky to get a pretty good education and whilst at school, I joined the Hitler Youth."

"Herr Hitler had just become the new leader of Germany and he had some excellent ideas. He wanted to make Germany great again and put behind it, the humiliation wreaked by the allies. He pinpointed the problem of the Jews, who had such an influence on business, especially finance. He told us that they were the main cause of wars as they always profited from them. My father agreed with him, without question."

Helmut was changing before their eyes. He became more self–confident, even arrogant. His answers were given in a clear, clipped voice with a definite guttural, Germanic accent.

"I enjoyed my time in the Hitler youth – we played many sports and went camping and shooting and had trips to the country. I had been brought up in a smoky industrial area and had never enjoyed the beauty and peace of the countryside. Do you know, I never realised how clean the air could be. In addition, we were taught about the glorious history of Unser Vaterland, sorry, Our Fatherland. The organisation was similar in structure to your Scout movement, but there, I think, the similarity ceased."

At this Helmut began to quietly laugh.

"My father was very proud of my achievements with the Hitler Youth."

As he said the word father, he hesitated and stopped talking for a few moments. A strange look crossed his countenance.

"Were you happy at home?" asked Dr. Quenby.

"Naturlich, of course!" he replied in a clipped and dismissive tone.

"Did your father treat you well?"

"Ja, er…" Helmut paused for quite a while, before explaining.

"My er, father, was not well. As I said, he was wounded in the war, not only physically, but his spirit and his pride were severely damaged. He could not help doing, what he did!" Helmut was now beginning to sob as he opened his heart.

"He did ill-treat me, but that was the fault of the allies and the Jews!" As he said this, he almost spat the words out – there was definite hatred in the words expressed. Whether the hatred was directed at his father or the allies and the Jews, it was hard to ascertain.

The doctors observed that Helmut was now becoming very agitated and spoke with a more pronounced, German accent, his words spoken with a vehemence that surprised the interrogators. He also imperceptibly began to assume an arrogant demeanour and began talking to the doctors as if they were his inferiors.

"What happened after you left school?"

"I got a job in an office, as a humble clerk, again not well-paid, in fact it was very demeaning. This was compensated by my work with the Hitler youth and I began to attend rallies. I remember being honoured by being selected to represent my local unit at the big rally in Nuremberg. It was held in this enormous outdoor arena – the parade ground called Zeppelinfeld, which stretched over one hundred and forty-eight acres, ringed with twenty-eight towers each forty metres high. At a previous rally, Hitler reputedly addressed some 1.6 million followers. Can you believe that! At the rally I attended, there was line after line of German troops in their smart uniforms and in front of each line was a standard bearer, proudly carrying their banner. In addition, there were ranks of Hitler's Youth and a large crowd of supporters. When we arrived, there was a fantastic atmosphere of excitement and the cheering became deafening when our beloved leader arrived to address us, He stood on this raised podium at the end of the arena and when he began to speak, there was utter silence from the vast audience – his words were so inspiring and moving. Next door was the Congress Hall, where Nazi party conferences were held and also nearby, the church where the Imperial Jewels were kept, after being brought back from Vienna. I felt I was in the very centre of the universe at that time. It was truly an unbelievable experience." Helmut had a look of pride on his face and his chest seemed to swell out.

"In 1938, I was asked to take part in a special demonstration on the 9th November. I should explain that the previous week a German diplomat had been shot by a Jew and the authorities informed us that this was part of a Jewish plot against the government. We all rallied round and that evening became known as Kristallnacht, – the night of broken glass, I think you call it. We were led by Stormtroopers and set out to smash the windows of Jewish shopkeepers, businesses and homes. In fact many homes were broken into and the contents destroyed. In addition, we attacked many synagogues and a number of these were burnt to the ground. The bystanders were shouting "Juden heraus" and the polizei, sorry, police, looked on, giving us encouragement, so we knew that what we were doing was right. To me at the time, it seemed to be a logical operation; after all they were the cause of our many problems!"

"Were you happy with this?" asked Dr. Fitzgerald.

Helmut was silent for a moment before replying.

"Yes, we wanted Germany for the Germans – the true Aryans! The Jews were one of the main causes of the hyper-inflation and the unemployment."

"Carry on with your story," said Dr. Fitzgerald.

"Well, in 1939 I joined the Reich Labour service for one year, before joining the army to help with the cause."

At this point, Helmut sprang to his feet, clicked his heels together, and raised his arm, shouting "Heil Hitler, Sieg Heil!"

Slowly he resumed his seat and his story. His personality now exhibited a distinctly militaristic quality, and a rather arrogant attitude. Dr. Quenby bit his lip and refrained from commenting on this attitude, although he was plainly annoyed by the patronising tone of Helmut.

"After my training, I was eventually sent to the Eastern Front – June 1941 I think it was. I enjoyed the camaraderie in the army and the fighting, but gradually, I began to hear rumours about the camps where Polish Jews were being sent. In fact, I myself was sent to a camp, where I was ordered to assist the doctors. My superiors told me that they were doing extremely important medical research."

"But when I got there, I was appalled by the work that was being done. They treated the Jews, Slavs and gypsies as sub-humans and the research was similar to that normally carried out on rats and mice. In fact, it was even worse, as there appeared to be no medical benefit to be derived from most of the research – no cures to eliminate painful diseases. A lot of the research seemed to be just for the gratification of the doctors. On my return to my barracks, I questioned my conscience – I set out to try to find out more about the regime. I discovered that countless Jewish men, women and children were disappearing and heard rumours about trains being despatched to far-off places, to the east, loaded with civilians. I began to question my commanding officer, who was very non-committal. He told me, in no uncertain terms, that it was none of my concern. My job was to fight the enemy and win the war for the Third Reich and Germany.

I regret now that I did not take his advice, as I continued to question and to protest about the rumours and the medical research. Two days later, there was a knock on my door in the middle of the night. I opened the door with dread in my heart. There were two Gestapo officers standing there and before I could protest, I was bundled into a black Mercedes car. This sped through the deserted, dark streets to their headquarters, There, I was taken out of the car and frog- marched into the building for questioning. I was thrown into a cell and each day for about a week, subjected to intense interrogation and torture. This went on for hours on end. They thrust lighted cigarettes on my skin, hit me repeatedly with batons and whips and numerous other procedures to make me confess. They even accused me of being a Jew, myself or alternatively, of being a Jew-lover. I was beaten repeatedly, but still I refused to give in and continued to argue against some of their policies."

The two doctors were visibly moved by the harrowing story. They could see that Helmut was in a bad way.

"I think we should leave it there," said Dr. Quenby as he counted to ten and brought Helmut back.

Helmut sat in the chair, visibly shaking, with tears in his eyes.

* * *

The following day they resumed the session.

"Helmut, yesterday you were telling us about the torture and interrogation by the Gestapo."

"Please continue – what happened next?"

"The torture got worse and worse. I even began to believe that I was really guilty of treason against the state. I was almost ready to confess that I was a Jew lover, just so the pain would cease, but somehow I held firm. I kept repeating that Jews were people, just like us and deserved to be treated as such. Naturally this did not go down well."

"Well, after about a week of this treatment, they became tired of me and I was put up for trial. It was an absolute travesty. I was marched out of my cell and bundled into the dock. I had no-one to represent me and the judges did not even seem to be listening to my arguments. The so-called trial lasted barely an hour and the result was a foregone conclusion. Naturally, I was found guilty of treason and sentenced to death the following morning."

"There were no niceties like a last request or a special meal. I was taken back to my cell and left to consider my fate. It was such a long, long night: I couldn't sleep and yet I prayed for it not to end, knowing that come the morning, my life would be over."

"Of course, the following morning inevitably dawned – it was bright and sunny as I recall. Before I could collect my thoughts, I was duly taken out to the yard behind the cells, accompanied by four officers and strapped to a post. Facing me were a group of soldiers all carrying rifles and looking distinctly unhappy at their task. A blindfold was put over my head and I heard the rifles being loaded. As I stood there, with my legs shaking, my whole life seemed to flash before me. There was a moment's silence, before the Officer shouted out "Heil Hitler – Feuer!" I heard the sounds of an explosion and then nothing."

Helmut finished his story in tears – he was sobbing uncontrollably.

After Helmut was sent back to his room, the psychiatrist and the hypnotist sat in the office, visibly moved and unable to discuss the case.

Chapter 5

About a week later they arranged another session, again the subject, Paul/Mustapha/Helmut, was hypnotised. They began by asking him about his schooling.

"Where did you go to school, Helmut?"

"Who the hell is Helmut, my name is Mustapha, I have already told you that I went to school in Hackney." He said this with a definite edge to his voice. As the interview progressed, he began to display the personality traits that had been evident in his earlier interviews as Mustapha. The session did not reveal any further information that was of consequence.

At the hypnosis session, the following week, they again began by asking about his youth.

"Where and when were you born? They asked, not knowing whether he would be Helmut or Mustapha.

"I was born at Dover in Kent in 1765. My father was French, but my mother was English. They moved to England just before my birth. As I grew up, I regarded myself as French, even though I spoke perfect English."

"I beg your pardon, what is your name?"

"Je m'appelle, Jean-Paul Lafortune. Pardon, my name is Jean-Paul Lafortune."

The psychiatrist and hypnotist again exchanged puzzled looks.

"Tell us about your life, Jean-Paul."

"I was educated in England, but my heart was in France and I became very upset at the way the French peasants were being treated. The rich were under-taxed, in some cases paying no tax at all, whilst the tax burden on the poor was unbearable. In addition, the ordinary people suffered in many other ways. I followed all the news in the newspapers and eventually when I was twenty-two, I decided to flee to France, despite the objections of my mother. There I met some young men, who were mainly students from the university, who wanted to change society. I became friends with them and eventually they asked me to join their group. We planned how we could bring about this change, hopefully without too much bloodshed. We used to meet regularly in a small café in Montmartre, where we drank cheap wine and smoked Gauloises cigarettes, whilst making our plans. They were good times as we built up a wonderful camaraderie. Sadly, some would later be killed in the fighting – killed by fellow Frenchmen! Oh, we were young idealists then. We made plans to erect barricades to cause disruption in the capital and thereby pressurise the government to make changes; but sadly the government did not listen. In consequence we planned to storm the Bastille on the Quatorze Juillet, pardon Fourteenth July, 1789. I was enthusiastic, as I felt this would accelerate the change and limit the bloodshed."

At this point, his face broke into a broad smile

"The fourteenth of July was a glorious day; all the young idealists joined up with groups of peasants and gathered in front of Les Invalides. It was later estimated that there were about sixty thousand of us. Firstly we all seized muskets, together with some ten cannons, but we were short of cartridges and powder. In consequence we then had to march to the Arsenal to obtain the necessary ammunition, before setting off for the Bastille, that accursed prison. Perhaps I should explain that the Bastille had been built as a fortress in the Fourteenth century with towers some eighty feet high. It had been used as a state prison for centuries and had acquired a sinister reputation. For us idealists, it symbolised the power of the aristocracy. We had been warned that the governor had heavily armed the prison, anticipating our arrival. Large paving stones had been hauled up to the top of the towers, to drop on our heads, if we attacked. We were not afraid and this did not deter us. We chopped down the ropes which caused the outer drawbridge to be lowered and gave us entry to the main yard. After some negotiations, we destroyed the inner drawbridge. Eventually the governor surrendered and we all celebrated a famous victory, with only a small number of casualties. Our group went back to the café and we drank many bottles of wine, that night. How we got drunk."

At this point, Jean-Paul, jumped up and shouted out "Liberté, Égalité et Fraternité," before resuming his seat and sitting with sweat pouring from his forehead.

As Jean-Paul was telling his story, his personality seemed to change. He became rather reserved, but with a certain Gallic charm. His words were spoken in a quiet manner, quite unlike the rather forceful manner of Mustapha or the militaristic demeanour of Helmut.

"So the revolution began and I played a full part. I even became friends with several of the leaders, Danton and Marat, but later, I became increasingly disturbed by the levels of violence being proposed and especially the guillotining of the aristocrats. The rise of that evil fellow, Robespierre, who proposed the Reign of Terror, was the moment when, I became completely disillusioned with the glorious revolution. Certainly, some of the aristocrats deserved to die for their actions in persecuting the poor, but a lot were innocent. When women were also executed, I decided to protest and had many arguments with other revolutionaries. In consequence, I was asked to explain my beliefs before a tribunal who accused me of betraying the glorious revolution. They did not really listen to my arguments and accused me of being an English spy. They even said that I was the Scarlet Pimpernel, the Englishman who had rescued a number of aristocrats from execution. The following day, I was summoned to another meeting, where I was again subjected to a stream of insults and threatened with violence, if I persisted in my opposition to the Reign of Terror. On my way home, I had to walk through a wooded area, where I was set upon by a gang of youths, some half-dozen of them. I tried to fight back, but there were just too many of them. They beat me with sticks and kicked me till I lost consciousness. When I came to, I was lying in a filthy cell with two other prisoners. My legs were manacled to the wall and I ached all over. One of my companions informed me that my head was bleeding and I had severe bruises all over. He admitted that he had murdered a man for money and probably deserved punishment. He was friendly, but the stench from him was overpowering, he had probably not washed for months. After an uncomfortable night, I was dragged out of the cell, the following morning and led into the court. After being pushed into the dock, the Magistrate read out the charge – Treason. The so-called trial was a farce, I was not even allowed to call witnesses and I swear that the judges had decided the verdict, before the trial even started. Naturally I was found guilty of treason and sentenced to death."

The two doctors sat bemused at this tale, before asking him to continue.

"Well, the following morning I was dragged out of my cell and thrown into a tumbril. In the cart with me were two rather elderly aristocrats, who seemed to be suffering from some sort of senile dementia and were certainly no danger to the state. They kept mumbling, 'they will pay for this treason.' They were so pathetic. Also in the tumbril was a very beautiful young lady, the daughter of a French duke. She had gorgeous blonde hair, but her beauty was marred by the mud that had been thrown at her and had stuck to her face. In addition, she had cuts and bruises all over her face, arms and legs, obviously inflicted on her after her arrest. The tumbril shuddered as it started to move and we were driven slowly through the streets, lined with rowdy, violent peasants, shouting abuse at us and hurling stones, rotten fruit and other objects, which I am sure were excreta. After what seemed an age, we reached the square and there in the middle stood Madame La Guillotine, looking strangely beautiful and awe-inspiring, with the blade glinting in the morning sun. The upright posts framing the blade, seemed to be pointing to the heavens, where no doubt the souls of the victims were hoping to go. The structure was surrounded by a cheering and jeering mass of people, all pushing and shoving to get the best view of the expected gory spectacle."

"I had read that the guillotine was designed by a certain Doctor Joseph Guillotin as a humane method of execution, that was quick and painless, but in prison, I heard reports that it could take up to thirty seconds from the time the blade struck the neck till the victim lost consciousness. One by one we were hauled out of the tumbril and forced to mount the scaffold. It was a lovely sunny morning and we watched enthralled as the blade travelled ever so slowly up the structure, accompanied by a roll on the drums. There was a moments delay, when an official shouted 'Vive La France' and then the blade travelled swiftly down, followed by the sickening noise as it sliced through the neck and the head rolled into the basket followed by a river of blood, again accompanied by a roll on the drums. The mob cheered excitedly and shouted "Vive La Nation, Vive La République!" I must say that the beautiful young lady met her fate with great dignity and I prayed that I would be equally brave. She stood proudly and defiantly on the platform, the sun glinting on her golden hair. After the blade separated her head from her body, and it rolled quietly into the basket, I could not suppress tears, and even the crowd were somewhat subdued by her death. My tears had to be short-lived, because my turn came almost immediately afterwards. I moved forward trying to maintain a dignified ascent, on legs that had turned to jelly, reached the scaffold and resignedly bent my head on the block. The pulley pulled the blade slowly upwards, then the delay – the cry of 'Vive La France' followed by the drumming and the rushing noise of the blade travelling towards its target and then nothing!"

"The doctors sat perfectly still as Francois sprawled on the floor with tears pouring from his eyes, before the hypnotist counted down and snapped his fingers, to release him from the trance and his agony. He sat on the chair shaking terribly as tears continued to pour down his cheeks. The doctors were again amazed by his detailed knowledge of the period.

So the hypnosis sessions continued on a regular basis. The doctors, however, never knew which personality would manifest itself. Some days it was Jean-Paul, at others it would be Helmut, whilst at others it would be Mustapha. Each personality denied all knowledge of the other two personas. Gradually more and more details of the three personalities were elicited from the subject, but the doctors were no nearer solving the mystery of this enigma.

In fact, it got to the point where the staff would have a sweepstake on which of the three personalities would appear at the next session. The Registration and Appointments clerk was quite lucky or clever and made some very useful pocket money from the betting.

Chapter 6

After this practise had been proceeding for about a month, it was decided that there should be a conference to discuss this extraordinary case. The police, Anti-Terrorist Officers, doctors and psychiatrists were called in and there was a long and at times heated discussion of the case. What was the truth of this man? Was he a charlatan, who had invented these fantasies? Was he a person with disassociative identity disorder? Was he a person living the lives of ghosts of the past? Or was he a person who proved the Eastern belief in Rebirth or Reincarnation?

One of the eminent doctors present maintained that it was definitely disassociative identity disorder or Multiple Personality Disorder, as it is more commonly known. He explained that it manifested itself in several patterns of behaviour, each of which is completely forgotten by the patient, when another personality is present. Each pattern of behaviour is a complex and integrated scheme of emotional responses, attitudes, memories and social behaviour. He reminded those present of the book about Eve, which was later made into a very successful film entitled "The Three Faces of Eve".

He then asked whether the patient had shown signs of anxiety and depression and whether there was a history of childhood abuse in this case. Dr. Quenby confirmed that the patient had admitted there had been abuse in at least two of the personalities and also confirmed that the patient had shown symptoms of anxiety and depression, during the interviews.

After a long debate the conference ended, but they could not arrive at a conclusion. They all wondered whether there were any further personalities to be discovered – any more stories set in critical periods of history. What they did, finally, agree on was that he should be kept in an institution and his mental and physical condition monitored carefully.

* * *

So John, Paul, Helmut, Mustapha, Jean-Paul, whatever we shall call him, was taken to a secure mental hospital, where further tests would be carried out, including more hypnosis sessions.

About three weeks later, he was visited by a new Eastern doctor, who was introduced as an expert on cases of rebirth. After he had left, the resident doctor went to give the patient his drugs. As he unlocked the door he found Mustapha lying on the bed apparently in a coma. The regular doctor tried to raise him, but there was no pulse, no heart beat and no sign of breathing. He was dead!

Naturally there was a post-mortem, but this did not reveal any signs of foul play- there were no wounds, no sign that drugs had been injected and the contents of the stomach did not reveal any poisons administered. As a consequence, a verdict of death by natural causes was returned by the coroner. Perhaps the abnormally low blood pressure and temperature, which had never been fully corrected by treatment, had finally taken its toll.

After his death, he became a national celebrity as the newspapers, especially the red-tops, printed article after article about his life. Various theories were expounded and many experts gave their opinions. In addition, questions were asked in parliament.

There was an official enquiry into the case and his sudden death and again this failed to reach a satisfactory verdict. So, in his death, this man had left behind a mystery that was as strange as his life. Was he the definitive example of the Hindu belief in reincarnation and would he be later re-incarnated in a further life, again in a time of trouble or would he now have reached Nirvana? Or alternatively was he a charlatan or a fantasist with an extremely vivid imagination?

His funeral was, of necessity, kept secret – only doctors and some officials attending.

As the funeral procession wended its way to the graveside in the bleak South London cemetery, with an icy wind blowing from the North, the mystery remained. The man with no name, who became the man with many names was buried and with him his true identity. No doubt many books and articles will be written about him in the future, but I fear that no-one will ever know the real truth.

No Way Back

By Jessie Hobson

Unseen, and slithering serpent-like
The tiny signs are there
The misplaced name, the phrase half-thought
The sudden vacant stare.

The foot that falters on the step
The wobble in the walk
The listless inattentiveness
When other people talk.

As time goes on, one cannot read
Or keep one's concentration
One fumbles trying to turn the page
To find an illustration.

The food goes in, the food goes out
All dignity is flown
Dependence on another's care
No power of one's own.

A raging tantrum may occur
Like writhing of a snake
In protest at one's impotence
Such shackling to un-shake.

No sci-fi this, but sinister
The mindless downward slip
Oblivion only can release
Dementia's vicious grip.

The Day That Changed My Life

By David Shaer

I loved my job. The work was second nature. But…

All I had to do was to make a choice – twice a day. Choose a route. That was all: Fenchurch Street station, London, EC3, to Bermondsey Street, London, SE1. And back again in the evening.

How difficult was that? Not at all, but it had to give me pleasure and satisfaction. No time pressure. No surge against rush hour commuters swarming from London Bridge Station. In the morning I was too early; in the evening, too late. Not being confronted by an oncoming, head-down army offensive. Well, not every day.

My choice was simplicity itself; should I cross Old Father Thames by Tower Bridge or London Bridge? I was influenced by the seasons. No, I wasn't. It was by London's weather.

My preference, the Spring season Tower Bridge route. I loved those cool, sunny mornings. They commanded me to stride past the rarely noticed, open green spaces of the moat of the Tower of London.

In the early morning harsh light of the rising sun, I could relax surrounded in regal pageantry as I almost drifted across Tower Bridge. Below me, below the bridge, Old Father displayed proudly his fresh, untarnished new day, on his glistening, dew-soaked waters and everything was smiling happy, crisp, clean and cheerful.

By total contrast, a wet, windy or drizzling morning cast this open space aside and to fight the head down challenge of the early morning, northbound and demented London Bridge battle troops was Hobson's choice; the parapet, my only real protection. Braced with clenched teeth tension, against the advancing nomadic tribes, I shouldered my way past the landmark Monument to counter the umbrella charged masses, totally oblivious to us southbound stragglers. Barging each City bound parapet hugger, no matter what size or gender, gave me pleasure. I always seemed to be at the head of a single line of like-minded marauders, all set up for the day ahead with an aggressive mind set and soon-to-be bruised shoulders.

A keep dry alternative, the number forty bus appeared not to break any of my unwritten rules.

An added challenge was to avoid the use of an umbrella, a singularly useless piece of equipment that serves only as a mediaeval lance when rolled and possibly sharpened.

With a few sidesteps and hand-offs, it was possible to exit stage right Fenchurch Street station main entrance and, mostly under cover, slip into Fenchurch Street where commuter coaches halted to disgorge daily miserable travellers. Interspersed with these carriers of misery, was my number forty red double-decker, sucking up bedraggled queue waiters.

But not for me, mingling with furtivers in the entrance of Prêt à Manger food emporium, none of whom had any intention of purchasing the overpriced wares. Each was merely timing to perfection the leap from store to the opening door of the arriving Clapham Omnibus.

Then the bus stop just short of London Bridge Station and 20 scampered paces into the revolving doors of Price Waterhouse Towers. Escape down into the underground corridors to Hays Galleria and the solace of further weather shielding canopies pointing towards the wine cellar smelling railway arches of Bermondsey Street. Only fifty paces more of unprotected exposure. Taxi drivers still don't want to go south of Old Father Thames.

Then came the return journeys, interrupted occasionally by adjourning to an hostelry after work and thus needing to find the fastest route to an acceptable (to one's spouse) not so early train.

For this, a cab was sometimes acceptable – they want to come north, the route dependent upon the driver's ability to earn payment on condition of my catching the designated train or if he lived in Ilford; or both.

My ready made excuse – the raising of Tower Bridge to accommodate the passing of a Thames Barge laden with partying sots thus just missing the 19.00 and catching the 20.30.

But, one Spring morning, with an early morning watery sun burning its way slowly through the visible dawn clouds of pollution, all of this changed dramatically and forever.

The worst form of pollution stealth every day, no matter which route chosen, was noise, be it the hammering piston of a two-stroke grossly underpowered little motorcycle, the growling clatter of a three tonne delivery truck or the self asphyxiating howl of a diesel double-decker Routemaster, the journey always totally polluted by the decibels of progress.

My particular beautiful, but still eardrum busting morning, I was striding purposefully across Tower Bridge, admiring the full sails of a Thames Barge that was shortly to inflict its bridge opening disruption to traffic flow, taking a group of awestruck Japanese lens-clicking tourists on the experience of a lifetime downriver to the empty Dome and the raised Thames Barrier, God bless them. Long before O_2 and cheap Tesco value mobile telephones had been conceived.

Suddenly, above all of the usual sounds of a London day beginning there rang out a metal screeching, stomach rending, unbelievably slow, laborious and heart-stopping, deadening thud, followed by a split second's silence that exaggerated and

highlighted the intensity of this new, different and appalling sound.

I could only imagine this was similar to the sound of an enormous bomb landing on its target, the deafening noise in the sky somewhere above me. Everybody around me heard it, felt it, even the drivers and passengers of the motorised vehicles emitting their own noise pollution, and everybody turned their heads upwards.

Immediately there followed the rumble of an horrific explosion and there, about ten thousand feet up appeared an enormous ball of fire. Around me was, for a few seconds, the blast of dumbstruck silence. The traffic all around had stopped instantly and everybody was standing, gaping, staring upwards at the unbelievable sight.

Travelling-much-faster-than-sound sight meant everybody had all missed the cause of the reverberating explosion still bouncing around the tall buildings of the City and echoing back towards the River.

And then, from the vast ball of fire, debris began to fall, to float, to twist and turn. At first, it was just debris but then it began to become distinguishable to the discerning eye. In slow motion, a large, silver, tapered platform of metal began to float and flip. Slowly it rolled and, as I looked, it began to disintegrate further in the now harsh light of the sun. I recognised the outline of another, smaller tapered wedge of silver metal and, with a sickening stark moment of realisation, I knew I was witnessing the breaking up of an enormous aircraft. Everybody around me all reached the same immediate conclusion and a communal sharp intake of breath sounded like the roar of a jet engine being thrown into reverse. Everybody stood motionless as the reality registered and a further explosion became inevitable as we watched a second ball of fire ignite – this time pushing out all sorts of different debris.

A penetrating scream came from all around me, an almighty "Oh, my God!" A frozen to the ground, powerless, useless and feeling totally inadequate sensation came over me and all the crowds around me. A mixture of commuters, tourists and all sorts were united as one, grasping together what was happening, what dreadful phenomenon was taking place in the skies above us and how unprepared and useless we all were. The debris was real – we really were witnessing the mid-air collision of two large civil airliners and the world around us had seemingly come to an abrupt, horrific end. The screaming and running started. The need to shelter was paramount but where? We were all in danger. Where to go? Where to hide? Where was safe? Understanding what 'rooted to the ground' meant. Nothing at all could make me move. Speechless, frozen, transfixed, terrified – all of those sentiments and more grasped me by the throat and started to choke me. I could do absolutely nothing. I wanted to look around for guidance from others but I was mesmerised, they were mesmerised, still looking upwards. As more and more debris continued to fall from the sky, I thought that I was not in immediate danger because I was far enough away from the direct path – so why did I suddenly start to run towards it? And the lemmings around me were doing the same. Just as suddenly, "what on earth did I think I was going to do?" hit me. Nobody needed help, nobody was going to survive that, either up there or down here. The best place not to be was anywhere near the ground under this dreadful event.

I turned and started to run back, away, left, right, in circles. I didn't know what I was doing. I was obviously panicking along with all the other lemmings. And just as suddenly, just as unexpected, just as unannounced, I threw up. I don't know why or where or how. It just happened. Shock I suppose. No matter how much you think you've got your life under control, you do not, at all. It takes moments like this to make you realise how small and ineffective you really are. If I was to gain any consolation, it would be that I might have been the first around me to realise how inadequate I really was. Perhaps that made me throw up first. I was setting a trend. I was now surrounded by screaming vomitors. And bits of debris.

Everywhere was painfully apparent that distance from safety meant nothing. Large chunks of unrecognisable metal were falling around us. I saw what looked like an aircraft engine land straight on top of a bus and just cut through it like the proverbial knife through butter. Ignition was instantaneous and I could hear the screaming searing of flesh and minds. I threw up again.

Under Tower Bridge itself seemed to be the only safe haven. I noticed that I was close to some steps that went down to somewhere. I didn't care to where – I just shot down the steps and cowered under the arches. I was shaking, trembling uncontrollably. I was genuinely very, very scared. This was just not happening to me. But at least I was now safe. Nothing was going to get me now. But just as I started to calm down, I was followed down the steps by a violent crash and an aircraft food trolley. I looked at it and suddenly realised that it had an arm attached to it. From the shoulder down – a whole arm. With a watch on the wrist and a ring on a finger. I suppose that this was when I passed out.

It cannot have been out for long because when I came to, nothing had changed. Alone – just me, an arm and a trolley. But not for long. As suddenly as the trolley had appeared, I became smothered, with something dark blue and soft. A blanket, a coat? I didn't know and I didn't want to find out. I just gathered up my mind, my briefcase, my self esteem and decided that I was not going to be there anymore.

I leapt two at a time up the steps I had just come down and ran breathlessly back towards the City. I put my head down and just charged. I was going home and never coming back. Well that was my plan – until, of course, my legs challenged me and changed my mind. But by now I was passing the moat of the Tower heading towards the tunnel under the Highway. There was nothing more to fall out of the sky.

And there it was – an inviting bench. My salvation. My resting point. Never before or since had a park bench been so welcome. As I sank onto it, I went straight back into freeze mode. And there I stayed, for possibly ten or twenty or even thirty minutes – until I started hearing sirens. At last it was no longer my responsibility. I could now relax. Never again would I have to cross the Thames via Tower Bridge. I should never again see the sunrise over Tower Bridge. In fact I probably even won't venture into Bermondsey again.

Other people work from home. I resigned from home.

All this time later, I cannot contemplate leaving the protection of my home. After nearly a year, it took a new found courage just to put my empty milk bottle out on the doorstep each night. But that was as far as I could go. One day I shall pluck up courage to go out again but not yet. I am frozen in time. If I can never think further ahead than ten seconds, maybe I shall stop being interrupted by the screeching crunch, the heat, the explosion and the deafening roar that still invades my head. I wake up sweating, shaking and screaming. I dream of planes falling out of the sky. I lie at night either sound asleep with my eyes open, or wide awake but too scared to open my eyes lest I see the falling bodies, the falling debris or the bus being scythed in two.

Even three years on, or possibly six, or more, I still cannot go out. Other people have phobias about trees falling on them. I don't. This is no phobia. Everything has fallen on me. It is not safe out there. Even sleeping isn't safe because dreams fall on me.

But still the worst thing is the watch-wearing arm. Somebody will never reach 8:26 a.m.; will never need to know that time ever again; I shall never be able to sleep at that time. No matter what I do, I am always awake at 8:26 a.m. Usually it is from about 3:00 a.m. People come to see me. They are going to help me. Then they go away and the dreams start again. The noises in my head get louder. The screaming. When eventually the people come back, they have a new idea or they have forgotten the last one. I can't handle this. I need help. I no longer have a plot to lose.

A Letter from the Grim Reaper

By Simon Woodward

You don't know when you'll come across me.
But... without a doubt... you will.

When you decide to take gun in arms,
you don't know when you'll use it.
But I do.

That person from the other gang.
Do you know them?
Perhaps not.
But I do.

I walk along the streets, cognisant,
waiting for my pray.
R U the 1?
Have gun or knife ready – be worried.
This could be my harvesting day.

What goes around comes around;
many people say.
R U willing?
I am.
This could be your special day.

Your measure draws you closer to the end,

when you walk around the corner or next street
bend.
Who will be there?
Waiting and watching?
– I WILL.

Be wary young traveller,
and understand the decisions you make,
makes your choice whichever option you take;
for good or bad.

Life is for the living,
but tooled up,
U R the walking dead.
And I'm here... waiting,
just 4 U.

I have no job without the foolish and stupid.
But I'm happy to say,
I'm gainfully employed, in this age and this day.

Yours always,
The Grim Reaper

P.S. Watch out!

The Night of the Hag

By Paul A. Bunn

Chapter 1

I stirred for the fourth time that night as I heard Tom crying again. Lucy, my wife lying next to me mumbled something unintelligible as I climbed out of bed.

"I'll see to him, love," I said, putting on my dressing gown.

Tom was six years old and didn't usually wake up this many times in one night, so something was disturbing his sleep. I made my way to his room across the hall, thinking of my early start the next morning and the mountain of paper work I had to get through at the office. I hoped it was a "one off" and he got back to his normal sleep pattern the following night.

"Come on, Tom, what's up?" I pushed his door open and peered into the half-light trying to make out his tiny frame on the bed. I didn't bother with the light this time, feeling that it was only disturbing him further. As I got closer, his crying became more of a wail of anguish and fear. Sitting gently down I reached across, wanting to comfort him and try and control his sobbing. He was as stiff as a board, head now tossing from side to side.

"There, there, Tom, sssh." I lifted him up cradling him in my arms. "What's the matter, son?"

He didn't answer; still in a state of semi-sleep, he gripped me tightly around the neck, tears now running down my shoulder where he had buried his head. Reluctantly, I decided to take him into our bedroom to sleep with us. Lucy wouldn't mind, just for the one night if it helped us all to sleep. An icy cold draft brushed the side of my face as I groped for the door in the darkness. Turning, I thought I saw a deeper shadow move swiftly out of my peripheral vision and let out a yelp of surprise. I held my breath, staring in the direction it had been, but saw nothing.

"Seeing bloody ghosts now." I was surprised how nervous my voice sounded. Waking up a number of times in the night was obviously making my mind play its own little tricks and giving me the jitters. Still, I didn't want to stay where I was any longer, so swung the door open and walked, probably a little too quickly, back to my own bedroom. Placing Tom onto my bed, he was now sound asleep again breathing deeply. Sliding in next to him, I kissed him on his still wet cheek and saw a smile cross his lips.

"Love you, little guy," I whispered, pulling the quilt up to his chin. I rested my head on the pillow studying his delicate face, wondering what dreams he was having that troubled him so much. Sighing, I closed my eyes.

Chapter 2

I couldn't sleep. I kept thinking back to how I had felt in Tom's room, as if someone else had been there. It was ridiculous but the sense of being watched had been strong. I stared at the ceiling, eyebrows knotted together in a frown. Sleep had fled, for the time being at least, and my mind was racing, unable to relax. It was then I heard the crash from the hallway. Startled, I sat bolt upright, my heart leaping in my chest like a trapped bird. I glanced at Tom and Lucy but they were still asleep, undisturbed by the noise.

My mouth was dry as I climbed out of bed, trying to pinpoint in my own mind what could have made such a noise. I looked around the room for some sort of weapon; maybe someone had broken in and knocked something over. There was nothing useful to hand that I could see and I was loath to turn on a light, it would only wake my family and let the intruder know someone had heard him. Reaching for the door handle I hesitated, concentrating on opening the door as quietly as possible. Standing with it ajar, I listened intently for any further sounds, footsteps or any other signs of someone moving about. There was nothing.

Feeling bolder, I moved out, shutting the bedroom door silently behind me and heading for the stairs. I reached for the landing light and switched it on, squinting as the bright light briefly dazzled me. As my eyes adjusted, I saw what had happened and was glad I hadn't walked much further. At the top of the stairs had stood, hooked to the wall, a full-length mirror. It was now in hundreds of tiny slivers on the floor. The odd thing was, the frame still hung, only the glass had shattered, covering the carpet.

"Jesus," I muttered. This was going to take a lot of cleaning up and it couldn't be left until the morning. The broom was in the kitchen so I carefully made my way through the glass and down the stairs.

It took the best part of an hour to get most of the shards out of the carpet; every time I thought I'd finished I found another piece winking at me in the reflected light. Eventually though, I was confident it had all been cleared and carried the dustpan out to empty straight into the bin. I was still trying to work out how on earth the mirror had broken like that without the whole thing falling off the wall. My guess was that the frame may have given way and made a mental note to check it before throwing it away.

Chapter 3

Lucy's screams stopped my deliberation in its tracks, making me drop the dustpan, spilling all the glass. I flew back up the stairs, terror coursing through my veins like ice.

"Lucy?" I shouted. The only response was more screaming, hastening my sprint to our bedroom. I hit the door like a sledgehammer but bounced off it, coming to rest in a heap by the opposite wall, my shoulder awash with pain.

Scrambling to my feet I grabbed for the handle, twisting fiercely but it wouldn't budge.

"Lucy, open the door!" I banged on it with the palm of my hand. There were footsteps and I saw the handle moving but it wouldn't budge.

"I can't open it," Lucy's frantic voice came from the other side. I looked around trying to find something to break it down.

"Hold on!" I shouted, but couldn't see anything that was going to help and felt a tide of panic start to envelop me.

Bang! Bang! Bang!

I jumped as the walls shook under some unseen onslaught, reverberating around the house.

Bang! Bang! Bang!

The sound seemed to be moving around the house at speed, unlike anything I'd heard before. What the hell was going on? It suddenly stopped almost as soon as it had begun. I could hear Lucy whimpering from the other side of the door and tried to break in one more time. Taking one step back I shoulder barged the door with all my might and it swung open this time without resistance. Lucy was standing in the far corner, a petrified expression on her face and both hands covering her mouth. The room was a mess, as if a hurricane had hit it. The bed had been moved half way across the room, covers thrown back and lying half on and half off. All the wardrobe doors were open, along with the chest of drawers with clothes strewn everywhere.

"Where's Tom?" I grabbed Lucy by the arms, probably a little too tightly as she winced. There was no answer; her eyes were glazed in shock. "Where is he?" This time I shook her, demanding a response. Her cheeks flushed and she gasped as my actions had the desired affect.

"Oh my God," she wailed, pulling away from me and making her own hurried search around the room.

"He's not here, Lucy."

She didn't appear to hear me; and was now on her knees looking under the bed. I was about to grab her again when her body stiffened and became still.

"She's got him."

Lucy spoke so quietly I wasn't sure I'd heard her at first.

"What?"

"She took him, she took him." She was sounding hysterical and started shaking as she stood up staring at me with pleading eyes. This was making no sense at all as I tried to control my own rising alarm.

"Who's taken him?" I wanted to shake her again but knew it would waste more valuable time. I needed to find out what Lucy had seen and more importantly, where Tom had gone. For a moment, she said nothing, a deep frown the only sign of any activity in her mind.

"The old woman," she said, and then fainted.

Chapter 4

I caught Lucy as she fell so she didn't hurt herself and laid her head gently onto the carpet. She was pale, and a faint sheen of perspiration had appeared on her forehead, but her breathing, although shallow seemed regular. I stood, feeling lost and uncertain what do next. What had Lucy meant by *"the old woman?"* Surely, no person of that description could have taken him? I was tempted to try and revive her but felt it might do more harm than good, the way she was looking at the moment. Tears sprung into my eyes as the frustration built within me, knowing I had to do something. What was it Lucy always said to me? *"The trouble is you think too much and don't spend enough time doing.*" She was right; the new extension to the house was still in its planning stage and that project had begun five years earlier.

A thud downstairs brought my mind back into focus and I dashed along the landing to the stairs again, still not comprehending what the hell was going on. At first, everything seemed in place, unlike the mess upstairs, as I searched room by room. Then I noticed the back door ajar, moving back and forth slightly in the breeze. I knew it had been locked when I'd gone to bed, as I had been the one to lock and check it. As I cautiously approached it, I could hear voices coming from outside, speaking in whispered tones. My hands were sweaty as I reached for the doorframe and opened it fully. The light from the house cast only feeble amounts onto the garden, and, even then, for only a few feet. Beyond this was just a pool of inky blackness, leading into what I knew was about a hundred feet of lawn with a small cherry tree, bought a couple of years earlier, down near the end to the right hand side.

"Hello, Tom?"

I could still hear something, but now wasn't sure whether it was just the breeze blowing through the hedges on either side. The torch was under the sink in the kitchen so I went back in and quickly retrieved it. "He *must* be out here," I thought. There seemed no other logical explanation; the front door was still locked with all the windows shut. A shiver ran through me and I pulled my dressing gown closer around my body, pointing the torch onto the grass ahead of me. Taking a deep ragged breath, I moved cautiously off. The garden sloped shallowly downwards after only a short distance, so I couldn't rush on this wet ground in case I slipped. The light from the torch cut swathes through the night but I saw and found nothing. I was about to give up when something caught my attention in the far corner where the tree had been planted; a lighter shadow that didn't seem to fit in to the uniformity of its surroundings.

As I raised the torch in its direction, it moved. A sharp, cackling laugh exploded from it as my torch found an old, wizened face.

My legs almost gave way at the sight and the torchlight visibly shook as my hands trembled.

"Hello, dearie," she said.

As I widened the angle of the beam I saw that she was sitting, not on the ground but on the chest of my son, Tom.

Chapter 5

I couldn't move. Tom, even in this light, looked pale and was ever so still; too still. The old woman was looking at me with luminously green, challenging eyes. Her clothes were drooped over her like rags, flowing in long tassels from all parts of her body. The heavy wrinkles in her face were offset by long, shockingly white hair, which reached down to her waist. Her legs were gripping Tom's body like a vice.

"Who are you and what do you want?" My voice sounded dry and cracked and I was ashamed at the fear I felt at that moment.

"I've got what I want dearie, so no need to worry." She flashed a smile, showing a set of teeth that looked like crumbling tombstones. "I don't have a name although some people call me a hag, which doesn't show much respect do it? Now leave me be." At that she turned away from me and focused herself onto Tom, staring intently at his face. I was still rooted to the spot, my legs refusing to move. The hag's expression had changed; her thick bushy eyebrows were arched in concentration. Initially, nothing happened but then there was a thin bead of ghostly light coming from the centre of her forehead, making its way inexorably towards Tom. When it touched him, Tom's body shook violently and his head thrashed from side to side just as it had earlier but now much more violently. Despite this, the hag hung on, appearing to enjoy it, as a cowboy would enjoy riding an untamed horse. This forced my unwilling legs into action. My son was everything to me and no-one was going to hurt him. Without thinking I leapt forward, arms outstretched screaming like a banshee, wanting to tear her apart. A cold blast buffeted past me just before I landed in a heap beyond my son's body, dropping the torch in the process, which went out. I couldn't see anything apart from the dim lights from the house. One thing I sensed immediately though was that Tom and the hag were gone.

"Shit," I shouted, fumbling for my fallen torch, which seemed to take an age to find. Grabbing it and switching it on I scanned around the garden again but this time there was nothing to be found. Running up the garden back towards the house I had a hunch where they might be, Lucy's sudden scream confirmed my suspicion and I picked up the pace. I remembered from something I'd read years before that a hag attacked its victim by giving them nightmares, sitting on their chest and holding them down. This in turn made the poor soul concerned unable to breathe properly and have a feeling of paralysis. No permanent harm ever came to them though. What didn't make sense was the abduction element; this I hadn't heard of before. I just knew that Tom was in danger of more than just having a few bad dreams.

Back on the landing, my bedroom was suspiciously silent and in darkness, Lucy's cries had stopped abruptly whilst I was still climbing the stairs. With increasing trepidation, I approached the door, pushing it gently open and peering in, the dull thud of my heart the only thing I could hear. The light from the hallway illuminated Lucy, lying on the floor, but in a different position to the one I'd left her in. She was on her side with an angry red mark just above her left eye; then I noticed her arm. Feeling the bile rise in my throat, I could do nothing more but vomit onto the carpet, continuing to retch until my stomach was empty. I closed my eyes to try and shut out the image, but it stayed like a scene out of a horror movie. Her arm was twisted at an impossible angle, bent completely the opposite way to a normal bend at the elbow, with bone protruding through the skin.

"Lucy." I rushed over to her, not looking at her limb, just concentrating on her beautiful face. She moaned softly as I held her head, tears stinging my eyes as I thanked God she was alive.

"It'll happen to you, dearie, if you don't leave me be."

That ancient, evil old voice cut through the gloom as it had in the garden moments earlier and I felt a surge of anger. However, I didn't move as I had outside, letting my mind become calm, knowing I couldn't just rush her, needing to know more before deciding what to do.

"What do you want?" I could just make the hag out, sitting on the bed with Tom lying behind her. I was relieved she wasn't astride him as she had been.

"You know what I want. I told you." She turned, stroking Tom's hair gently with her withered old hand. I felt my skin crawl, imagining her touch. Thankfully, Tom didn't stir.

"I needs his body, I needs his soul." She began to rock, humming tunelessly to herself. "Only then will I be re-born; time is short."

For just a moment I saw a sliver of fear cross her face, like a fleeting shadow, before it was gone so quickly I thought I might have imagined it. Lucy began to stir again; I could only imagine the pain she must have been feeling.

The hag gave a guttural laugh. "See what happens when you interfere," she said, pointing at Lucy on the floor. "This boy is mine, he will feed me for the next hundred years, so's I can give more people nightmares." She threw her head back and shrieked in wild delight.

Hearing her plan for Tom tied my stomach into knots of terror, time was indeed short. If I was right in sensing she didn't have much time to carry out her scheme then I had to do something now. I was surprised how quickly I moved, leaping forward and grabbing Tom from the bed. The hag was incredibly fast though, grabbing at my arm and tearing a large gash into my forearm. It felt like it had been doused in flames and I roared in pain. I didn't let Tom go though, gripping him tighter in my desperation not to lose him.

"Give him back, he's mine." The hag towered over me, hovering three or four feet off the floor, arms outstretched with hands extended like claws. A chill wind blew out of nowhere, whipping the contents of the room into a tempest of flying objects. I stood firm, staring into the witch's wrath filled eyes in my own defiance.

"You will not have him." Tears fell down my cheeks as the hag edged closer, her image filling my vision.

"Give him to me, I needs him," she thundered. I noticed a subtle change in her voice though: a hint of pleading perhaps? She reached towards Tom and me but got no closer than a few inches away. Screaming her fury and frustration she sank back towards the bed, arms now loosely held by her side.

"I needs him." Her voice had changed to a whimper. "Gives him to me or I can't carry on." She didn't appear to be talking to me now, but to herself. The air in the room had stilled as immediately as it had begun. As I watched the hag began to diminish, shrinking like a wilting flower until nothing was left.

"Dad?" The sleepy voice of Tom came from my shoulder where his head rested. My heart soared; it was the most wonderful sound I'd heard in my whole life. He still looked very pale but a little colour was coming back into his cheeks.

Chapter 6

Once every hundred years a hag changes from a nuisance giving human's nightmares to a killer keeping themselves in existence by taking just one life.

Only one hag had gone, her inability to regenerate using the body and soul of a human child proving her undoing. This is a rarity; there are thousands more out there. Tonight it could be your turn...

She Was Cool

By David Shaer

She was good, she was cool, she was nobody's fool
And she gave off an air of good grace
But the one thing she lacked, an unpleasant fact,
She never could talk to your face.

Her charm was her smile, 'twas there all the while
Her beauty grew deep in her eyes.
The call of her lips, the curve of her hips
The Princess who would tantalise

So pretty to some, her features could numb
Her laugh was infectious and kind
Whatever she did, that innocent kid,
She always took over your mind.

We loved her for sure, her body demur,
Her giggle the image of love
She drew us all in, her favours to win
Our aim to find heaven above.

Her delicate hands, not one person withstands
The pressure she put on all men
Her indirect look our confidence took
Yet we all came to do it again.

We thought we knew best, took a glance at her
chest
We could handle our looks with disguise
Discretion our aim, not up to her game
Her hand she would pat on our thighs.

Her thought was now set, her target to get
Each boy to succumb to her ways
Her devious plan to control every man
For all of their forthcoming days.

The plot was not quick, but twisted and slick,
She knew that all men were the same
The slowly approach, within mind to encroach,
Then offer to take half the blame.

So simple the plan, lead on just the man
And flatter his ego, the fool
His weakness exposed, the prey now enclosed
Administer one final tool.

Still looking elsewhere, she knew how to dare,
She never looked full in the face
Our man's cause was lost, her eyes turned to frost
As flash from the camera took place.

The blood curdling scream, his now shattered
dream
He knew that his fate had been sealed
The blackmail began, the guilt of the man
His savings would now be revealed.

She was callous and hard, the Queen of the Guard
She squeezed the blood out from the stone
No man escaped, his mind had been raped

And his wallet was bared to the bone.

Each man cast aside, with shame and no pride,
And hoped that she'd finish the job
But the Queen was severe, she'd sever an ear
Or anything else she could rob.

Now broken and sad, he tried to be glad
She'd actually spared him his life
But little he knew, she wasn't quite through
She'd now get in touch with his wife.

Whatever your plan, pathetic small man
Forget it, it's nature that wins
You thought you were strong, Boy, how you were
wrong
She'll kick where it hurts - on your shins.

How could you not remember those stilettos, eh?

A Quiz Night in the Sticks

By Simon Woodward

"Are you sure we're on the right road?" Paul asked his wife, after what had already been two miles travelling along something that was hardly a road, and more like a rarely used track only wide enough for a car. The scraggy tufts of grass along its centre and high hedgerows on either side were telling him they must be off the usual tourist routes.

Jane didn't answer and after quickly glancing at his wife, and seeing the look on her face, Paul decided not to push the point any further. She'd always been an excellent navigator and because the *road* wasn't what he'd expected, he should have known better than to question her skills. Jane ran a hand through her thin blonde bob, as if conscious her husband had been observing her.

They'd left booking their holiday, for the New Year, too late to get a place on the coast of Cornwall. So they'd accepted the fact that the Swedish style lodges they'd found advertised on the Internet, in the grounds of Eastcutt Farm, well away from the coast, was where they would have to stay if they were going to carry on with their Cornish breaks over the festive period.

Moments after Paul's comment, a large beige sign attached to an oak tree, loomed out of the hedgerow. "Eastcutt Farm & Lodges" it indicated in very visible maroon lettering; a small black arrow pointed to a concealed entrance on the left. Paul indicated and turned the car into the lane that was somewhat smaller than the vestigial road they'd been travelling. He shook his head wondering where they would end up. Jane didn't notice, the views of the frosted countryside outside the car keeping her attention.

A quarter of a mile further on, another sign appeared; "Reception" it declared. No matter how much faith Paul had in Jane's incredible navigation skills, he was always stunned when they ended up where they ought to be and he was envious, though he could never admit it. He pulled up on the gravel laid parking area, crunching to a halt next to a wooden planked reception building.

Paul and Jane got out of the car and stretched their legs; the four hour drive from their breakfast stop at Stonehenge, taking its toll.

As Jane pulled her blue and grey Berghaus jacket tighter, to fend off the cold, she gave Paul an "I told you so" look across the car's bonnet. Paul shrugged knowing he shouldn't have questioned the route his wife had chosen.

Though there was a sign hanging on the glass panelled door to the reception stating it was open, the only light inside was seeping from another room behind the reception's desk, its door slightly ajar.

Paul was about to comment that the reception looked deserted when a small head, with long lank mousy brown hair, quickly peeked out and disappeared again.

"Looks like there's someone in," Paul said to his wife and the couple walked the short distance from their car and entered the bare reception area.

As per the outside, the interior walls were of thin pine planks; the flooring was the same. On one of the walls hung a cork notice board, bereft of any notices. The reception's counter was surfaced in nondescript Formica.

Paul and Jane looked around, trying to find something to summon someone so they could book in for their short break, but there was nothing.

Jane called out. "Hello?"

The door behind the counter opened slowly and a woman in her late thirties, wearing an obviously old, baggy brown woollen knitted jumper, entered the reception. Paul recognised the lank hair.

"Ah. Good," the woman said. Paul noted a peculiar reluctance in the woman's few words. "Mr. and Mrs. Johnston?" the woman asked.

"Yes," Paul said.

The woman began to explain the general rules of the holiday site and what should be done in case of any problems. Once she'd finished her spiel she reached under the counter and retrieved a set of keys. Without meeting Jane's gaze the woman handed the keys over, her hand trembling almost imperceptibly.

"If you would like to take your car to the cabin, to unload, then there's a small gap between the trees over there," the woman said pointing to a gap that wasn't visible from where they were standing. "You can only take the car when loading and unloading. The rest of the time you must park where you are now."

"Thank you very much," Jane said.

Jane and Paul left the woman in the reception and got into their car. Paul didn't mention the peculiar demeanour of the woman as Jane hadn't indicated she'd picked up on anything out of the ordinary.

As soon as Paul had reversed their car a little way out of the parking area, he spotted the gap the woman had spoken of. "Ah! There it is," he said and drove the car through the gap, then down the gravelled slope that had been cut through the thirty foot wide strip of fir trees. Exiting the manmade track way Jane and Paul saw the woman from the reception beckoning them, insistently, toward a log cabin that was raised from the ground on breeze block stilts. It was almost as if the woman's life depended on them reaching their cabin, and no other by accident or folly.

Paul frowned as he pulled up next to the wooden cabin. He couldn't imagine how the woman had got there before them.

Turning off the engine he looked at his wife and could just make out the smile on her slightly round face, hidden beneath the hair of her blonde bob, as she looked out of the passenger window at the lodge. He smiled too, happy that she was happy. They got out of the car.

The woman from reception stood on the veranda that fronted the lodge and opened the cabin's wooden framed glass panel door, as the couple walked up its few steps, and showed them in.

The inside was impressive and had all mod-cons. Apart from the huge expanses of glass making up the front; the cabin was entirely of wood, planks for the interior and logs for its exterior.

Before leaving Jane and Paul to unpack, the woman said, "John, the farmer who owns this site, is having a quiz tonight in the pub about three hundred yards further on from the reception." Again Paul felt the woman was giving information against her wishes.

"Thanks," Jane said. "That'll be nice." The woman left.

"Well. Wasn't that strange?" Paul said.

"Strange?"

"Oh. Nothing," Paul said. "Shall we get the stuff in?"

"That'll be a good idea."

Before going back to the car to unload Paul and Jane stopped on the veranda and looked around. The place felt isolated and calm. The iciness of the last few days had glazed the surrounding vegetation and the small fifteen foot wide strip of grass that separated cabins from the line of fir trees hiding the entrance to the site. It was ideal.

As they made their way down the frost covered steps to the path and their car, a voice called out, "Hello?"

They both looked up. A man in grubby overalls, who had seemingly appeared from nowhere, was striding quickly towards them across the crystal sparkling grass in front of the lodge next to theirs.

"Hello. It's Paul and Jane I take it?" the man said.

Jane nodded.

"I'm John and this is my farm. It's great to have you here. I hope the cabin is to your liking."

Paul was dumbstruck. Where had this guy appeared from and how did he know their names? How had he known they'd arrived? It was only a mere few minutes since the woman had left them and Paul hadn't noticed a mobile phone on her belt or any tell tale bulges in her pockets. He was certain she hadn't had enough time to let the farmer know they were here.

Jane said, "Hello."

As the man got closer Paul saw how grubby his overalls were. Little pieces of straw covered the navy blue dungarees and dotted amongst them were spatters of something deep red in colour.

As if reading Paul's mind, John said, "Sorry about my clothes," the farmer made a sweeping gesture down his front, "but I've just been feeding the sheep."

Paul thought, *Feeding the sheep to what?*

Jane said, "That's alright."

"Anyways," John said, "I was wondering whether you'll be popping into my pub a bit later, for the quiz night. It starts at eight p.m. You *will* be there?"

"Of course we will," Jane said. She enjoyed her quiz nights.

"Good. Use your torch on the way. The path to the pub is very dark this time of year."

Paul pressed the button on his car's key fob to open the boot, the boot unlocked and as Paul was about to echo his wife's acceptance of the invitation, the words stopped in his mouth. John was gone. Paul froze for a moment, attempting to work out what had happened to the man.

After half an hour they'd finished unloading and Paul stood on the veranda to have a cigarette. Although it was now only five thirty and early evening, the site was utterly silent – no wildlife could be heard clucking, tweeting or cawing. Nothing rustled in the bushes and nothing scampered across the grass strip in front of the twelve or so Swedish cabins on the site. It seemed, at this moment, the world had become devoid of sound.

Paul shuddered. He couldn't understand how something that seemed so idyllic could also seem so ominous. Shrugging the thoughts off, he finished his cigarette and went back into the cabin to help Jane finish setting up their temporary home, unpacking the food and loading up the pine cupboard in their bedroom with their clothes for the next few days. Paul then made his way to the kitchen and pumped all the coins he could find in his pockets into the electricity meter. The place would need a lot of heating if they weren't going to freeze overnight.

After a snack of cheese on toast and the time now six forty five, the couple got ready for the quiz night. Paul and Jane left their cabin and walked up the short path between the trees, to the lane that led to the site's pub. Paul now knew why John had mentioned the use of a torch; it was unfortunate they hadn't brought one with them. There was no moon and no light pollution; the site was truly out in the "sticks" and as still and as silent as a... Paul didn't finish the thought. Jane hugged her husband a little closer in the darkness, as if she'd been infected by the notion that had passed through his mind.

Turning a corner in the lane the festive New Year lights of the pub came into view and at last they could see the path they had been tentatively following. Like moths to a flame Paul and Jane made their way the final hundred yards to its entrance and entered the pub.

The converted barn had a low ceiling and Paul had to stoop as he entered, his six foot two stature not allowing him to stand upright. However Jane was okay, being almost a foot shorter than he.

To Paul's mind the pub's décor was eccentric, if not damned weird. Although the walls were whitewashed and its ancient wooden beams painted black, the two goats' skulls and a single sheep's fleece pinned to its walls, gave the place an otherworldly feel.

As the couple walked further into the warm pub, towards the bar, the ceiling got higher and Paul was able to stand. Everyone there welcomed the couple as they walked in, saying such things as; "*Good to see you, Jane*", "*Nice to see you, Paul. Hope you like the place*", and "*Glad you could make it*". Paul and Jane nodded their acknowledgments.

A wood burning stove halfway between the door and the bar against the left hand wall provided the heat. Jane sat down at an empty table against the wall opposite the burner.

Next to the stove sat a large bellied man who leant back against the pub wall behind a small mahogany table, not a single hair covering his head. At the same table, two teenage girls and an older woman sat, the trio still wearing their outside coats, the girls' ones more fashionable than the one the other woman, presumably their mother, was wearing.

At the bar on a stool was another man, also in an outside jacket, a dark blue one this time, compared to the light colours the teenagers wore, with a woollen hat pulled down to his brows and a beard that covered his face in its entirety.

On the surface everything *seemed* right to Paul; the amicable introductions, the lack of prejudice from the locals and a general feeling of "rightness" – a happy atmosphere all in all. But no matter what his perception, the whole circumstance had an edginess lurking somewhere beneath the good-humour, and Paul couldn't figure out why. Possibly it had something to do with the fact it wasn't New Year's Eve – a time when people might behave like this; it was the day before. And the more he thought about it the more he couldn't shake the feeling the whole situation had an overtly embracing wrongness about it.

Paul continued to the bar and ordered himself a pint of the local cider and a Bacardi and Coke for his wife. Then made his way to the table Jane had sat at.

"Isn't this lovely?" Jane said quietly. The room was small and didn't lend itself well to private conversations.

"I suppose, but don't you find this all a bit peculiar?"

"Peculiar?"

"Well... you know... the décor? The way everyone knows our names, for instance."

"Don't be silly, Paul. It's their way of making us feel welcome. I'm sure the woman from reception let them know."

Paul wasn't so sure. The woman from reception wasn't even in the bar. He might concede the point, later, if she ever turned up. He supped his pint and looked around. Everyone seemed genuine enough though, sitting in their small groups, around the other five tables, all chatting happily to one another. The bearded man chatted to John whilst he pulled a pint for himself.

After half an hour the quiet background music got even quieter and John picked up some sheets of paper. "Okay," John said, and the conversations hushed. "Right. Round one of tonight's quiz will be the general knowledge round."

John made his way from behind the bar and walked over to where Paul and Jane were sitting, past the tables that were nearest to the bar, the people sitting at them not even noticing they'd been overlooked in favour of the newcomers.

John winked at the couple. "Don't worry if you lose, we've got a professional quiz team in tonight." He handed Jane one of the sheets of paper, there were lines on it numbered one to twenty. "Do you need a pencil or pen?"

"No thanks," Jane said as she took a pen from her handbag.

John smiled, and before leaving them he took a tooth pick from the breast pocket of his tweed jacket and began to dig at something stuck between his teeth. Once satisfied he walked away handing out the remaining sheets, then returned to the bar to start the quiz. "Don't forget to write your team name at the top of the sheet. And here we go, question one; which of these continents has the greatest landmass. Is it a) Britain, b) Australia, or c) Antarctica?"

"Oh, that's easy," Jane whispered as she wrote down Antarctica.

After half an hour of delivering questions, John said, "We're half way through round one and time for a little breather I think. If you need a break or a drink now's the time, part two of the general knowledge round will recommence in fifteen minutes."

"Do you want a top up?" Paul asked his wife.

"Yes please."

"Same again?"

Jane nodded and Paul took their empty glasses to the bar to order another round. As he waited for their drinks the man in the woollen hat finished scrutinising his answers, turned his sheet over and started to roll himself a cigarette. Paul glanced at the man out of the corner of his eye; his beard really did cover his whole face. *Weird*, Paul thought.

"That'll be four pounds eighty please," John said.

As Paul took the money from his pocket, the man in the woollen hat and dark blue jacket got up and made his way out of the bar to have his roll-up.

"Thanks," Paul said and went back to his table, putting the drinks down. "I'm just going outside for a cigarette," he told Jane.

"Okay. See you in a minute," she said.

Paul pulled open the door to the pub and stepped outside, then shivered. The temperature had dropped considerably and a mist was beginning to develop. As he shut the door behind him he realised the furry faced man was nowhere to be seen.

Paul took his packet of Marlboro Lights from his coat pocket and placed one in his mouth as he leant back against the railings surrounding the large top step of the bar's entrance. Putting his hand into his coat's pocket, seeking his lighter, he looked around.

There were four outhouses of differing sizes, but no sign of the bearded man.

Pulling the lighter from his pocket, he flicked its flint. A flame sparked and, as he craned his neck forward to light his cigarette, a movement in his now diminished night vision stopped him. He looked up, away from the flame, toward the bushes that lined the furthest edge of the lane, and frowned, shaking his head.

"You didn't see that," he told himself, trying to rid the idea that he'd seen someone in a dark coat leap from the ground, over the hedge and into the lower branches of the trees that lay beyond. A sound of snapping branches drifted across the silent farmscape. Paul took a couple of deep puffs. "You're just tired," he tried to reassure himself. "You've been on a long drive and you're *just* tired." Paul finished his smoke quickly and went back into the pub.

He sat down and finished half of his pint in one go.

"Paul, you okay?"

"I'm just tired. Six hours is a long drive."

"Okay, ladies and gentlemen. And locals of course," John said and quiet laughter broke out. "We're now starting part two. We're still on the general knowledge round and question eleven is; which of the following chemical symbols represents diamond. Is it: a) C, b) Di or c) H_2O?"

Jane looked at Paul. "I don't know this one. What is it?"

"It's C."

"Are you sure?" Jane asked. "I thought H_2O was water."

"No, it's C for carbon."

"Oh! A."

"Yes," said Paul a little too forcedly. He was finding it hard to relax, his thoughts elsewhere.

"Don't get cross."

"I'm not cross. Just tired. That's all," he said.

The questions carried on and Jane continued to fill in the answers.

As John was about to read out question seventeen Paul crashed his pint onto the table as a thought struck him.

"You alright?" Jane asked, concerned, seeing her husband had paled.

"Yeah, of course," Paul said. But he wasn't. Whilst he'd been concentrating on the questions his subconscious had proposed an answer as to why he felt something wasn't quite right. *"They're afraid of scaring us away,"* it had posited. Why that should worry him, he didn't know.

"Are you sure, Paul?" Jane pushed.

"Of course I'm sure. Don't worry. Just answer the questions and make sure we win. We can't be beaten by a professional team; especially not on holiday."

* * *

"Okay. That's the end of the general knowledge round. Please exchange your answer sheets and after you've done that, don't forget the bar is still open for drinks and snacks."

The bald man with the paunch walked towards Paul and Jane's table, answer sheet in hand. He rubbed his stomach in a circular motion as he made his way and mumbled, "Yum, yum, yummy," then winked at Paul.

Paul blinked. "What?" he breathed.

"I said; Jane, here's our answers, how do you think you did?"

Jane looked up from her answer sheet. "Okay, I think," and swapped the sheets. The man nodded and walked away with Team Jane's answers.

Paul thought about asking his wife whether she'd seen what had gone on, but looking at her he realised it would be pointless. He stared into his empty pint. "Do you want another drink? I think I could do with one."

"Yeah, but just a Coke this time."

"Okay." Paul got up, giving the fat man's table a wide birth as he returned their empty glasses to the bar. Whilst he waited to be served he noticed that the furry faced man had not returned; the guy's answer sheet remained face down. Paul glanced around the pub, the man was not there.

John filled Paul's glass and got a fresh one for Jane, topping it up with Coke only.

"How are you doing?"

"I think we're doing quite well," Paul replied.

"Reckon you'll like the next round – it's a little bit different."

Paul handed over the cash for the drinks but didn't respond. *A little bit different*, Paul thought. *This whole place is a little bit different.*

Paul sat down next to Jane. "John thinks the next round is going to be a little bit different. Is that possible with quizzes?"

"I suppose he must mean the subject."

"I can't imagine any subject that hasn't been used in the quizzes we've been to."

"Let's wait and see. You never know."

The large bellied man got up from his table after a short conversation with one of the teenage girls. Picking up a scuttle next to the wood burner he opened the burner's thick glass and metal doors, and using a scoop, he shovelled short chopped logs into its centre. Once satisfied he replaced the scuttle, closing the wood burner's small doors and returned to his seat.

"Right people, the final round," John said.

Paul looked at Jane and whispered, "Final round? I knew it was going to be a bit different but only two rounds in a quiz?"

"It must be the way they do it here."

"Get your pen or pencils ready. The last round in tonight's quiz is… religion."

"Not that different then," Paul said to Jane.

Jane smiled.

"Okay," John said, "the first question of round two is; in the Christian belief system which one of these is said to be present in devil worship?"

Paul gave Jane a quick frown.

"Is it: a) Christ with a thorny crown, b) the donkey from the nativity, or c) an inverted cross?"

Jane wrote "C" on their piece of paper.

"Can you believe this?" Paul asked Jane tersely beneath his breath.

"It's only a quiz on religion."

Paul nodded twice. "Okay, okay. I'll go with that – just until something more weird happens."

"Question two," John said. "Which of the following numbers is said to represent the anti-christ? Is it: a) 999, b) 118, or c) 666?"

Jane scribbled down her answer.

Paul looked sternly at Jane. "This is mental," he hissed. "Can you believe these questions?"

"Paul, it's a quiz. That's all," she whispered back.

Paul conceded. "Okay, it's a quiz. But if this goes on for much longer, I'm out of here. Okay?"

Jane didn't respond, she'd had enough of Paul's wild assertions that there was something untoward going on.

The quiz carried on and Jane, after every question, wrote an answer on the paper.

"Okay, that's the end of round two. Please exchange your answer sheets for marking."

As Jane checked everything she'd written down the fat man from the other table got up and walked across the room to their table.

Smirking as he approached the man said, "Here's Team Reficul's answers." He thrust his sheet towards Jane.

"Thank you. Here's ours," Jane said, swapping the sheets again.

"How d'you think you've fared?" the man asked, resting both hands on the table as he bent over so his head was level with theirs.

"Quite well, I think," Jane said. "I used to be a Catholic, so this round was quite easy."

The fat man stood up abruptly and as he walked back to his table, he shuddered.

Paul studied the back of the receding man, then turned to his wife. "You can't tell me that wasn't weird."

"Paul, he shuddered, that's all. You really must be tired, all these crazy thoughts you're thinking. I'm glad it was a short quiz."

"Ladies and gentlemen, all the sheets have been handed in and the scores have been calculated." John paused for a moment, then said, "I'm very happy to announce that Team Jane, albeit coming second to our professional team, have won, with thirty three points."

All the people in the pub nodded their appreciation of the result, a few clapping as well.

"Well done, Team Jane," John said, leaving his position behind the bar. "Here's your prize."

John walked over to the couple holding out a blue circular tin of chocolates. "Not a lot I know, but it may fatten you up." The farmer smiled.

"Thank you very much," Jane said laughing, accepting the Cadbury tin.

Paul was nonplussed.

"Can I interest you in another drink? One for the road, so to speak."

Before Jane could respond Paul answered. "Sorry, not tonight, John. It's been a long day. Need to get some shut eye if we're going to make the most of tomorrow."

"So be it," John said, his demeanour darkening as he walked away.

Jane and Paul put their coats on and before exiting the pub turned to say their farewells, but no one was looking their way and John was talking quietly to the bald fat man.

Standing on the top of the steps outside the pub's entrance Jane pulled her coat closer. "Wow. The temperature's really dropped." Vapour formed as she spoke.

"Can we hang on here a moment while I have a cigarette in the light?" Paul asked.

"As long as you're not going to be too long. It's really cold," Jane said.

"Just a few moments." Paul retrieved a cigarette and before he lit it he quickly glanced at the bushes across the lane then struck the flame.

Inhaling deeply Paul looked at his wife and breathed out. "You didn't find anything remotely odd about that?"

"Not really."

"What about the second round?"

"It was only a round on religion."

"Pretty specific though."

"It wasn't general knowledge."

"I suppose," Paul said, dropping his cigarette into the water filled, white plastic container on the ground. The cigarette glowed for a moment on the surface ice before going out. "It's cold. Let's get going," he said.

"Good idea."

The couple walked along the lane then Jane stopped and listened. "It's very peaceful isn't it? Listen. You can't hear any cars at all; nothing like it is at home."

"You can't hear any wildlife either," Paul said.

"It's winter. There's probably not a lot of wildlife around."

Paul and Jane started walking again and as they got to the bend, when the lights from the buildings behind would diminish, they all went out. Paul looked back at the pub.

"Looks like the pub's finished for the evening. The only light they've left on is the one above the steps; not a lot of light really." He turned back. "Bloody hell! You can't see a bloody thing. It's pitch black."

Jane was now worried. Her night vision had always been atrocious. "Should we go back to the pub and ask for a torch?"

"Wait a moment, my eyes will adjust." The last thing Paul wanted to do was to go back to *that* place. He was glad his mother had always insisted he should eat carrots, though he had doubts as to whether that was the real reason for his good night vision. "Okay. I can make out the path," *just*, he said and thought. "Hold on to me."

Paul started walking and Jane followed with her arm firmly looped through her husband's.

Paul stopped. "I think we're nearly at the cut through the fir trees."

The cold mist wasn't helping any; all Paul could really see was a grey wall surrounding them. If they were near enough to the path through the trees Paul could press his car's key fob and the lights indicating its alarm was off, would flash, giving them a little light to determine exactly where they were.

As he fumbled for his jacket pocket and his car's key a sudden loud cracking, in what could only be the branches around them, rang out in the still and chilled air. All the hairs on his neck and forearms stood on end, the skin across his forehead tighten and he shuddered; goose bumps prickling his skin. Jane seemed to sag, pulling on his arm.

"Paul. What was that?" Jane's voice was feeble.

Paul drew a deep breath trying to calm himself. "Dunno. Probably a badger in the undergrowth or something like that." He was pleased his voice was steady, not giving away the dread he felt inside.

Paul found the key and the car's indicators flashed. He had judged it right; they had stopped in line with the path down to their lodge. Quickly Paul turned to the right and shortly after entering the cut, through the line of fir trees, the outside light of their lodge illuminated the sparse strip of frosted grass in front of their cabin.

The wooden steps to the veranda creaked slightly in the freezing night as they made their way up them, the frost covering the planks hardly affected by their footfalls. On the veranda Jane took the cabin's keys from her handbag and unlocked the door.

Inside Paul said, "I must admit I've never had to walk along a lane that dark, ever before."

"Let's get a torch when we're out tomorrow," Jane said.

"Good idea," Paul said holding out his hand.

"What?"

"Keys please," he said.

Jane handed Paul the keys and he locked the wooden framed glass door.

"At least it's warm in here," Jane said.

"That's because I charged the electric meter and turned on the heating before we went out." Paul pulled the thin curtains across their cabin's front windows and door.

"Time for bed?"

"Yeah. In a minute. Going to have a can."

Now they were in the cabin Paul started to relax. *The holiday begins here*, he thought. Entering the kitchen he checked the meter and seeing it was almost full he went to the fridge and took out a can of cider, then sat down on the sofa in the lounge next to the cabin's front door.

"I'm going to bed, to read," Jane said.

"Okay. See you in a minute."

Jane opened the door to the master bedroom and went in; its entrance was also in the lounge. The wooden bed creaked loudly as she got under the duvet, blankets and the extra blankets they'd taken from the other bedroom.

Paul listened to the nothingness as he supped from his can; the silence only being broken on occasions by Jane turning in their bed. Paul was happy with nothing to think about and no signal for his firm's mobile. The more he relaxed the further the weirdness of the evening and their arrival moved from his immediate thoughts.

Paul finished his can and got ready for bed. In the bedroom, he found Jane already asleep, though she'd left the bedside light on. The bed creaked as he got in, but Jane didn't stir. As he flicked the light off, he smiled. There was something special about the air in Cornwall, and he couldn't wait for its effect to take hold of him.

Thirty minutes later he was still lying there, wide awake, wondering why the sleep he was used to in Cornwall had eluded him. He looked at the clock; twelve thirty, and then succumbed.

Gradually Paul's consciousness came to the fore. What had woken him? Had he heard a noise? He twisted his head and looked at the clock again. Its red digits blazed twelve forty seven. *Oh God*, he thought. *Was that it? Seventeen minutes?* He turned onto his back, the bed creaking, and he listened. Nothing. He turned onto his side facing the clock and the dressing table, but his body was telling him sleep was not the right thing to do.

Paul tried one of the tricks he'd learnt a long time ago that would always bring sleep; he imagined a desert island with a blue sea surrounding it and a beach of soft beige sand, the waves gently crashing upon the shore. He imagined sitting under a palm tree on his idyllic island and he began to drift off.

Then he was wide awake again. This time he'd definitely heard a noise. It was either the creaking of the veranda or the brass handle to the front door being gently twisted to free the catch. He was glad he'd locked it. He turned onto his back and lying still he listened more intently. Nothing. Still he listened and as he did his body began to feel cold, though sweat was now running off it. His body started to buzz, adrenalin coursing through him, and the hairs on his arms prickled to attention. Still he listened, still nothing. He tried to relax. Something cracked lightly. It sounded like the door to the cupboard in the room coming ajar. Paul lay frozen to the bed, cold, with the hair on his scalp bristling. Then no noise, the alertness in him receded. Then nothing and his tension dissipated. And finally, calm. Paul breathed out slowly, chastising himself for the fool he was, and again drifted off to sleep.

* * *

Paul's eyes flicked open and he glanced at the clock, it was gone three a.m. He pulled the duvet down so his head was completely clear. The noise started. This was a real noise; a pointed claw dragging its way along the grain of the wooden panelling. He could imagine the natural swarf curling out of the rut being driven into the logs that made up the walls of the lodge. And the noise continued as it vibrated through the cabin's wall. Then a loud crack of glass, from the lounge, a pane almost giving way, and Jane awoke.

"Paul, what's happening? What's that noise?" she said, the depth of sleep she'd come from not allowing her to form the questions clearly.

Paul remained silent, his fear stonewalling his ability to speak.

"Paul?" Jane implored. He could hear the tears in her voice.

The handle to the front door rattled and clacked as it was forced viciously up and down.

"Don't leave me," she said.

Paul couldn't move, he couldn't do or say anything.

"Paul!" Jane wailed.

The clawing on the logs multiplied. Jane, in her fear, turned to face her husband then slapped his face without holding back. The noise of shattering glass resounded around the lounge and Paul blinked. His left cheek burnt and he looked at Jane. Something within him grew; he couldn't let Jane become a victim of whatever it was that wanted them. He got out of bed and lifted the cupboard, with all its contents, off the floor and placed it against the bedroom's door, then pressed his back against it, arms splayed outward next to his sides, holding the cupboard in its new position. There was a final cracking and crunching before the hammering on the door started. Paul could see in his mind's eye the smashed entrance to the cabin. Using his legs Paul pushed harder against the cupboard.

Heavy thumps threw Paul forward and the gouging of the bedroom's outside wall continued, though it didn't give way like their cabin's front door had.

And on it went, THUD. Paul pushed back. The noise sounded like a shoulder muffled by something. *Hair?* he thought.

Then a rattle – the handle to the bedroom door being tried again.

THUD. This time the force jarred his neck as his head was thrown forward.

A quiet squeak – the bedroom door's handle being tested carefully – THUD, THUD, THUD.

Paul gritted his teeth as he leant against the cupboard with all the force he could muster. Holding back whatever was coming for them; hoping he could, wondering what would happen if the bedroom door caved in, leaving only the cupboard between him and whatever it was that wanted them.

He knew, if it came to it, he would do everything he could to protect his wife for as long as possible. He looked at Jane cowering beneath the duvet she'd pulled up under her chin, as she sat against the headboard, arms around her drawn up knees, and prayed she would not suffer when they got through.

After an eternity the thumping and crashing on the back of the cupboard subsided, then stopped. Paul looked at the clock; only an hour had past, but he knew this respite was no reason to lower his guard. And his fear was confirmed.

BANG. The floor beneath his feet shuddered. The force lifting the floorboards he was standing on. It was now under the cabin, attempting another way in.

Another bang jolted him upward. The bones in his heels felt like they'd been pushed through the flesh of his bare feet. Slowly, ever so slowly, the floorboards lifted, retching their complaints, creaking against their new form, as the nails holding them fast

were eased from the beams that held them. Ignoring the pain Paul stamped down hard; once, twice, then three times. The floorboards returned.

* * *

Jane stopped sobbing and listened. There was silence; another half hour went by; still silence.

It's now or never, Paul thought and moved away from the cupboard, then eased it back from the door. Whatever the reason why the onslaught had stopped, he had to take advantage of the opportunity; it may be the only chance they had. He waited for a moment. Nothing tried to push the door open. Paul reached for the handle and pulling it down he opened the door slightly. After a few minutes he peered through the gap between the door and its frame. There was nothing to be seen.

He shut the bedroom door quickly and manoeuvred the cupboard away so he could get out into the lounge. He opened the door fully and looked out. The lounge was as pristine as when they'd arrived. There was no broken glass on the floor and the front door remained invisible behind the curtains he'd closed when they'd got back from the pub. Pulling back the drawn curtain he saw thin cracks in the door's upper most pane. Then he jumped back, shocked, as a flashlight's beam, coming from somewhere in the fir trees, picked out a dead barn owl lying motionless on the veranda. Its beige speckled wings were splayed out, old nails pinning them to their position. Viscous blood pooled beneath its beak and its large eyes were glazed, clouded by death's exclusive privilege. Paul was certain they'd been left some kind of gruesome message and although he didn't understand it entirely, its grimness spoke volumes.

"That's it, Jane, get dressed. Forget about anything else. We're not staying here a moment longer."

Jane dressed. "What's going on?"

"I don't know. I *really* don't know. Are you ready to run? Because we're going to have to run for our lives, I think. Just stay close and don't think."

Paul unlocked the door and waited for the inevitable. Nothing happened. He looked at the tree line – whoever was holding the flashlight was still there, waving it around in sudden jerks.

Good, he thought. "Ready?" he said as he looked at his wife. Jane nodded.

Paul pulled open the door and grabbing his wife's arm dragged her onto the veranda and then onto the path next to the cabin, then started running.

Within moments they were across the grass strip and through the thin strip of fir trees. He pushed the button on his key fob and their car unlocked. Paul got in the driver's side and Jane made her way around the back of the car to get to the passenger door. Time seemed to drag. Paul twisted around in his seat to see where Jane was, but the outside was too dark. *Where the hell are you?* Paul thought, shaking his head. They'd got this far, surely she was about to get in. He was on the verge of getting out when the passenger door was wrenched open. Jane jumped in and quickly closed the door. Paul hit the central locking and started up the car; slammed it into reverse and turned on the headlights. He swung the wheel to the left and steered for the lane, shifting the car into first. In the headlights Paul thought he glimpsed the woman from reception, madly waving a flashlight about as humanesque shadows circled her. Then the flashlight went out.

Paul drove down the lane as fast as he could, but if he was to avoid crashing the car in this miniscule lane, he had to take it easy. The last thing he wanted was to be marooned and at the mercy of whatever it was this *holiday* site harboured.

The hedgerow had been unmoving in the windless night, but as the car's headlights picked it out, it began to shake violently. Then at the limit of the beams Paul saw man-shapes, leaping over the bushes, flying through the air across the lane. Light coloured jackets becoming visible. And then *he* was there, the bald fat man, standing in the middle of the lane – except, somehow, he was less man. Paul's brow furrowed as he tried to make out what it was between the man's out stretched arms and waist. Questions fired through his mind. *What is that? A cloak? Black skin of some kind?*

"Paul. Stop!" Jane screamed. "You're going to hit that man."

Paul glanced at his wife and shook his head. "Whatever that is, it's not a man." Risking all he pushed the accelerator down and before the fat man-thing could get out of the way the car clipped it, throwing it hard into the hedgerow. Momentarily the car lurched.

* * *

To this day Paul and Jane can't explain what they'd experienced during their curtailed time away and resolved never to go anywhere without checking the details. They would definitely never go to a place one could call "in the sticks" again.

* * *

A few weeks after their nightmare break, out of morbid curiosity, Jane looked up the place they'd stayed at, but her Internet search failed to return any results.

I Am Nothing

By Paul A. Bunn

Can you see me?
As I walk along the street
Hiding my face.
In a grey, lifeless world

You seem so far away
But somehow within reach
If only I could touch...
Then maybe I would feel warm again.

My mind is drawn,
To a darkened room,
There are others there,
Who share my sadness.

This time I can reach you,
For one final time,
We say our goodbyes,
For I am nothing.

Don't Mess With Mildred

By Jessie Hobson

Chapter 1

The bus purred quietly along the coastal road, and Gloria looked out across the shingle beach of the estuary at the curly grey waves topped with spits and spots of froth. The serenity of the graded blues of the sky seemed to belie this minor tumult, until she looked up at the wispy wind-driven clouds in the heavens above. She knew very well that it was cold. She had waited in middle-aged misery at the bus-stop, her features pinched and drawn, in spite of a multitude of scarves wrapped in abandoned fashion round her head and shoulders.

Gloria felt grateful that her seat by the window was in full sun, as the warmth through the glass comforted her after her chilly stand. She could begin to think about what was in store for her at the end of her journey.

Gloria had realised from a young age that she was a lumpy, dumpy sort of person, not likely to merit a second glance from people. Self-esteem was foreign to her nature – she neither expected nor received much in the way of praise for her actions. Nevertheless, she plodded through life with a dogged determination which satisfied her own expectations. This sometimes led to a grudging respect from work colleagues, as she seldom let situations defeat her.

On this occasion, however, she had decided it was necessary to approach the Citizen's Advice Bureau to solve her problem, and she had made an appointment to see one of their advisors. She alighted at the lower end of the High Street and went for a coffee, as she had spare time before making her way to the C.A.B. offices. For Gloria, coffee was a rare treat – her usual choice was strong, sweet tea – but she felt she needed a boost to her nerves before the encounter, and she had read somewhere that coffee was good for that – what did they call it? A stimulant? She felt quite proud to have remembered this word. She sipped the beverage appreciatively and sat for a while, unobtrusively in the corner of the cafe before gathering her bag in her arms and venturing into the street. She noticed a tall young woman in a full-length brown dress, and thought it strange that she was wearing pale kid gloves, as they looked rather dressy, more for evening wear, but then, people would be very boring if they all liked the same things. The lady's hair was full and hung round her shoulders in soft blond curls. Gloria wished her own straggly strands looked half as pretty. In this, she was being hard on herself, as it was only the wind which had disarranged her hair from its usual neat coif of a pleasing shade of chestnut. She pushed her hair off her face and wondered what sort of hairspray the lady used, because her tresses seemed smooth and unaffected by the wind.

Thinking these thoughts, Gloria had walked briskly, almost to the C.A.B. building. As it came in sight, she began to plan what to say. It did not turn out at all as she meant, because she found herself facing a man to speak to. Her mental conversation had been with a woman, and this threw her completely off course. She was very conscious of her disordered hair and wrapped- up appearance, which would not have bothered her if she had been confronted by a woman.

The C.A.B. assistant introduced himself as Jim Baxter, and he saw her discomfort and did his best to put her at ease

"Miss Mariner, isn't it? How can I help you?"

Gloria never quite knew how she managed to explain that her trouble was with not just one, but three different electricity suppliers, all dismissive, none of whom had found anything wrong with her wiring or appliances, although she herself found curious occasions when things just did not work, without apparent reason for malfunction.

Jim listened patiently and watched sympathetically as the tale unfolded. Gloria did not seem to be the kind to make difficulties, indeed he found himself warming to this gentle, self-effacing woman.

"How do you think we can help?" he asked. "Do you think perhaps there is some chemical imbalance in the structure of the house which might be behind the anomaly?"

Gloria had no idea what an anomaly was, but gladly clutched at the suggestion put to her.

"Can you find someone who knows about things like that?" she queried.

Jim pursed his mouth and looked thoughtful.

It might be an idea if you tried to find out who lived in the house before you, in case there have been alterations. Have you lived there long?"

"At least ten years."

"I'll give you an introduction to the local authority, who will have details of previous occupants. Maybe we can then trace what has happened."

Gloria was much comforted by the response to her problem, and resolved to follow up the details of who had been living in her home before her. What she did not know was that Jim was not just an assistant at C.A.B., but that he was a spiritualist, and that he had an inkling that the electrical interference might have a more supernatural cause than a chemical one. He made a new appointment for Gloria to come with any results she might find from her search, and watched her leave the office with interest, thinking this could be a more intriguing case than most.

Gloria hastened to the Civic Centre after her appointment with Jim Baxter, as she only had the one day off work, and she sought to follow up the lead she had been given as swiftly as possible. In this, she was fortunate; she was able to trace that one Arthur Sanders had lived in her house with his partner, Janine Drummond. The unusual name of Janine struck a chord in Gloria's memory. Surely someone of that name had been in the papers when she was younger? Still, first she would try the telephone book to see if she could find either of the names at another address. If lucky, she might be able to find out from one of them if there had been changes made to the electrics at her house. She would start searching when she got home, she decided, and queued up once more for a bus on the homeward journey. She was rather surprised to notice the young lady in the brown dress among the passengers. It's a small world, she thought, with amusement.

Chapter 2

Mildred Elderton sat demurely on the bus behind Gloria, smoothing her delicate kid gloves over her elegant brown dress. She had no wish to alarm Gloria, but she was keeping a close watch on her activities, as her great-great-niece was her only surviving relative. Mildred's brother (who had been Gloria's great-grandfather) had always warned her not to fiddle with newfangled electrical equipment, but, silly girl that she had been, she had contrived to light up a faulty lamp and had been electrocuted in the full bloom of her youth. In the World Hereafter, she had discovered that she could contact her former existence in the Present Life by means of the electrical attachments belonging to later relatives, and had followed the loves and lives of her descendents with interest ever since. However, she did not wish to see her family die out completely, so she wanted to do a little match-making for Gloria. Jim Baxter would do nicely, she thought. It was clear to her that he was wise enough to realise that Great Aunt Mildred was behind the disturbances in Gloria's electrics, although he had no knowledge of who she was, or why she was involved.

"Excuse me, Mildred," said a young woman's voice from behind her. Mildred sat bolt upright, looking straight ahead with eyes wide with astonishment. No-one had ever spoken to her so familiarly since she had entered the World Hereafter, and she certainly had not known that she was visible to anyone except Gloria in the Present Life. She turned round slowly and looked into the face of, well, she would have said a 'fast' young woman, definitely not a lady. The heavily made-up girl with frizzy brown hair grinned cheekily back at her.

"It's OK," she said. "I'm in the World Hereafter, too, you know. I thought I'd better let you know that I'm Janine Drummond. Your Gloria won't find me, of course, because Arthur Sanders murdered me. But if she tries to trace him, she might be in danger."

"Tell me more!" said Mildred, her curiosity aroused. "Is he still in the Present Life, then?"

"Yes, he's getting on a bit now, but still nasty."

"Getting on a bit? In what way? Has he made a fortune?"

Janine realised she had used a more modern phrase than was familiar to Mildred.

"He is getting old is what I meant. And no, he is living – er – in poverty."

She had been going to say 'in a squat' but realised she would confuse Mildred even more.

"How did he come to kill you? Was it in Gloria's house?"

"Not only killed me there, he buried me in the garden under the compost heap, which is why the police never found me."

"How disgusting. So he succeeded in convincing the police that he had no idea what had happened to you, is that it?"

"Yes, I'm afraid so. There was a nine-day wonder type of story in the newspapers, but then it all died down and got forgotten."

"We will have to see if we can bring this villain to justice. Perhaps I can contrive something through Gloria."

"Well, just be careful she doesn't end up joining us here in the World Hereafter before her proper time."

Of course, no-one on the bus, not even Gloria, was aware of the conversation between Mildred and Janine, as although Gloria knew that Mildred was behind her, when she heard her talking, it was not clear enough to distinguish the words, which Gloria assumed were taking place on a mobile phone, as what Janine said in reply was only audible to Mildred.

Gloria got off the bus at the bottom of her road without a backward glance, her head bowed against the wind. Mildred and Janine continued unseen to the terminus, discussing ways and means to make reparation for Janine's death and to foster a romance between Gloria and Jim Baxter.

Chapter 3

Once home, Gloria tried, without success, to find a telephone number for either of the former occupants of her home. This was hardly surprising, with Janine under the compost and Arthur living in a dingy run-down house with a small group of equally destitute individuals, who had broken in and taken over the place. The appointment she had made with Jim Baxter was for a week hence, and she knew she needed to ask for time off yet again, something which would not be popular with the management.

The next day, she set off for work wondering how to ask her boss, and on the way, she met Harriet, a fellow-worker in the little factory, who noticed Gloria's worried expression.

"You look as upset as I feel," she said. "There was a break-in at my place yesterday, and I've had police all over the house."

Gloria immediately put all thoughts of her own problems on the back burner to concentrate on Harriet's distress.

"Did they catch anyone? What did the burglars take?"

"Fortunately, my husband was home and scared them off, and one of them dropped a jewellery box he had taken, in trying to escape. They must have been real amateurs, because everyone knows these days to wear gloves, from watching TV, and the police said they have got some fingerprints they hope to match with a known villain."

"Did you see who they were?" asked Gloria.

"Not to say I could recognise anyone, but one was a young lad and the other was a much older man. I did my best to describe them to the man who came from the police."

The two factory girls carried on talking as they walked into work. Naturally enough, the topic became the subject of the day, and Gloria decided to leave it for another day to arrange time off. When she got home, she was irritated to find that her hall light was on, as she was sure she had turned it off overnight. Her irritation gave way to anxiety, as she wondered if she, too, had been visited by burglars. Had someone broken in at the back? She grasped an umbrella from the stand in the hallway, and began cautiously to make her way round the rooms downstairs, thankfully finding no-one, nor signs of forced entry.

"It's those rotten electrics again," she muttered crossly as she put the umbrella away. "It is getting on my nerves."

She jumped nervously as the hall light flickered and went out.

"Don't do that!" she told it severely.

Wearily, she checked that the switch was truly off, then concentrated on preparing her evening meal, wondering what she could now do to find out whether anything really had been altered in the electrical circuit. Perhaps a free-lance electrician, a local man, had done something? The trouble with that was that even if she could find out who he was, he might have retired after all these years and moved away.

After her meal, she settled to watch the news on TV and was about to turn off the local news when the volume suddenly increased almost to deafening proportions, and she realised the item was about Harriet's burglary, and that two men had been arrested, one of whom had been identified as one Arthur Sanders, a small-time crook known to police, and whose fingerprints had been found on Harriet's jewellery box. Understandably, the police were crowing a little at such a rapid arrest, but Gloria's interest was in the man's name. Could it be the particular Arthur Sanders she was seeking – it was rather a common name. Maybe Harriet would get to know more about the man. She would ask the next day. For once, she was pleased with the sudden electrical interference, as she might have turned off the TV and missed the item. Strange it should have happened just then, she thought.

Chapter 4

Mildred felt rather smug that she had contrived to alter the TV volume just in time to alert Gloria. Janine said, "Now we need to make sure she knows it's the right Arthur Sanders."

"I can only influence the electricity in the house, not elsewhere, except I do sometimes find that I can affect static electricity in other people. I have only ever been able to make proper contact where my relatives actually were, although I think Gloria may have heard me talking to you on the bus, as that was something I have never done before, only in the more private areas of the World Hereafter."

"Where Arthur lives in the run-down house with the other old geezers, he has some past papers identifying him," said Janine. "If I can get to them when the police search the place, maybe I can push things around a bit with spirit wind and whisk something away at a time when they interview Harriet, so she gets to show it to Gloria."

"Perhaps," said Mildred doubtfully, her mind more on this new word 'geezers' which she rightly assumed was a latter-day one for 'men'. "It's worth a try," she said more positively, feeling that Janine would think her efforts were not being properly appreciated.

So it came about that the two spirits sat in on a visit to Harriet's home, where police asked if she knew Arthur Sanders (showing her a 'mug shot' of the man), which she vehemently denied.

"Why would I have anything to do with such a villain?" she cried.

"Well, madam, from papers we have here, it seems he lived hereabouts some years ago, so you might have come into contact at some time," answered the CID man. He pulled some papers from an inside pocket of his jacket, and Janine leapt into action, puffing and huffing so that the sheets flapped and fell out of his hand. Harriet helped to pick them up and noticed Gloria's address was on one piece.

"That's my workmate's address," she exclaimed. "She lives alone. She rents a two bedroom semi, a Victorian place in the main village street. Are you sure that is right?"

"He lived there over ten years ago," said the policeman. "Before her time, perhaps. We will need to check up on that."

Janine and Mildred looked at one another, and nodded their satisfaction. Things were going according to plan. They trotted after the CID man and his colleague as they left Harriet, and when the men set off by car, the spirits levitated and arrived before them at Gloria's house.

Gloria was astonished to see two policemen on her doorstep, but dutifully allowed them in as they requested. Once she heard who the villain in the picture was, her face lit up with pleasure. This was not at all what the police were expecting, and such is the mind-set of the constabulary, they were instantly suspicious.

"Do you know this man?" this in a stern voice which wiped the smile from Gloria's expression.

"Well, er, no, not exactly. It's just that I've been trying to find him, because he used to live here."

"Now why would you want to do that, madam?"

Poor Gloria got quite flustered.

"It's about the electrics. They keep going wrong."

"He's not an electrician, he's a vagrant."

"It might help me to know if he altered anything when he lived here. Can I see him and ask?"

If this sounded peculiar to the CID man, he concealed his thoughts, and wondered whether there might be a more significant reason behind Gloria's request to see his prisoner. Could she be a 'fence' for the goods? Had she lived with him in the past?

Aloud, he said, "We'll see if that can be arranged," his benign look hiding his motive of hoping to learn more about Sanders' other activities, and perhaps clear up a number of other crimes in one go.

Chapter 5

Next day, Gloria hurried to work to talk to Harriet about the police visit, and they exchanged news.

"I think you are mad, wanting to see him," said Harriet. "If he is a regular criminal and does burglaries often, maybe he went to prison, which is why your house was vacant. He might have left something behind he wants to recover, something which affects your electrics."

"The police said I could talk to him. I didn't say I wanted to invite him to my home, Harriet. That would be mad, I agree."

"He might invite himself," said Harriet ominously. "Like he did when he burgled my house."

"But he's under arrest."

"Suppose they bail him? You don't imagine the police have got time to keep watch on him all the time, do you?"

In this, Harriet was wrong. Such were the suspicions of the policemen who had visited Gloria, they had every intention of keeping a close watch on the activities of Arthur Sanders once released.

"Harriet, whatever happens, I must see the boss about time off to go back to the Citizen's Advice place, to let Mr. Baxter know that I have at least found the man who lived in my house before me."

Gloria refused to be pessimistic about things, unless they proved to be hopeless, and in any case, she was quite looking forward to seeing 'that nice Mr. Baxter' again. At work, she was lucky to find her employer in a compliant mood – the burglary had provided him with good conversational material at his golf club, a bit of one-upmanship to be able to say that one of his employees seemed to be the victim of the crime.

Gloria and Harriet had no idea that he knew any of this, but the factory girls had been chatty within his hearing.

In the World Hereafter, Mildred and Janine had returned to base, in accordance with angelic instructions. They were debriefed about their activities and their intentions applauded, but both were reminded not to interfere more than absolutely necessary. It was understood by the Higher Souls that Mildred had limited control over her access via electrical equipment; also that creating spirit wind was about as much as Janine could manage. They were advised to use both with discretion.

Gloria had been given a time to call at the police station to see Arthur Sanders, and in her normal manner, set off by bus for the town. Mildred and Janine sat further back on the bus this time, so Gloria did not see anything.

When she arrived, Gloria was ushered into an interview room and Arthur Sanders was brought in to speak to her. They were kept under surveillance throughout, and Arthur's blank denial that he had altered anything electrical in the house depressed Gloria.

"Could you have put up shelves or built cupboards or something which might have had an effect?" she pleaded.

The police were quick to notice a wary look appear on Sanders' face, but all he said was "No, nothing like that."

With this, Gloria had to be content. She left, baffled, and the police went into conference about the possibility that Gloria's talk of cupboards might have been a coded message that something was hidden. Sanders returned to his cell with a thoughtful face. He most certainly did not want size eleven boots traipsing round Gloria's house looking for clues. They just might find more than they bargained for. True, the real problem was in the garden, and he thought it unlikely they were seeking bodies, only stolen goods.

Until now, Great-Aunt Mildred had been discretion itself, and she forbore to ask Janine what her relationship had been with Arthur Sanders. She was understandably curious, nonetheless, to know what had caused the man to kill her companion. Janine did not seem to her to be a dishonest girl, even if she was of an inferior class of person, judged by the values of Mildred's generation.

"The house Gloria lives in is not very big. I assume Mr. Sanders did not employ servants?" she asked Janine.

"Servants?" hooted Janine. "The man was on the dole, couldn't pay his rent, never mind servants. People mostly don't have them, nowadays," she explained, in acknowledgement of Mildred's dismayed grimace. "Not unless they live in big posh places. He was separated from his wife and I used to give him a bit of company now and then." Janine said this coyly, as she realised Mildred would not have understood if she had brazenly said she was his 'bit of stuff on the side.'

"Not a very good way to thank you for your attentions, to kill you. Was he quarrelsome?"

"He didn't like it if I didn't cough up any brass when he was skint."

"Pardon?" said Mildred.

"Sorry – he expected me to pay for things when he had no money."

"Disgraceful. Definitely not a gentleman."

"Ooh, no. He was a bad'un through and through, but in those days he was good-looking and had a way with him women found attractive, which was my downfall."

"Yes, well, being a cad is one thing, murder is something else."

"That was because I found out about his thieving, and threatened to go to the police. I didn't want to end up in jail on his account. Instead, I ended up under the compost heap. He never did keep things he had stolen on the premises, so the police will be disappointed."

"They are quite wrong about Gloria, of course, but I think it may be as well if they are keeping an eye on her, even if for the wrong reasons."

Chapter 6

Little happened for a day or so, as Arthur needed to appear in court before being bailed, and Gloria was not yet due back to the Citizen's Advice Bureau. From time to time, Mildred made her presence felt by disorganising the odd lamp or making Gloria's steam iron spit water after she had placed it on its stand. Once bailed, Arthur Sanders decided to make his move on Gloria. This coincided with her visit to see Jim Baxter, which confused the police assigned to watch the pair, as she went out before Arthur arrived. He wanted to talk to her, to see how much she really knew. He wandered round the back of the house to reassure himself that the compost heap was still intact, then gave up and went away. Meanwhile Gloria went for her appointment, which did not seem to her police followers quite the action of a guilty 'fence'.

Gloria explained to Jim Baxter that she had found and spoken to the man who had lived in her house, but without progress. When she mentioned the name Arthur Sanders, Jim's hands clenched. It was the only sign he gave that he remembered the disappearance of Janine Drummond. He had no reason to suspect she had been murdered. But if Arthur Sanders was in trouble with the police at present, it might have some bearing on earlier events occurring at Gloria's house. Jim looked at Gloria's disappointed face and decided to take things outside his remit as an assistant at the Bureau.

"Would you permit me to come and take a look round your house?" he asked diffidently.

Gloria's face brightened.

"Would you?" she said eagerly. "You must have realised from what I've told you that I am not clever with electrical things; I would so welcome your help."

"That's settled then. When would you like me to come?"

"We both work, and I expect you have a family to go to in the evening, so perhaps if you can spare the time at the weekend?"

"Saturday. Ten o'clock – would that suit you?"

Gloria nodded, speechless at the prospect of help from – Jim. She allowed herself to think of him by his first name. She chided herself for unfamiliar feelings of attraction towards him. He must be married, or surely he would have said.

Jim, although only a year or so older than Gloria, was a more experienced man where relationships were concerned, his employment by the Bureau requiring his ability to discern the qualities of the people he helped. He thought it wiser not to tell Gloria that he was single, unattached and especially not that he felt drawn to her, in case things did not work out. But he, like Gloria, looked forward to getting to know her better.

Mildred watched the pair with a proprietary air, pleased with the turn of events.

"He will give her a measure of protection," she said to Janine.

Don't Mess With Mildred

"What's more, the police can't suspect him of skulduggery." said Janine brightly. "Do you think he knows about me?"

"Not that you are in the World Hereafter, no. But he thinks Arthur Sanders is a bad lot."

Chapter 7

Jim was still of the opinion that there was an occult aspect to the trouble with Gloria's electrics, so he went to call on a friend who shared his spiritualist views. They discussed the possibility of contacting the spirit source through a séance, and arranged to meet with a like-minded group before the weekend.

Mildred got quite excited when she realised she might be summoned to give account of herself, but Janine was more scornful.

"They're amateurs," she said. "They might get hold of quite the wrong people.

"Then it is up to us to see they don't," said Mildred with enthusiasm.

Just then, the pair got a buzz from the Higher Souls, reminding them that what was about to take place had its dangers from wayward and mischievous spirits trying to interfere and cause mayhem.

"They had better not mess with me!" said Mildred with tightening of her lips. "I'll – I'll –".

"No, you won't," said Janine. "Behave yourself or you might end up in the Wilderness. It is hard to get back from there, you know. You are neither ghost nor ghoul there, just a poor Wandering Entity. Higher Souls do not want us going there."

Mildred stuck her nose in the air and sniffed disdainfully. "Can't we even have a little bit of fun?" she pleaded.

"You may think it is all fun, but for me it is a very serious business. I need you to introduce me to these Present Life people;

that way, perhaps they will realise they should look for my mortal remains."

Mildred was immediately contrite.

"Yes, of course – how frivolous of me. The most important aspect is to see justice done for you. I'm sure we can sort out a match for Gloria and Jim by the wayside."

The two spirits agreed to meet at the house where Jim and his friends intended to look for answers.

"Do you think they will go into a trance? They look so comical sitting in the dark, holding hands." Janine pretended to moan and groan.

"Perhaps we can encourage them to use the table method, with letters and numbers, and a glass they all hold on to. Maybe that would produce static electricity I could use. That way would be more reliable, provided no unruly spirits get involved."

Mildred had no real knowledge of what might happen; only hearsay from when she had been in the Present Life – it had acted as a party game in those days.

Fortunately the spiritualist group felt the way Mildred had hoped, as they had little time to rig dark curtains because they were meeting in the early evening when it was still light. Six men and women grouped themselves round a polished circular table, and the host produced Lexicon cards and laid them reverentially round the edge together with numbered playing cards and a tall, sturdy glass in the centre.

"Is anyone there?" asked the host when all fingers met on the glass.

Janine huffed and puffed to guide the glass to Y E S.

"Do you know Gloria?"

Truthfully, Janine puffed, N O.

"That's not a lot of use!" said Mildred. "Let me have a go."

She found she could use impulses, gentle ones, but enough to influence the movement of the glass.

M I L D R E D D O E S, she spelt.

The spiritualists got so excited they let go of the glass, and had to reorganise themselves.

"Who is Mildred?" asked Jim.

G R E A T A U N T, replied Mildred.

"Have you played with her electrics?" pressed Jim.

N O T P L A Y. Mildred was indignant.

Just then a gruff voice behind her said, "BOO!"

She jumped and turned to see an ugly poltergeist grinning wickedly at her. Before either she or Janine could stop him, he had thrown all the letters and numbers in the air so that they landed in a great untidy heap. He then fled, shrieking with mirth.

"We haven't even reached telling them about you," said Mildred, aghast.

With desperation, Janine began huffing and puffing until, finally, at the point of exhaustion, she had contrived to form J A N I N E H E L P from the jumbled letters.

Jim remembered the connection between Gloria, Arthur and the missing Janine.

Gravely, he said, "Does this mean you have Passed Over?"

Janine was too weak to do anything more than nod, so Mildred guided the group to Y E S. She had to concentrate so hard that to the delight of the group, she manifested over their heads. "So, Mildred, you have been doing some detective work for Janine, through Gloria's electrics, have you?" asked Jim.

Mildred was too truthful to answer 'yes' to this, but she thought it better to say nothing at all rather than give away her matchmaking plans.

At this moment the poltergeist returned, and Janine and Mildred both grabbed him before he could do any more damage, and hustled him away, disappearing from sight.

"They've gone," said the host when no new message came through. The group broke up with thanks for one of the best sessions they had ever had, and Jim went away with plenty to think about. Could Arthur Sanders be such a villain as to have killed Janine? Surely her cry for help made it look that way. How much did the man think Gloria might know? Jim decided to risk the scorn of the police, and went to tell them that he had information that Janine Drummond was dead, and that there was a probable connection with Arthur Sander's tenancy of Gloria's home. He mentioned his concern that Gloria might be in danger.

To Jim's way of thinking, the police made light of what he told them, so he decided not to wait until the weekend, but to go straight to Gloria's house and warn her.

Chapter 8

Gloria had returned home to begin a tidy-up ready for Jim Baxter to visit. She felt he should be able to have the run of the entire house, so she decided that she ought to open up the attic room. This was situated at the top of a flight of stairs reached through a stout door which Gloria normally kept locked, as she did not have enough possessions to justify storing anything up there. She had previously taken the electricity people up to examine the electrics, but they all came down saying there was only a dim light bulb, no sign of power cables, and therefore unlikely to be the site of the problems. She climbed the flight and looked around. Unknown to her, both Mildred and Janine had joined her, and Janine began to shake.

"What's the matter?" whispered Mildred, aware that Gloria could hear her if she spoke aloud.

"It is where I was killed. I dropped my diary in the struggle, because I had been writing about the thefts, to take to the police – I even wrote that he had threatened to kill me – and he wanted to destroy my evidence. The diary fell into a crack in the floorboards, and he never found it. If only we could lead Gloria to it, perhaps she could..." Janine sat down sobbing miserably on the floor by the loose floorboard, and peered into the narrow slit alongside it.

Mildred began to make the little light bulb swing in circles, highlighting the crack each time it came round. Gloria jumped with fright, but spotted something white in the hole, and went down on her knees to pull it out. The little book was heavily stained with blood. Gloria sat there, opened the diary and read it. The full horror of what had happened to Janine became clear, and she slowly rose to her feet, clutching the diary.

At that moment, she heard the front door bell and innocently went to answer it, the diary in her hand. Arthur Sanders stood on the doorstep, and when he saw what she was holding, he shoved his way in, roaring as she fled before him. She ran up the stairs and through the attic door, trying to pull the door shut behind her. Janine huffed and puffed to help her push, whilst Mildred clutched at Arthur's hair, causing static to make it stand on end and making him pause.

Unluckily for Arthur a passing police constable, with his wits about him, spotted the well-known man going to Gloria's door, and pushing his way in when she answered. The policeman heard raised voices, then a shriek from Gloria, and immediately went to investigate. The front door was open, and he could hear angry hammering coming from upstairs. He ran up to the first floor, to see Arthur Sanders trying to smash down a door which seemed to be locked against him.

"I'll kill you, just like I killed Janine," Arthur bellowed.

"Oi, Sanders, on the ground, now, legs spread," cried the constable.

Arthur spun round to face him, ready to strike out. At the same moment, Jim also ran into the house, and after an instant but very brief struggle, the two men overpowered the intruder, the policeman handcuffing him and leading him away.

Chapter 9

"Gloria," called Jim gently by the locked door. "He's gone. It's me, Jim."

A scampering of feet came down the flight of stairs from the attic room, and Gloria unbolted the door, retreating to the floor above, tearful and shaken. Jim grasped Gloria in a close hug, and kissed her on the forehead, to Gloria's surprise and secret delight.

"You're safe now," he murmured huskily. She looked up into his face and knew from the expression in his eyes that this was the beginning of a new phase in her life.

In the dim shadows of the attic, the two spirits watched as Jim took things a step further and kissed Gloria roundly on the mouth.

"Thanks, Mildred, I can go home now," whispered Janine blithely as she quietly slipped away to the spirit world where she belonged. Mildred watched a little longer, then chuckled, turned out the attic light, and with a crackling and spluttering, began to slide down the electric cable.

"Go away, Great Aunt Mildred. This is private," yelled Jim joyfully, "but thanks for your help."

When the report of Sanders' arrest was issued, it stated he'd confessed to murder and the full force of the law had swung into action. And Janine, in an advanced state of decay, was unearthed from the compost heap and given a proper burial. After the proceedings, Mildred reached into the meter cupboard under the stairs, and patted the mechanism fondly in blessing.

"It is time to go," she said, and vanished, well satisfied, to the upper echelons of the World Hereafter.

The Ferryman

By Colin Butler

The stygian gloom presses all around
Punctuated by ominous growls of thunder,
With intermittent flashes of lightning
Threatening to blow all asunder.

On the shores of the river Styx,
Forlorn figures wander in their plight,
Lumbering in the perpetual darkness
Of a land never visited by the light.

Their eyes endlessly searching the river
Till the outline of a boat appears,
Bringing the lost figures swiftly to life,
Kindling their excitement and their fears

Out of the thick, sulphurous, choking fog
A spectral figure is seen, skeletal and tall,
Propelling the boat – dressed in funereal black,
With an appearance guaranteed to appal.

The figures beg a passage to the other side.
The ferryman enquires, "Can you pay the price?
If not, you must wander for eternity,
In darkest oblivion as a sacrifice."

"What happens on the other side?" they ask.
"You must get past the three-headed beast,
That prowls ravenously, eager to devour,
Then await judgement with the myriad deceased."

Only a few receive a judgement, evil-doers
Descending to the depths of the bottomless pit,
Whilst most will wander forever in limbo,
Only a few ascend to the heavenly ambit.

At this, silence fell over the waiting throng
As the corpses considered their fate.
Gripped by a sense of fear and dread,
As they lumber in their catatonic state.

And so death goes on and on,
The souls performing a sinister rite
As they wander in their torment,
In the land of perpetual night.

Something I Never Told Anyone

By David Shaer

I began by being confused, stressed and resentful of those whom I viewed as being cleverer than I. And when they worked out that they had the upper hand, they were wicked and always took advantage. But, one day, as a five and a half year old, I sorted it out. I used to go to a school that was over two miles away and had to walk initially nearly one mile to a bus stop. There I joined other "*little tearaways*" and we played some magnificent games on a dangerous and exciting piece of waste ground until the bus turned up. Often the games took precedence over the stupid bus and it left without us. The walk to school was then more of a group run because the teachers would lie in wait with muscular crossed forearms at the school gates to see who did not use the bus. We were duly reprimanded and told that our parents would be extremely unhappy when they found out. So we learned how to grovel, make up stories about the bus leaving early, being too full or sometimes just driving past the bus stop without even slowing down. Oscar winners all of them but they were fuelled by commerce because, even as five year olds, we rapidly learned that not travelling on the bus gave us cash in our pockets. So we began to dupe the teachers.

Then we worked out that we could double our assets by walking home in the evening too. That was much easier because parents were usually even more gullible after "*their little darlings*" couldn't get on a bus that was full or failed to stop and we had had to wait for ever for the next bus. Parents naturally fought for the honour of *"their little darlings"* and mostly leapt to our defence, threatening all sorts of retribution, which we just knew they would not enforce because of their personality disorders and weaknesses. Sure they made a lot of fuss and noise but only ever to friends and relatives, never to bus companies or their employees. So, as youngsters, we already held power and short term investments. Short term because the assets became dangerous to retain. One day we found an old petty cash tin still with a key but no contents – probably the remains of a burglary haul – and pooled our secret assets and buried them in the Silver Birch Woods in Belfairs Park. At the age of five we already had a treasurer who maintained records, although even in those days, I felt that this exposed us to inadequate audit procedures and potential money laundering risks. But the records were hand written and were not subject to file corruption without collusion between two or more people so initially we felt safe. Nobody had heard of Enron in those days.

What the grown ups didn't know didn't hurt them.

But inevitably, insider dealing and greed became our downfall. Five year olds didn't do wealth where I came from and so, when it came to *"divi up"* time, you can imagine the horror that arose when we discovered that we had been milked. Sure there were funds available but most of us had an idea that we had pooled far greater resources than were now available for distribution. We felt swindled but had nowhere to turn for retribution. To say that the treasurer needed to be dealt with once and for all was a mild understatement.

Unfortunately, I was one of the oldest, having a September birthday, and it also seemed that I was also one of the biggest. It was assumed, therefore, that I would have more influence over the treasurer and his misdemeanour and I was democratically volunteered to terminate our financial operation, liquidate the remaining assets and to declare a final dividend to the shareholders under section 238, clause B(ii) of the Companies Act 1948. Annulment of the operation had to be carried out and it was also my role to advise the treasurer that he was deemed not to be a suitable person to hold a directorship within our gang until full restitution had been made. I was instructed by the committee to inflict the appropriate punishment.

The effect of this on me was akin to the total shattering of my faith in mankind. Not only was I viewed by my siblings to be an executioner, but it also seemed that they all thought of me as being a strong guy who had no feelings whatsoever. Sure I had older contacts, like a seven year old neighbour, who could be drawn upon to provide knee-capping and other such services but, come on, Man, I was only five. I mean, I wasn't that big, either physically or even mentally. Good God, I still had that little plank of wood put across the barber's chair so that he didn't have to stoop to cut my hair.

I was mortified. My whole life changed instantly and I had nowhere to turn for help. I couldn't go home crying to Mum as any normal lad would have done. I couldn't even ask my Dad to go round and sort out the treasurer's Dad. Neither did I have any older brothers in whom I could confide as in matters intimate or perverse. I was too young to be able to share pillow talk with a lover, although there was a girl in the class ahead of me who was a real stunner and already six years old.

So, not being able to call upon the 5th amendment, I decided that the punishment would be meted out in my time and when it was convenient to me. I had a fairly full diary for the next week but would revert either with a proposal within a week or with confirmation that the deed had been done. I then ran home on my own and probably started my life of high blood pressure and tension.

As I reached home, I was so distracted by my fears and thoughts, that I even forgot to make up an excuse for being home over an hour late and went straight to bed without any tea. Oh,

Boy. You would think that I would have had that much sense but I didn't and within just a few minutes my Mother had appeared in my bedroom to ascertain what the excuse for today was. I was so absent minded that I almost began to tell her about the judicial review that I had attended and the findings of the kangaroo court. But much worse than that, I gave myself away because I just hadn't prepared my case for the defence and could say nothing. My Mother assumed, therefore, that I was ill and threatened to take me to the doctor the very next morning. She could see that I was shaken and indeed shaking but because I couldn't communicate, she had no herbal or old wives' tale remedy at her disposal, although, given time, I am sure that she could have created some sort of heathen potion. I was ordered downstairs and presented with a cold plate of beans on toast and a cup of tea which had obviously brewed and stewed for many an hour. This was, as usual, totally unpalatable but abstention was not an option. Trying not to choke, I disposed of the uninviting repast and shot back up to my room, climbed fully clothed into my bed and lay there trembling. What was I to do? Why me? How was I going to explain this one away?

After what seemed like hours, I heard the front door open and realised that it was way past my bed time and I was still awake. That man who visited us at weekends, my Father, had come home from work at his normal time and I was still not undressed. Oops. Clutching the bedclothes up to my neck and squeezing my eyes shut, I hoped that he would not drop in to see me, as was his wont, and I could just pretend that all was under control.

Lady Luck was with me for the first time that day and I was able to wait for his passing footsteps as he changed out of his suit and went downstairs to dine giving me the opportunity to leap quietly out of bed, throw my clothes in a heap on the floor, don pyjamas and leap back into bed. But my thoughts were still racing. There was no respite and my fears were still ever present. Sleep was elusive, my mind racing to the extent that I felt I could hear it rushing around inside my head trying to find a way out.

Finally I must have dozed off but the brain was still charging around. Suddenly the solution hit me between the eyes and a warm glow came all over me. I dropped into a deep sleep and only the voice of my Father cursing as he poured tea from his cup into his saucer to cool, so that he could dash out of the house to catch the ten past seven bus, woke me from the dead the next morning.

With a positive skip in my pace, I raced around to get ready to go to school with my problem resolved. As I left to make my way to the bus stop, even my unperceptive Mother remarked that I must be keen to get to school today, because I was actually leaving early. I apologised and implied that I was feeling so much better that I just wanted to race back to school – today we had Puppet Theatre, which I hated really, but the teacher lived in the flat under my nasty Great Aunt Bets and I'm convinced that she based the wicked old witch puppet character on her neighbour, that aunt.

So off I raced to the bus stop and today I paid my fare and travelled in style. As soon as I got into the school, I set up a vantage point and waited for the arrival of the 'Honorary' Treasurer. He was unaware about the 'night of long knives' meeting and had duly walked to school, planning to invest his fare. I sidled up to him and whispered from the corner of my mouth that I needed a meeting with him by the caretaker's gate at noon and come alone. I then sloped off to the Puppet Theatre and paid particular attention to the scene where the policeman beat the crap out of Mr Punch for being a bad man.

By noon, I had already been three times to the lavatory and the adrenaline was flowing. With a confident gait, I strode round behind the outside toilet block, taking care not to walk too close to the wall because some of the big boys thought it was fun to try to wee over the top of the wall to prove their masculinity. As I approached the caretaker's gate, I could see that the Treasurer was pacing up and down nervously, perhaps already calculating that I was not going to be discussing the merits of ISAs or Post Office Savings accounts.

"Right, Sunbeam," I started immediately, "the game's up. The Audit Committee has discovered examples of impropriety, accounting inconsistencies, and 'teaming and lading'. As elected representative, I am empowered to advise you that a fair trial would not be likely or even constructive and I have, therefore, been instructed to advise you that, as of now, you have resigned, will have nothing further to do with the investment fund, other than to pay back the unaccounted *'despondencies'*," – I knew what I meant – "and you will be required to fall on your sword. If perchance you fail to do this, the consequences will be dire and the full wrath of the Committee will descend on you. I am doing you a big favour here because you, yourself, are going to mete out the punishment on yourself, thereby saving you considerable pain and anguish because I would be none of kind, understanding or considerate should you not inflict a sufficiently heavy level of beating. I suggest that you simply go quietly home tonight, run and trip somehow and come back tomorrow covered in bruises and some dried blood. How you do it is up to you but if I find that the level is deemed to be inappropriate, woe betide you. And don't think that you will be let back into the gang until the funds have been re-instated."

Without hesitation, I spun on my heels and stormed off round the back of the toilet block and threw up.

When, the next morning, the ex-treasurer limped into school, he looked a mess. He had a black eye, a graze down his cheek under the eye and a split lower lip. Everybody in the gang looked at him, looked at me and went slightly pale. "Good God," one of them said, "we didn't think you'd be that brutal! It's a good job that he hadn't hurt your little sister." Little did they know.

Something I Never Told Anyone

From that day on, everybody treated me differently and most days, except when I was off sick or doing music lessons, I was the leader of our gang. When, six months later, I was six and the class got closed down because of a polio outbreak, some of us got transferred to another school and when we arrived, I got the distinct feeling that I was being treated with respect and with an element of reverence. I have never told anybody how I got that, until today. And the ex-Treasurer is going to tell nobody.

I Love the Night

By Simon Woodward

The sun is due to rise and I know I have to leave
you.
The night we spent together meant everything to
me,
I hope it meant the same to you.

When dusk arrives later, woman of my love, don't
despair,
don't believe what we have is nothing – you are my
life.
You keep me beyond death and I hope you feel the
same.
For now — I'll let you go.
Though through your protestations you know you
need me, as much as I need you.

Later — we'll be as one, but as it's time, your time
is done; as much as mine.

Farewell woman of my dreams, we'll be together,
later.
But tell no-one of our tryst.
It wouldn't be good for you, or I, and we know the
best is yet to come.
Leave me now and I'll wait your return.

But if you can't, I'll still be here, looking to hold
you in my arms,
my mouth upon your neck, to help you on your
path.

I see the confusion in your face, as I say these
words.
But it's a confusion without base.
You let me in and although, to your community, it
may be sinful.
Believe me — *it is not.*

When dusk rises I'll be here, I'll be here waiting for
you, my consort, my life's breath.
If I could die, I would, just for you, woman of my
dreams, but it is not possible for me.
And in our time together I don't doubt *you* would
die for me, when the time comes.
We are committed in death, as you once were —
committed in life.

Go home now, and say your goodbyes.
The next time we meet we'll be together again,
forsaking all others, to be with each other, in our
universe.

Don't worry, young woman. The universe you'll
enter is nothing like the one you came from.
There is no suffering. There is no death, no pain
and no ill.
With me you'll experience a life forever extended
into infinity; watching feeble humanity suffer
through all their ills and their diseases.

I Love The Night

And we'll be without.

I love the night — and so will you.
Soon.

Underground

By Colin Butler

Chapter 1

It was just another Monday, or so I thought, not realising the problems I would encounter before the day was out. I never did like Mondays – then I suppose no one does. But I could never have envisaged the problems that I would encounter on this Monday.

Just as I was approaching the station, on my way to work, there was a loud screech of brakes, just behind me. I turned around startled and saw a black Ford Mondeo heading straight towards me. The driver had obviously been travelling too fast and was desperately trying to stop. As I jumped on to the pavement for safety, I caught a quick glimpse of the driver, a young man with a baseball cap. The Mondeo just about avoided me, but succeeded only in careering into the back of the stationary car, just ahead of me. There was a sickening sound of metal striking metal and the cars were a complete mess. I wanted to stay to see if I could help, but then I remembered my important morning meeting. What should I do? The man next to me was already on his mobile, phoning for the police and ambulance, and there were a number of witnesses. I asked them what I should do and explained about the meeting and they all agreed that there was little I could do to help. So I wrote my name, address, telephone number and mobile number on a piece of paper and handed it to the man who had phoned the emergency services, asking him to give it to the authorities. The scene was one of mayhem, with commuters rushing for their trains, or else scurrying to see what had happened with the accident – the usual rubber-necking. Then, rather guiltily, I left to get my train, arriving on the concourse of the station, just in time to see my train disappearing into the distance.

As I awaited the next train, I thought back to the day so far. It had started disastrously when I had woken up and sleepily put my hand out to check the time – I peered at my watch through half-closed eyes and saw that it was only 6:00 a.m. – time for a few more minutes in bed. From the light coming through the half-opened curtains, I saw that it was a dull, miserable October morning and a Monday to boot. I noticed that my wife, Melissa, was already up, preparing the breakfast for the kids and me. She shouted from the kitchen, "Hurry up, Richard, you'll be late for work."

"It's only 6:15, I've got plenty of time," I replied rather tetchily.

"It's 6:35, the news has just finished," she yelled back.

What had happened? My watch said 6:15 and it was normally so reliable. I immediately began to rush, knowing I would probably miss my train. I rushed my shave and of course, managed to cut myself, I searched high and low for a plaster, but in the end settled for a piece of tissue. It was going to be one of those days! Then I hurried my breakfast and was rather short with the children, who wanted to talk – Peter, about football, and Samantha, about a new dress she wanted. This morning, breakfast was even more chaotic than usual, just like a three-ring circus.

"Sorry kids, I can't stop now, I'm late for work – I'll talk to you to-night," I said as I grabbed my briefcase, gave them both a quick hug and then I rushed out the door, giving Melissa a quick peck on the cheek and began to run down the road.

The running didn't last long – I was patently unfit and resolved, once again, to join a gym without delay. So the run became a walk and even then I had to stop a couple of times to get my breath back and I realised I would not catch my usual train. Then I thought, I am never late it won't hurt this once. Every one else in the insurance office was often late; but then I remembered that I had an important meeting at 9:30.

As I descended the staircase to the platform, I tripped and slightly twisted my ankle; fortunately it happened near the bottom. The ankle really hurt, but after a few minutes I was able to walk, albeit gingerly. It was certainly going to be one of those days!

Perhaps it is time that I introduced myself, my name is Bond – Richard Bond. Yes, I have to endure all the usual remarks and jokes – shaken not stirred etc. In fact, in the office, I am known as 007, and my secretary is, of course, known as Miss Moneypenny. I work in an insurance office in London – not an exciting job, although we do have our moments; but on the whole I enjoy my work.

I checked the indicator-board; there were only ten minutes to wait for the next train, just time to read the paper. I don't usually read the horoscopes – I always think that they are complete rubbish and you would have to be very simple to believe them. Today, though, my eyes happened to rest on the horoscope page and under Scorpio it said, you will have a day full of problems, you will travel, will meet several strangers, but you should not listen to their advice. Then I read the main news items and they did not cheer me up either, as I read about the troubles in Zimbabwe, bombs in Iraq, more British troops killed in Afghanistan and yet another teenager stabbed in South London. Then there were the problems with rising fuel prices and the silly antics of some celebrities who were obscenely overpaid and seemed to be in every magazine and paper, ad nauseam.

The train duly arrived and was not as crowded as usual, so I settled back in my seat, to prepare myself for the day at the office. I soon completed over half the Cryptic crossword and this always gave me great satisfaction. The journey was uneventful, but I did, however, miss my usual companions. There were a group of about eight of us who always caught the same train and tried to sit together. We would exchange banter as well as discussing last night's television, the weather and football. In addition, we competed to solve the cryptic crossword. Without them the journey seemed much longer. I glanced at the other occupants of the carriage – a mixed bunch, to say the least. Opposite me was a young lady dressed in black stockings and a black party dress, which seemed totally out of place on the early train. She proceeded to produce a metal contraption, that looked like a trap for spiders or other insects and in fact, it seemed to contain a couple of hairy black spiders. She then proceeded to apply these to her eyes and finished with a full set of false eyelashes. Next to her was an Arabian lady in Islamic dress, was it a burqa or another Muslim item of dress, I was never sure. Her face was visible, but she had her head covered. Also in the carriage was a builder, complete with dirty overalls and a stubbled chin and finally a young student with a severe case of acne.

Chapter 2

We arrived at Barking, where I always changed on to the underground. This involved a long walk down tunnels, usually packed with commuters of every nationality, all rushing to get their tube trains.

I realised I had missed my usual connection, but again it should not be a problem. I was only about fifteen minutes late and, provided the next tube was on time; I should be OK for my meeting. The first tunnel was, as usual, packed, but when I made my way up the slope towards the District line, the crowds mysteriously seemed to disappear – the next tunnel was empty and I was completely baffled. In all the years I had travelled up to town, I had never seen it like this during the rush hour. What was wrong? Had there been a bomb alert or some other emergency? I became rather scared, as I struggled up the deserted tunnel, feeling strangely vulnerable and wary.

At the end of the tunnel, I walked on to the platform – which was deserted – again a first. I looked at the indicator board which stated that the next train would arrive in ten minutes time.

After about twelve minutes there was the usual strange underground wind that preceded the approach of a train and almost immediately the tube train duly appeared, travelling rather slowly and the rolling stock seemed to be very old-fashioned. I remembered these carriages from years ago and had imagined that they had all been scrapped or sold off, when the new, more streamlined carriages began to operate. Oh well, perhaps they had had problems this morning and were short of rolling stock – just so long as they got me to work, without being too late.

I consulted my organiser for details of the meeting at 9:30 and saw from the station clock that it was already 8:45. I would struggle to make the meeting! Luckily, I had done some work at home in preparation. Strangely, soon after we started off, the carriage seemed to get colder and colder. It had not been a cold morning and even more remarkably, the windows began to steam up – I had never known this in all my years commuting. At last we came out into the open, but I could not see anything with the windows now completely steamed up. I vigorously rubbed the glass, but still was unable to see, as it appeared to be very foggy outside – as if we were travelling through a cloud. I began to worry, as the journey was very strange. Suddenly we drew up at a station and a disembodied voice called out. "*Allgit, Allgit – Allgit out everybody – the train terminates 'ere.*" But I wasn't sure where "'ere" was. It certainly was not the Embankment station, where I wanted to go – we seemed to be in a disused station somewhere. Everything was conspiring against me! I picked up my briefcase and the passengers all filed out of the train and marched down the platform, in a desultory fashion. I did not recognise the station, which looked as if it hadn't been used for ages – the film posters were torn and advertised films that were vintage to say the least – one was for 'Top Hat' with Fred Astaire and Ginger Rogers. At last I saw the name of the station – "St. Mary's" – Where the hell was that? – I didn't remember that name being on the tube maps, but the name rang a slight bell, (the Bells of St. Mary's? – I mused, but really, I was in no mood for humour). Maybe I had heard it on 'I'm Sorry I Haven't a Clue' in the Mornington Crescent game? Anyway we were guided down a corridor to another platform, where a train was waiting for us. By now I was getting quite annoyed – I certainly would miss the start, and possibly most, of the meeting. The other passengers were equally frustrated and there was a general murmur of discontent – not uncommon on Transport for London, I know, but this was more serious. Everything was working against me – perhaps the horoscope was right after all! There seemed to be only about half a dozen passengers for this train and we were being drawn together by our common frustration and bewilderment.

My eye was taken by a rather attractive young lady, wearing a smart black suit and teetering along on very high heels. She was walking beside another businesswoman, who was dressed in far more sensible flat shoes, a blouse and skirt, and had long rather mousy hair. There was an elderly rather scruffy man, who looked like an unsuccessful artist with designer-stubble and he was followed by a middle-aged lady with a scarf over her head and who gave the impression of being a cleaning lady, (Mrs Mopp)? Finally there was a young man in a baseball cap, jeans and a rather scruffy T-shirt.

Unfortunately I have this dreadful habit of observing people, giving them names and assuming their jobs or status, probably incorrectly. I have observed that passengers on the tube are reluctant to talk to other people and can be categorised into three types. First of all, those who sit stony-faced, staring into space; secondly the readers of newspapers, magazines and books. Their reading matter precludes them from making conversation. Lastly there are the busy ones, who knit, do office-work or crosswords. I was pleased that I had not been subjected to the usual squash in the tube. Normally you are thrust up against other passengers in a most intimate manner, with various smells of garlic and B.O. This was much more civilised. We shuffled along the platform, all moaning that we wanted to get to our destination and comparing notes as we expressed our annoyance and frustration. We were all puzzled as to why we had stopped at this god-forsaken station.

"Mind the gap," said another robotic voice. Mind the gap, he said and he wasn't kidding. The gap appeared to be about eighteen inches wide. So I helped the older lady and the young girl on to the train and then jumped in myself, but the doors snapped shut, catching my sleeve! I shouted and hammered on the door and eventually they opened to release my sleeve. We had all got on this train, with no idea where we were going – but at least we should get on to a recognisable station and hopefully meet a Transport for London employee who could advise us what was going on.

The train started off slowly with jerks and shudders, but gradually picked up speed and again we seemed to be going too fast. The air in the carriage was chilly to say the least and I began to shiver. Suddenly the train ground to a halt at a station. I looked out of the window and was amazed to see the station platform crammed with people – it looked more like Blackpool beach on a sunny weekend in wakes week. There was hardly a space between the people. Many were asleep on blankets and they had their pillows and other belongings with them. I then remembered seeing photos of the Blitz with people sleeping on the underground platforms to avoid the bombs – using them as an air-raid shelter. Had I travelled back in time to 1943 – was I in a time warp? This was becoming ever more bizarre. The doors did not open and we remained stationary. I just stayed watching fascinated. I looked around the people sleeping on the platform and there seemed to be many families – mothers, fathers and children, with a sprinkling of the older generation. They used coats as pillows and someone seemed to be leading a sing-song in the corner of the platform. Suddenly there was the sound of an explosion somewhere in the distance and some of the passengers jumped up in alarm.

We stopped there for about a quarter of an hour. By now, I had despaired of getting to work and decided to relax and, for a moment, enjoyed surveying the scene – looking at the fashions – the 40's hats and dresses. It seemed that, in the Blitz, Londoners had become like troglodytes. The platform resembled the crowd for a cup-tie, but they had been fighting for their very survival. Eventually the train pulled away and I looked back with some nostalgia as the wartime scene faded into the distance.

This train had re-started with a severe jolt that threw several of us on to the floor, but I managed to get back on my seat, which was fortunate as the train then accelerated until I felt that it was going dangerously fast. The business-woman was struggling to get up, like an upturned turtle, until a couple of us helped her. We all had to hold on tight to keep our seats. After what seemed like a quarter of an hour, the train stopped suddenly. Yet another disembodied voice called out, "All passengers out," – obviously no human staff were on duty. Where were we now, I certainly did not recognise the station? We crawled out to see an even more dilapidated station that smelled of damp and decay, as if it had not been used for years – the walls were covered in cobwebs, flaking paint and black grime – relieved only by torn, very ancient posters. This station was called "King William Street," – again I had never heard of it. The platform was very dimly lit and I could have sworn the lamps were fuelled by oil or gas. The young lady passenger, who introduced herself as Annette, was getting very emotional, as she had an important interview that morning and desperately wanted the job. I tried to calm her, but she broke down in tears and clung to me, sobbing. We embraced and I must admit to enjoying the warm embrace, until the cold fingers of reality dissipated any warm feelings.

I consulted my tube map and searched in vain for King William Street station. I stalked along the platform in quite a temper now, although I was usually very tolerant of delays on my journey. We were directed by a mechanical voice to wait on the platform for the next train. There were no indicator boards to inform us when the next train was due or where it was going. As we waited on the platform, I had a very uneasy feeling – the feeling that unseen eyes were watching me, from the gloomy recesses of the platform! I was very relieved when, eventually, a train appeared in the distant tunnel entrance and gradually drew up to the platform.

It was another very ancient train that had lumbered into the station, the doors creaking open – and I got into the nearest carriage and chose my seat. The doors closed noisily, obviously in need of maintenance and, after a short delay, the train started off slowly but soon gathered speed. I tried to see the names of the stations we passed, but we did not stop or even slow down at stations, even though, many were crowded with passengers waiting. I was now very worried, it seemed to be the journey of a nightmare and this feeling was obviously shared by the other passengers, as conversation ceased. At last we drew to what seemed a terminal halt, as all the lights in the train went out. It was yet another worse-for-wear station – more grimy walls, more torn, out-of-date posters advertising Camp Coffee and Sunlight soap and faraway the name of the station – "British Museum" – I made a joke, saying the trains had obviously come from the museum, but the other passengers failed to see the funny side, and I refrained from making a remark about the whereabouts of the mummy! Again I failed to find this station on the tube map. Was this a nightmare, or was I simply going mad. Had all the recent pressure and hard work started to take its toll – I was becoming ever more confused and ever more annoyed.

We all disembarked and walked to the ticket barrier, along the platform, in virtually total darkness; the only illumination was a very dim flickering light that gave off a very eerie, greenish light. A very old, bearded man was collecting tickets. He looked well past retirement age, unless of course, he had led a very hectic life! He reminded me of a character in a Will Hay Film like "Oh Mr. Porter."

I handed over my ticket and expected him to punch it and return it to me, but instead he tore it up. "Excuse me, but I shall need that for the next part of my journey," I snapped.

"Oh! You won't need the ticket where you are going," he said ominously, in a strangely quiet and yet somehow unnerving Scottish accent.

I was taken aback as he then guided me along a corridor, which stretched out to the right. I began walking slowly along this very long corridor and as I looked around, I realised that I was all alone. Where were the other passengers? They seemed to have vanished into thin air. I was now becoming distinctly alarmed, as well as frustrated and annoyed. I began to realise, perhaps for the first time, that travelling underground was an unnatural means of transport that should be reserved for moles and trolls. Underground was a separate land, disconnected from the normal world above. I felt so helpless, being shunted around the underground system, like an old shirt in a washing-machine. I had a vague recollection of reading about the ghost stations on the tube, but never imagined I would visit them!

The corridor was again lit by the strange greenish flickering light that added to the ghostlike atmosphere, reminding me of the ghost trains I had visited in my youth. It seemed endless, and as I plodded along, my only companions were rats that scampered around the floor under my feet. I had always had a fear of rats – their long tails and the way they scuttled about. I suddenly remembered Winston Smith in 1984 and his ordeal in Room 101.

The intense dark somehow seemed to magnify the noise of their scampering. Fortunately, the sound of my footsteps echoing around the long-deserted tunnel seemed to make them scurry away into the corners away from me. I was creeping along in almost total darkness and, every few minutes, I walked into a cobweb, which caught on my face, and in my hair. I began to imagine giant spiders crawling over me, whilst I sensed various other nameless creepy-crawlies in the dark. There was a horrible smell of decay and rotting matter. Was it rubbish, animals or even human corpses? The nightmare was becoming more and more frightening. I felt so alone, so helpless and was trying to resist the feeling of utter panic, that was beginning to take me over!

After what seemed an eternity, I reached the end and turned right to yet another platform, just as deserted, even more run down and unused, to await a train. In fact part of the wall had fallen down, and twice I tripped over bricks and rubble. I touched the wall by accident and found it was covered in wet, green slime.

Naturally, there was no clock and no destination boards, so heaven alone knew where my next destination would be, on this roundabout to hell. As I waited, I missed the other passengers – especially the young girl and wondered where they had gone. But I missed Melissa and the children, so much more – would I ever see them again, I began to wonder?

I looked to my right and saw a strange figure lurking at the far end of the platform. He had certainly not been there a few minutes ago and I could swear no one had passed me. Where had he come from? He was tall, thin and wearing very old-fashioned clothes – clothes you saw in the films of the 1920s. He turned towards me and his face had a strange, almost skull-like appearance as it broke into a kind of smile – an unearthly smile that sent shivers down my spine. I looked away in fear and when I looked back, a few moments later, the figure had completely disappeared! There was an old newspaper on the bench. I picked it up and saw that it was an Evening Standard for the 5th September 1943! What was going on – I was becoming more and more confused and frightened.

I was very relieved when, eventually, a train appeared in the distant tunnel entrance and gradually drew up to the platform. It was completely empty. In fact, I didn't notice a driver, but I assumed there must have been one – although on this nightmare journey, I would not have been surprised if the train had been driverless.

Where would we go next? It seemed like the perennial nightmare, where you seemed to be rushing, but not getting anywhere, as if your feet were trapped in treacle or concrete. Again I thought of the fairground ghost trains I had travelled on in my youth.

Chapter 3

The train rushed on for a while and then finally came to a stop. We had arrived at another station – again there was no station name, but this station looked more modern – it certainly was not dilapidated. It was built of shining metal and glass and was brightly lit, the antithesis of the mouldering stations I had visited on this nightmarish journey. The doors opened smoothly with a rather comforting whoosh. I got up and stepped on to the platform. After my tour of ghostly, long unused stations, cloaked in dust, spiders' webs and faded posters, I was now in a modern, futuristic station. The walls and ceiling were a brilliant white and the bright light dazzled my eyes, after travelling in the dim carriages and stopping in dismal, unlit stations. I walked forward, till I came to a barrier manned by a strange, skeletal figure, dressed all in black, his main garment being a type of black cloak, complete with hood. His face was skull-like and he grinned at me, revealing an almost toothless mouth.

"I need your ticket," he said in a husky, deep voice.

"I'm sorry, but it was taken at one of the many stations, I have visited this morning."

"That is very irregular – very irregular indeed," he muttered.

"Oh, dear, oh, dear – we shall have to look into this. You must come in here," he continued.

"But where are we? I have been travelling around the underground system for hours. Don't you realise that I had an important meeting to go to this morning?"

I looked at the ticket-collector, but there was no reply and no real reaction.

"You must come in here," he repeated with a threatening edge to his husky voice. So, reluctantly, I followed him into a waiting-room, also very futuristic in design with a high ceiling. The ticket – collector left and the doors shut slowly behind him, leaving me all alone in the large room. The noise of the door shutting echoed eerily around the room and then there was silence. It reminded me of a doctor's waiting room, but was much more scary. The nightmare was continuing. When and how would it end and in fact would it ever end? At each turn of events, my feelings of fear and panic increased.

I pinched myself hard, as I had done on a number of occasions that morning. Several times I had been convinced that I was dreaming, or rather, living a nightmare, to which there seemed no end; but each time, I felt the pain and convinced myself that it was not a dream.

I was left alone for what seemed an eternity – I was losing all sense of time. I looked at my watch – it showed 12:30 – presumably the same morning that I had set off for work. Then I remembered that my troubles had all started with my watch losing time before I got out of bed – had it now become even more inaccurate? As I looked, the second hand crawled ever so slowly around the yellowing dial. The room was sparsely furnished, just a table and three chairs, all made of glass and a silvery metal. There were no magazines in the room and no water dispenser – I was so thirsty – my throat was parched.

At last, the far door opened very slowly and I watched anxiously as another strange, tall skeletal figure entered. The figure shuffled rather than walked in and sat down in the chair opposite me. The face was emotionless and had a cold, icy look in its eyes. I shuddered with fear – cold fingers seemed to ascend my spine. I felt I was not dealing with a live human person. Was it a robot, or could it be a corpse – this idea filled me with dread – perhaps I was going mad?

The figure swung round in his chair and then the eyes seemed to bore right into my head.

"How did life cease for you?" it exclaimed in a cold expressionless tone.

I was taken aback and could not make a reply.

"When did you become life-redundant?" it said, as if to explain.

I was still unable to reply, as my mind was in a whirl.

"What caused your demise?" it stated with an edge to the voice, as it appeared to be losing patience.

"When did you die?" it shouted losing tolerance with me.

"I did not die, I am alive," I shouted back.

"Impossible," the voice snapped back.

"I left home for work this morning and have been travelling around the London Underground system for hours, getting more and more frustrated and failing to get to work. Now you imply that I am dead!"

"Well, according to our records, you died this morning and our records are never, ever wrong," the voice said, its tone now more soothing but with a quiet, authoritarian manner. "If you will wait here for a while, I will check with my superior." With that, he silently left the room. He seemed to glide out of the door and it left me with a very uncomfortable feeling. Where was I? Why did they think I was dead? My mind began to race.

I sat there for about half an hour – all alone with my thoughts. Gradually the idea formed in my mind, that it was a premonition: could this creature see into the future. Was I about to die in the next few days? Had they just got the timing wrong? All these thoughts whirled around in my brain and I began to sweat profusely – was it hot in this room, or was I about to have a heart attack? I felt my heart beat faster and faster and began to worry – which only succeeded in accelerating my heartbeat further.

My mind had been in turmoil all morning, as strange event followed strange event. I was now all alone in a room, God knows where, being told I was dead, by a strange robot or corpse.

The minutes ticked by and my panic grew. How would I ever get out of this? I began to believe that I would never see my wife or the children ever again! Just then the door opened and the same figure glided back into the room.

"Well, I have talked to my superiors and they have checked the records and have confirmed that you died this morning," the voice was a flat monotone, completely emotionless.

"I am not dead!" I shouted – to no avail.

"I am instructed to take you into the court for the hearing in approximately fifteen minutes; I will be back when the court is ready."

Again he glided out of the room and again I was left alone with my thoughts, my anxieties and so many unanswered questions. It felt like a dentist's waiting-room, only a thousand times more frightening. There was a futuristic clock on the wall, with strange symbols instead of numbers and it made a quiet ticking noise as the main hand moved slowly on. My heart continued to pump at an unnaturally fast rate and the idea came into my mind that I might die of fright here in this very room. What was this court that the creature had mentioned? The fear of the unknown increased my panic.

At last, after what seemed an eternity, the door re-opened and the figure glided back in, this time accompanied by another very tall, thin figure in a cloak.

"The court is ready for you now – please follow me," it said in a quiet, matter-of-fact voice.

Reluctantly I got up, my heart still pumping, and walked to the door. My legs felt like jelly and, for a moment, I had to hold on to the chair to avoid falling. After we went through the door, we came into an extremely long corridor with a high ceiling – was this just another tube corridor – just like all the others, I had visited that morning?

My companions did not speak, but just glided silently along. I had difficulty keeping up, as they did not appear to be actually walking. At the end of the corridor, we turned into an ante-room. The first figure tapped on the big shiny metallic doors and almost immediately a deep booming voice called out, "Enter!"

The doors opened automatically and I was ushered into a very large room, again with a high ceiling – obviously the courtroom. The walls, floor and ceiling were all white and my eyes were dazzled as they tried to adjust to the extremely bright light. I was completely overawed by the size and design of the room. At the far end was an exceptionally high dais at which there were three seated figures – all dressed in white robes, which made them hard to distinguish from the background. I assumed these were the judges or inquisitors. Around the room were seated various figures dressed in grey or black. I was motioned to move forward, to what looked ominously like the dock of the Old Bailey, except that this one appeared to be made of white shining marble. The sounds of voices echoed around the high building and I then realised that there was a vast audience seated in the upper tiers of the room. They were all dressed in dark robes like monks and had very pallid skull-like faces. At my entrance, there was a quiet murmur, just like the rustling of leaves which went around the galleries. I was obviously the star attraction, at an event that I would have given anything to miss.

The central figure of the Inquisitors looked up and spoke in my direction. "What is your name?"

"Richard Aloysius Bond," I said in a quiet faltering voice, which illustrated my nervous state.

"We cannot hear you – please speak up," the inquisitor said.

"Richard Aloysius Bond," I repeated in as loud a voice as I could manage.

"Well, Richard Aloysius Bond, you maintain that you are still alive – is that correct?" the Inquisitor intoned in a voice that oozed with authority and gravitas.

"Yes – I left for work this morning to travel to my office – I had a very important meeting at 9:30 a.m.," I added.

"Tell us in your own words what happened on your journey to work," the Inquisitor now spoke with a slightly more friendly tone.

I then proceeded to recount all my adventures that day, starting from the time I woke up. To their credit, the court listened attentively. When I had finished, the chief prosecutor got up – at least, I presume that was what he was. He began to ask me questions in a belligerent manner, so typical of prosecuting counsels everywhere. He was a tall, very pale figure dressed in a dark grey cloak. I answered all his questions satisfactorily, I believed, and avoided being tripped up by one or two trick questions.

He still seemed to be under the impression that I had had an accident that morning on my way to work – an accident involving a car.

"Were you involved in an accident with a car this morning?" he asked.

"There was a car accident near the station, just as I arrived there, but I was not directly involved," I said and went on to describe the events at the station.

"Someone had called the police and the ambulance, but I don't know whether any one was hurt or killed," I explained.

"Didn't you enquire?" the prosecutor asked.

"No, I am afraid that I didn't, I was in a hurry to catch my train and in any event, I felt I could not assist," I said rather guiltily.

"That was very irresponsible of you and hardly to be commended. Perhaps, if you had stayed, all this may have been avoided," he observed rather sarcastically.

The prosecutor then slowly rose to his feet and began to recite the main events of my life, occasionally asking me for confirmation. It was uncanny, as he seemed to have a detailed biography of my life. At the end, he enumerated the good things I had done in my life, my work for charities and my local church. He then proceeded to list the many bad things I had done and I ashamedly looked at the floor as the list went on and on. Some of my misdeeds I had conveniently forgotten and was now regrettably reminded of them.

The questions continued for quite a while. Then a witness was called, who turned out to be a data collection officer in the expiry division, whose job was to record all fatalities or life cessations as he put it.

"According to my records, the life of Richard Bond ceased this morning at 7:30 a.m. at Leigh-on-Sea station. He was involved in a collision with a vehicle. A Richard Aloysius Bond of 15, Acacia Road, Leigh-on-Sea, aged 45," he stated categorically.

"What car was Mr. Bond driving?" asked the defence officer.

"According to the report, it was a Ford Mondeo with the registration number of EF59 THY."

"That's not my car," I said quickly to the defence officer. "My car is a Peugeot."

My defence officer hastily jumped up and reported this to the court. There was a definite buzz that seemed to go round the large amphitheatre, just like a sound version of the Mexican wave. The enquiry or trial, whatever it was, continued for another quarter of an hour. Then the three judges announced that they were adjourning to consider their verdict.

They filed out, gliding rather than walking, just like the usher (if that is what he was) who had led me to the court-room. I was left to look around the court and marvel at the beautifully sleek, white walls, which appeared to be made of some sort of metal. After about fifteen minutes, the judges glided back into the court and sat at their dais.

We were all requested to rise, until they had taken their places, before sitting. The chief judge then beckoned me to stand up, which I did.

"Well, Mr. Richard Aloysius Bond, we have considered all the facts and the evidence and have concluded that your life has not ceased and that you are in fact alive! There has obviously been a serious administrative error or, in your parlance, a 'cock-up' and there will obviously have to be a judicial enquiry into what has gone wrong with our system. Those responsible will face severe action," he said with a distinctly stern edge to his voice. "In the review of your life, the balance is good, but I must inform you that it would be most unusual to send a person back to earth. Have you anything to say?"

I was lost for words for a moment, before I could gather my thoughts. "Your honour, I left home this morning to go to work, leaving my lovely wife and two children. Please allow me to go back – I implore you to be reasonable," I said, the emotion rising in my voice.

"In the circumstances, we will adjourn for a short while and I will consult the Supreme Judge on your behalf," he said with an authoritative voice, but with a hint of geniality.

Again, I was left in the court-room for what seemed a very long time, my mind in a whirl. Eventually the three judges filed back and I looked anxiously at their faces, to try to determine their decision. Their faces were, however, inscrutable.

Finally the chief judge spoke. "Mr. Bond, I am pleased to inform you that the Supreme Judge has decided that you will be sent back to earth. I can only apologise to you for the inconvenience you have suffered, including the trial that has just ended."

I breathed an enormous sigh of relief and relaxed for the first time that day.

"If you follow the usher, you will be allowed to take a shower and be given a meal, and set back on your journey," the chief inquisitor said in a quiet, friendly voice and smiled at me.

"Thank you, sir," I replied. I followed the usher – the original gliding man – and had my shower in a very modern, futuristic bathroom and was then led to a large restaurant. Again everything was dazzling white or metallic. There were about a dozen tables, each one set for potential customers, and had gleaming wine glasses, white plates and silver cutlery. It looked like the dining-room of a stately home awaiting a banquet, yet I was the only customer. A tall, thin waiter, dressed all in black, sidled up and asked me what I would like to eat. I was really starving, as I had not eaten since my hurried breakfast of wheatie pops, toast and marmalade – God knows how many hours earlier. "Could I have a sirloin steak, well done, with sautéed potatoes, peas and asparagus," I said more in hope than expectation.

"Certainly, sir, and to drink?"

"A nice bottle of Merlot, please, and could I have spotted dick and custard, to follow." This was a particular favourite of mine, which my wife refuses to give me, thinking I might as well go for the full works. "Oh, and a coffee with Cointreau, please," I added, with my tongue set firmly in my cheek.

Within a few minutes the meal and wine arrived and it was most delicious, a truly heavenly meal. Soft, ethereal music was playing that sounded like an angelic choir. As I ate and drank though, a phrase came into my mind – 'the condemned man ate a hearty breakfast' – and this gave me cause to think. Perhaps I was being over-dramatic – surely the ordeal was over now? As I ate, I thought back to the day's extraordinary events and admitted that the review of my life had been humbling. I was still totally bewildered by the day's events and wondered about their significance

After the meal, I thanked the waiter, but felt that a tip was inappropriate and was then ushered through the corridors, back to the futuristic underground station.

"Have a good journey," said the gliding man with a smile.

As I went through the barrier, the ticket collector gave me a strange look, followed by a toothless grin. The train set off and I was the only passenger. We did not stop at any stations, until we drew up at a normal station platform – again it was deserted, but there in the familiar roundel was the name *Liverpool Street*. I silently whooped with joy, I was back in familiar territory. I got out and followed the signs to the westbound Central line. I felt in my pocket and there was a ticket. I glanced at my watch, it said 12:30 – presumably the same day, or was it? I had missed the meeting, but all was well. I walked along yet another corridor, turned right to meet a crowd and happily joined them to be jostled along till we reached the platform. I was back in the normal hustle and bustle of commuter life. The train drew up – packed as usual – but I did not complain, I was just pleased to be with normal human people. We soon arrived at Holborn station and I joined the throng, which surged this way and that and resembled a school of fish in the ocean. I was pushed and jostled towards the escalator and the exit. I got to the street and reached the kerb, looked up, saw a double-decker bus approaching, and stopped.

Unfortunately the people behind did not stop and I was pushed forward and lost my balance. I couldn't stop myself falling forward – the large red, London bus was bearing down upon me. I saw the drivers face contorted as he struggled to brake in time, but to no avail. I let out a scream......

Chapter 4: Epilogue

Melissa was just relaxing with her feet up, reading the morning paper and sipping a cup of coffee, with a chocolate biscuit. She had completed the children's school run, washed up the breakfast things and done some chores. She always enjoyed this time of day, alone, and today she planned to go shopping, which was one of her main pleasures in life. She needed a new outfit for her friend's wedding the following week. She had told her husband the previous night, that she had nothing to wear and he had rather unkindly said that if that was so, she would be the sensation at the wedding! Eventually, however, he had agreed to her shopping expedition, pleading with her not to spend too much as the future financial situation was uncertain.

Suddenly the phone rang. She picked up the receiver – it was St. Bart's Hospital.

"Mrs. Bond – I am sorry to have to tell you that your husband Richard has been in an accident outside Holborn station. He was hit by a bus and is in a serious condition," the receptionist said in as comforting voice as possible.

Melissa's mind whirled – her legs seemed to give way under her and she felt sick as she replaced the receiver and slumped back in her chair. She began to sob, uncontrollably. Quickly, however, she resolved to pull herself together. She had to go to see her husband, without delay. She phoned her mother, asking her to pick the children up and then grabbed a coat and shoes and was soon on her way. She called a taxi to get to the station and fortunately she had to wait only ten minutes for a train. Throughout the journey, her mind was racing. What would she find when she saw him? What had happened? Richard was usually so careful when travelling. Arriving at Fenchurch Street, she called another taxi and was soon pulling in to St. Bart's hospital. Melissa walked in the front entrance and was directed by the receptionist to the Intensive Care Unit. She hated the antiseptic smell of hospitals and this one was no different, still she appreciated the cleanliness that was so necessary.

She approached the room with great trepidation. She didn't know what to expect. Her heart was thumping and her legs felt just like jelly, but she carried on walking. A doctor came out to greet her. He looked very young, but had an air of efficiency about him.

"Good morning, Mrs Bond. I am afraid that the news is not good – your husband is in a critical condition, he was hit by a bus and has sustained a broken leg and ribs, but, more crucially, severe internal injuries. He is, however, putting up a tremendous fight and I am convinced there is still a chance he will survive," said the doctor in a grave but comforting voice.

"Can I see him, for a moment," Melissa asked – her voice had a catch in it as she tried to hold back the tears.

"Well, you can go in for a few minutes, but he is still unconscious and I would ask you not to remain any longer. You can, of course, stay in one of our guest rooms tonight and for as long as necessary."

"Thank you, doctor," Melissa whispered.

She tiptoed into the room and saw this figure lying in the bed, swathed in bandages and with various tubes attached to his body. His face was cut and bruised and she hardly recognised him. She could not stop herself starting to sob, but quickly pulled herself together. Slowly she advanced to the bed and held her husband's hand, squeezing it gently in an expression of her love. She stayed like that for a few minutes before quietly slipping out the door. She went into the corridor and there her tears poured forth, as she gave way to her feelings. A nurse came up and asked if she was alright? She nodded and thanked the nurse for her concern. Eventually Melissa summoned up the courage to go to the restaurant for a cup of tea. This helped her to regain her strength and as she sipped the hot, sweet liquid, she began to blame herself for all the petty arguments she had had with Richard, in what had been a very happy marriage. I could have done more for Richard, she thought – I have been selfish on occasions. The next few hours dragged, as she waited for news. She couldn't concentrate to read magazines and didn't feel hungry. Time seemed to go so, so slowly – the hands of the clock in the lounge seemed to be on a go-slow. She paced up and down, walked in the grounds, but was scared to go too far in case there was news.

She was allowed to see him around tea-time – but there was no change; he was still unconscious, but at least his breathing appeared to be normal. So the afternoon slowly turned into evening and the evening into night. Melissa visited him again in the evening – still no change. The doctor confided that this was a hopeful sign, but that the crisis would probably come in the early morning.

Melissa undressed and went to bed in the guest room, which was quite comfortable, but she could not sleep. She was exhausted, after all the emotional and nervous tension, but the harder she tried, sleep refused to come. She kept thinking of all things she should have done and all those things she should not have done. She prayed hard for Richard. She had been a regular church-attender in her youth and sang in the church choir. Sadly she had, like so many others, lapsed as she grew up and only prayed in times of crisis. She may have dozed for a short while, but the night dragged on and on. When would it get light?

At last the first faint chinks of light filtered through the curtains and she got up, washed and dressed. Being a hospital, the routines started early and she walked slowly to the Intensive Care Unit. She couldn't see the doctor or any nurses and worried whether there was problem. After about half an hour, a worried Asian nurse appeared and explained that Mr. Bond had taken a turn for the worse and that she should come in to see him. The doctor indicated that she should sit by the bedside, as this might help. She looked at Richard with tears welling up in her eyes.

"Oh, Richard, Richard, don't leave me, I love you so much," she whispered near his ear.

There was no response, although Melissa was sure that she felt just the hint of pressure from Richard's hand. The doctor whispered that the next two or three hours would be critical and told Melissa not to give up hope.

Melissa sat holding Richard's hand as the clock moved, oh so slowly on and the green, lighted display moved across the cardiograph with a regular pattern. Eventually, she was asked to leave, while they performed some procedures. Was this their way of getting her out of the way, when his condition was going to deteriorate?

She waited outside in a terrible state. She was dying to spend a penny, but was afraid to leave the corridor. Eventually, nature won and she had to rush to the ladies. On her return, there appeared to be no change. A nurse brought her a cup of coffee, which she managed to swallow with difficulty. It was now lunchtime, but she was not hungry. What was happening? Why was she left outside with no news? Richard's life was now in the balance.

Eventually, after what seemed an eternity, the nurse beckoned her in. What would she find? Richard still lay there unconscious, but at least the green light still flashed across the screen – he was still alive!

The doctor came over and said, "I believe the crisis has passed and our hopes of his survival have risen. Don't expect a quick recovery, but we have good hopes."

Again she sat with him, holding his hand, exerting the occasional pressure as a sign of her affection and once or twice she was sure she felt Richard pressing back. In the early evening, Richard's eye slowly opened and the hint of a smile crossed his face. Melissa felt like jumping in the air and uttering a great whoop of joy, but managed to content herself with a smile and a quick, "I love you", whispered in his ear.

That night she did manage to sleep for a while. She stayed in the hospital for about five days as Richard made slow, but steady progress. Then he was released from the Intensive Care Unit and Melissa returned home, as she felt guilty about leaving the children with her mother, who had looked after them over the days since the accident.

On the Sunday, she went to church and prayed for Richard, giving thanks for his recovery. Strangely in his sermon, the vicar, the Reverend Timothy White talked about death. He reminded them that whoever we were, rich or poor, famous or infamous, we would all face death one day. We did not know when, but when we did, we would face judgement – we would be accountable for our deeds, good and bad, facing the ultimate judge. This sermon made Melissa think long and hard.

Chapter 5

Richard made a very slow recovery from his severe injuries and would never again be able to regain his old life-style but he was grateful for his survival. He had to take early retirement. Many times, however, he relived his nightmare journey on the Underground and his subsequent accident. Had he been meant to die that fateful morning – had he cheated death? He kept recalling a phrase he had read in a book – "Remember you have a life, which no one ever gets out of alive." He vowed now to live life to the full and to help other people, whenever possible, because he realised that one day, maybe very soon, he would return to that courtroom to face the ultimate judgment, yet again.

The Weird Interview

By... Doh!.............. Anon

The telephone rings, a number withheld
My day's in a mess before noon
My plans all set out but nothing has gelled
Keep ringing, he'll go away soon

He won't go away, I'll have to pick up
"Finance" I'll just say with deep sighs
I know the routine, knock over my cup
Hot drink in my lap, bloody cries

But this time it's weird, he's done it before
He's been there and faked it, the scam
"I know that you're pushed but hear me some
more
You'll talk when you know who I am

It's not you I want, I need you to help
A reference is how, hence your name,
Could affect many lives, much more than your yelp
Important's the risk. Play the game!"

"I'm listening," I say, "but what can I do?
Accounts, I've got deadlines to meet
This better be good, so just who are you?
Cold call? That sounds so indiscrete!"

"My name is John Brown, and General's my rank
Support MOD, would you mind?
I need to meet you, you're close to the Bank?
Central Line and your office I'll find."

"I'm on the third floor." "I know where you are,
your title, your background, your weight.
Can you find some space, should I bring a car?
This won't take too long, won't be late."

"I'll spare just one hour, at lunchtime is good
I've time. Do I have any rights?"
"Why would you need them? There's no way you
should
feel guilty or have sleepless nights.

I'll be there at one, it won't take me long
I won't need a roll or a bap
I'll just need some coffee, dark and quite strong
Which I'll try not to spill in your lap!"

I waited with fear, a room I'd prepared
And hoped that the coffee was strong
It's not about me he said, like he cared,
I don't think I've done any wrong?

"Your visitor's here," Reception announced,
"you'll be down to fetch, he looks tough."
Confidence weakened, I'm already trounced
I run down the stairs to look rough.

I get to the ground, through doors open wide
There's no-one, oh shit, he's right here
He's six foot fourteen, I've nowhere to hide

The Weird Interview

He's solid, a gut made from beer.

His handshake is fearsome and full of such pain
He towers with head in the sky
I'm not giving references ever again
He's bloodshot in one bloody eye!

He smiles rotten teeth, his hair is too long
His shirt is too tight but well pressed
This interview lark for reference seems wrong
A job won if I pass the test?

We start with the drink – I hope strength is good
No biscuits but that seems just fine
This won't be as easy as I thought it should
I'd rather have whisky or wine.

We move on at pace, about my mate, C
With details about his wife, A
We switch to their daughter, who's married to G
But race past the daughter who's K

The third daughter, M, was married to P
Who liked on occasions to drink
We've glossed over daughters, seemed odd to me
But asked about what would I think

If we would find P prostrate on the ground
And seeming the worse for his drink
Would C help him out, this mess we had found
Or beat him and treat him like stink?

And what about G, who's married to D
Despite being twice of her age
Has he ever fought or argued with C

Has either of them had road rage?

Do politics ever come up in our speech?
Do I know which way C would vote?
No, never, such subjects are all out of reach
We'd go to the Ship or the Boat.

To discuss matters male we talk over ale
Or sometimes a glass of fine wine
The topic we choose over which to regale
Would never step over that line.

Politics bores us completely to bits
We don't talk of footie at all
Sometimes we might note a pair of fine tits
But oval's the shape of the ball.

Our spirits are few, a gin twice a year
There's Ricard in France we like too
As drinkers we stick to pints of real beer
And wine is all that we might do.

C is quite soft, a family man
Who loves his three daughters and wife
He controls his thoughts much even more than I
can
Monogamy fits in his life.

'Tis you and I, Sir, cannot with him match
for we are the Devils in here
however we try we'd not have a patch
on integrity, honesty, fear.

He outshines us both, a man who is good
Whilst we try to sit here and judge

He's better by far and I know he would
Forgive all, _not_ harbour a grudge.

Just give him the job, for which he's worked hard
He'll do it, without any fear
Let _us_ bend the rules, not deal a bad card
And nip down the pub for a beer.

Spiral

By Jessie Hobson

Foreword

*A cold clear night in 1925 stood still as the moon shone luminously over
the Schwartzwald. Even the owls and other creatures of the night were
silent, when, in a remote area of the forest, there was a flash of light and
a whooshing sound as a small meteorite made its descent through the
atmosphere, impacting the branches of a sturdy spruce before burying itself
in the forest floor*

*Perhaps far away, lovers watching the night sky saw it come, but no-
one took much notice of this momentous event.*

Let me tell you a story of four people

Number One – Art

Sarah Jane was a boisterous nine-year-old who was a middle-of-
the-road scholar whose termly reports often said "*Sarah Jane could
do better*", which made her mother tut and frown at her little
daughter, who was far too cheery and impish to care a hoot about
her mediocrity. There were only two times when she would sit
still for a reasonable amount of time. One, of necessity, was when
her mother insisted on brushing her unruly mop of chestnut curls,
during which she wriggled and chattered and escaped as soon as
might be. The other absorbed her for longer, and that was to sit

with a dot-to-dot book building up the pictures, number by number, until, with a triumphant flourish, she would complete the image and prance off to show whoever was available of her success.

One such was her Aunt Jennifer, who decided to buy the child a sketch book and a set of twenty coloured pencils for her birthday, to encourage her to develop an ability to draw. Neither Jennifer nor Sarah, Jane's mother, really expected much except doodles, but to their amazement, she soon began to show a flair for exquisite colour combinations and, as she grew older, her ability enabled her to pass her art exams with flying colours. Some children might have become haughty and proud of their talent, but Sarah Jane remained chirpy, amiable and occasionally mischievous, as always. She progressed to an art faculty at college, where she met a rather shy medical student called Timothy – not by any means her first boyfriend. The pair complemented each other as she greatly admired his earnest endeavours to complete his studies with honours, and he was hugely impressed by her colour harmonies and the delicacy of tint in her art work. Their friendship blossomed into love, and, although both went into the world to follow their chosen careers for a number of years, in the end the successful medical researcher and the talented dress designer came together in marriage and produced four children. Two were studious like their father, and to everyone's delight, one showed clear signs of their mother's wonderful ability with colour.

And for the moment, that is all you need to know about Sarah Jane.

Number Two – Music

The time was the end of August, 1939, and Gordon's father Martin had been to a music emporium in search of a good-class cello to give to his son for his 21st birthday. As all historians know,

Spiral

September saw the outbreak of World War Two, and before the gift could be delivered, Gordon found himself conscripted into the army and whisked away to serve his country. Martin never opened the stout case that held the instrument, as he was not musical, but had believed his son showed some of his grandmother's talent in that direction. To his great distress, son Gordon was killed in action, and the boxed cello was relegated to the loft. There it resided for many years, until Martin died in the mid-1980s. It fell to his daughter Elizabeth to arrange for the house to be cleared, as her mother had died several years earlier. She enlisted the help of her teenage son Michael, as her husband George had become an invalid from war wounds, and was not mobile enough to sort through his father-in-law's chattels. The mother and son worked steadily through the house, sorting, cataloguing, sometimes despairing at the vast quantity of goods to find homes for, and, with a degree of satisfaction, filling huge skips with items which were beyond redemption. Finally, they reached the loft, where large heaps of lumber, chests, cases, old tools and bric-a-brac of numerous kinds met their eyes. They heaved a sigh of resignation together, and burst into laughter, recognising how alike they were, then set to with a will to climb this final mountain.

In due course they came across the cello. Michael was instantly curious, as he was part of a small pop-group which had formed during his latter days at school. So he proudly carted the instrument, covered in dust but still safely protected in its case, down into the house. Elizabeth, glad of a break, followed him down and watched as Michael carefully extracted the gleaming cello from its shroud and stroked it ecstatically. He plucked at the strings, which were hideously out of tune, and grinned, at his mother.

"There is no way you will ever play that." exclaimed Elizabeth emphatically.

"Watch me!" replied Michael. "It's magic!"

Elizabeth was wrong. Michael took the instrument home and spoke to a boy in his group whose uncle worked with an orchestra. Grandfather Martin might not have known anything about music, but the retailer who had sold him the cello most certainly knew that the maker was first-class, so grandson Michael had just acquired a splendid instrument. He was able to take lessons with his friend's uncle and made astounding progress. He later employed his ability both in the popular music field and in more specialised classical works. His talents improved through the years so that he became a proficient professional musician, a fact which gave Elizabeth great joy, in memory of her long-lost brother. The cello sang with a deep, mellow tone under the hand of the young maestro.

Number Three – Disability

Karl hobbled from his great workshop with his hand to his eye, uttering pained groans as he stumbled across the threshold.

"Was ist los?" cried his wife Louisa. It was 1930, and the couple lived in a small German village on the outskirts of Schwarztwald – The Black Forest.

"I can't see," moaned Karl. "I think a splinter entered my eye when I put a billet of wood on the lathe."

"Lieber Gott!" Louisa answered. "We must get you to a doctor with all speed."

She grasped Karl's arm and together they made their way along the rough road to the doctor's home. Louisa had considerable difficulty in guiding her husband's steps, as she was a small, thin woman past her prime whereas he, who had been broad and muscular when younger had run to fat around the middle, although he still had the width in his shoulders from heaving planks of wood into stacks in his carpentry shed.

It was no easy matter for the doctor to extract the splinter, and at the end, he said sadly to Karl "It seems likely this will have impaired your sight, my friend. I can make no promises of a total cure. Keep the eye covered with this patch and I will make you up some drops to lubricate the surface frequently."

"Can you give him something for the pain?" queried Louisa.

"Well, – maybe some laudanum." The doctor was reluctant to make Karl too drowsy, in case he forgot to use the eye drops, which he thought likely to be the most effective remedy.

So Karl and Louisa had to be content with that, and they went home to a miserable evening. The wood stayed unworked on the lathe, and indeed it remained there for many a day, as the carpenter found his sight deteriorating, and what was worse, his other eye seemed to be dimming and losing vision also.

The pair were daily becoming more anxious as no money was coming in because no work was going out. Louisa did a little baking which she was able to sell to her sympathetic neighbours, and this just about kept them from destitution, but it left Karl feeling ever more inadequate and depressed. He finally admitted to himself that he was going blind, and with determination, he began to fumble with the lathe and other chair making work he had already started in a desperate attempt to learn how to do his work by touch. His first efforts were pitiful, but Louisa gave him all the encouragement she could. They had no children to whom they could turn, but a neighbour suggested that perhaps Karl could train a couple of local lads to take over, and he would be paid to take them on as apprentices. This he did, and for the rest of what should have been his working life, he passed on his skills to the best of his ability. Louisa built up her bakery into a fine little business, taking pastries to market, and the two lads were solicitous of their blind master, grateful to have a good trade. Karl, however, often wondered why a small splinter should cause such devastation.

Number Four – Insanity

The great lorry rattled and bumped its way along the roads from the logging yard where the trees had been stripped and cut into manageable proportions ready for the sawmill.

Otto and his men were awaiting the arrival of wood cut down earlier in the Schwartzwald which was finally due to be put 'in sticks' to season for a further two years before producing the planks and timbers needed in construction work, and for finer samples for craftsmen, to be carefully sawn into veneers which could be matched and mirrored and worked into specialised shapes.

This type of work was entrusted to the best of the mill's men, whilst Otto mostly acted as overseer in his senior position, only occasionally indulging in 'hands on' work when there was a shortage of workers.

The new trees were swiftly stored and the existing seasoned stocks continued to be used for the requirements of the various customers. It was only after a further two years, in 1928, that the time arrived to bring out the new batch.

There was pine, and some spruce would be set aside for the craftsmen for specialised cutting, for which Otto was needed to work alongside his men that day as there had been an outbreak of influenza affecting the entire area.

"Come, Friedrich," he said to one of the few men still unaffected. "We will separate the spruce first and set it up by the re-saw. It may have to wait until later to be worked, but then we can get on with the rest of the timbers, and at least bring some of the orders up to date."

The pair began to lift down the lengths of spruce, and Otto rubbed the surface with satisfaction, as he took pride in the quality work done by his men. After placing that wood neatly aside, he went on with hefting the pallets of wood and working to saw them to size through the re-saw.

For no reason that he could understand, he found himself chuckling. The wood was rolling smoothly on its way, feeding through the saw, when to his colleague's horror Otto began to slide his hand ever nearer the spinning blade.

"Sir!" shouted Friedrich. "Have a care."

"Hm?" said Otto, still moving his hand nearer the sharp teeth. "Heh, heh, wouldn't it be fun to slice one's fingers off!"

In alarm the workman rushed to Otto's side and pulled him away.

"Whatever is in your mind today?" he remonstrated. "You must be more careful."

He was puzzled to see a vacant stare on Otto's face, and a stupid grin on his face

"Gott in Himmel," he thought. "His mind has gone."

Carefully taking his boss out of reach of the saws, he called another worker to help him steer Otto into the office.

"Whee!" cried Otto, sweeping all the papers from his desk. He then sank into the office chair, opened a drawer and turned it upside down, laughing at the resulting mess with delight.

"Silly old records," he announced. "Don't want them."

His workmen exchanged worried glances, and Friedrich went to fetch a glass of water, in the forlorn hope that it would improve matters. Sadly for him, Otto bellowed with laughter and tipped it over his head.

The men decided it was safest to take their boss home and close the sawmill for the day.

Otto's wife called out the doctor, who could find no physical reason for the change in her husband. He gave him a sedative and promised to come back next day. But by then, it was too late. Otto had woken late in the night and gone out into the garden shed and swallowed a whole batch of rat poison, singing dementedly as he died.

Have you noticed that all these people have one thing in common? Probably you have, but there is more...... Do you remember the meteorite?

The Connection

Embedded in the meteorite were two minute entities, which were thrown out on to the tree. Not living organisms as you and I know them, but products of highly intelligent beings on a distant planet, able to use an alien version of telepathy. They were of different abilities, and their intended purpose was, if one can put it that way, to develop a colony for expansion of their own species. Landing in a tree had not really been part of their plan, but they were adaptable.

Unfortunately, they were not altogether compatible, as one was life enhancing, and the other was destructive. On the other hand, the violence of their arrival had rendered them both lethargic, almost inert. Perhaps they would in time have simply continued inactive in the tree, and nothing further would have occurred. But it so happened that the foresters were due to fell the spruce and transport it to the local logging yard. The vibrations caused by the loggers revitalised the two entities, and in panic, they fused together. As the tree was travelling, so the alien beings hastily produced clusters throughout the wood, a mix of their own properties, offspring of various kinds, the result of the fusion. The journey was, however, fatal to the original arrivals, as they had not been meant to be joined in this way, but to produce separate new entities of their own.

Many of the clusters were not successful in surviving either. Some found the new environment too challenging and perished. In so doing, they communicated their distress to the other clusters, so that some were able to avoid the same pitfalls, but most succumbed, and eventually, only four clusters held on. Two clusters were mostly of the destructive variety and two were principally life enhancing. Their mission in each case was to penetrate the bloodstream of a human and attach to the spiral of DNA, becoming a new gene and influencing the life and future of that person.

For this to be achieved, it would be necessary for the human to touch the wood at the point where the cluster lay. When the tree trunk was transferred from the logging yard where it had been split into manageable proportions before going to the saw mill, it was handled by many men but most wore leather gauntlets, and only Otto had the misfortune to touch one of the destructive clusters.

When Karl received some planks from the saw mill, the second of this variety of cluster was handled by him, resulting in his blindness. There was, however, in that cluster, a small contribution from the life enhancing entity, which enabled him to still make something good of his life.

The fine wood which was sent to the instrument maker was carefully cut, and converted into a high-quality cello, which eventually came into Michael's hands, its influence being almost purely life-enhancing.

Finally, the wood used for Sara Jane's pencils contained the last cluster, which was a complete mish-mash of both entities. As you have already read, she produced enchanting art, but the gene she passed on to her youngest child contained a high proportion of the destructive variety, and the youngster caused her parents great pain and hurt indulging in drugs and alcohol and descending further and further into a morass of debauchery.

All this from just two tiny entities.

We have no way of knowing how many more have been sent over the centuries to attach themselves to our genes, nor how many more are yet to come. But it does make some sense of the highs and lows of which humanity is capable, does it not? But why does a higher intelligence want to play such games with us? That is beyond my comprehension.

The Scam

By David Shaer

The barristers' clerk knew life, and much more,
but was treated like dirt all his days
Nobody cared when they walked out the door
Did he live in a flat, or doorways?

But he knew them all, their wives, their kids'
names,
Where they lived, where they loved, whilst away
To them he was nothing, was just known as James
His first name? His last? None could say.

For thirty odd years, he'd nursed them each one
He'd seen them grow up, – well – grow old
Through tears and through tantrums, they'd even
poked fun
But none of them cared for his stories untold

So the day that he broke was not off the cuff
He'd planned it for years and worked hard
He knew all their failings – they had enough,
They'd ignored him, his ego was scarred

His systems were manual, all written and old
They assumed he was quaint and was twee

But they'd missed his real progress, so strong and
so bold
This security king, a Lord in IT

Each night he had raided their PCs and found
What they'd really been up to – not nice
These barristers, judges, their secrets unbound.
Their senior partner – of vice

Surrounded by perverts, bestials and worse
His plan became crystal and sunny
He'd draw it out long, his blackmail and curse
He'd screw them each one for real money.

But first he would scare them and threaten their
lives
He'd crawl under skins, screw their minds
And show that he knew all their girlfriends and
wives
Anonymous emails of things behind blinds

Exposing their knowledge of vices and sin
Would distract their attention from him
Because he was "Old James" the workhorse within
Who knew only of work, nothing grim.

With emails he threatened to reveal all the facts
To societies, bankers and friends
To mistresses, wives, Inspectors of Tax
His skill at this fear knew no ends

Small bundles of cash they would post most
discreet
To PO Box numbers widespread
The sums mounted up, their targets to meet

Each one keeping their secrets unsaid

For months this went on but he knew it must end
His income must stay underhand
The thousands he'd gained so far offshore he'd
send
But to finish the show must be grand

* * *

The Senior Partner was after High Court
Lord Chancellor top of his list
But meeting young boys on Internet sought
Was a threat that our James hadn't missed.

A mere hundred grand in an envelope brown
Would avoid such a secret revealed
In used twenty notes to keep quiet from the Crown
His silence would always be sealed

Picked up from the post our James trembled true
The heavy soft pack in his hand
'Twas more than his mind could ever pre-view
Brown pack with its rubber red band

He took it straight home, his suitcase was packed
His plane ticket booked round the world
They'd see him no more, he'd never be tracked
False passport, ID now unfurled.

He opened it quick, loose notes caused him some
ire
He threw them down onto his bed
As he looked back within, he first saw the wire
Too late – the bomb blew off his head.

Ernie's Ancestor

By Jessie Hobson

Chapter 1

It was not Celia's intention to eavesdrop as she swung back and forth gently in her rocking chair, but the workmen outside her front garden who were repairing the pavement had raised their voices, and the conversation, complete with a larding of four-letter words, came clearly through the window of the small terraced house to which she had recently retired. One man was doing most of the talking, his companion contributing grunts and an occasional 'Yeah?' in query of a point. It seemed the noisy one was in serious difficulty with a relationship with 'his bird' as he put it. Celia had seen both men at work when she had gone to buy her Daily Mail, and as neither of them had impressed her as being attractive enough for a second glance, she was not surprised that the lady in question was not falling over herself with delight at being pursued by such a man. But then, Celia was elderly, a spinster; disapproving of men in general, she did not account in her mind for the strangeness of attraction between even the most unlikely people.

After listening for a while, it seemed to Celia that the complaining Ernie had suspected his girlfriend Maisie of making up to Don, who possessed a Ferrari, which was apparently way out of Ernie's league. This much Celia gleaned before the men moved away from the frontage. She could hear the whining, argumentative tone fading as they continued further down the road, until the rattle of machinery drowned out the conversation. A little later, the workmen returned to do the next phase of the work outside her property. Once again, the tale of woe continued. By this time however, Ernie was bitterly making plans to avenge himself on the usurper, mostly futile schemes to let down the tyres, scratch the paintwork, or, perish the thought, cut the brake cables. His colleague, Jack, mildly pointed out that he would probably kill Maisie if he did the last, and Ernie subsided into mumbles of 'serve her right. What does she want with a geezer like him, anyway?'

"Is he good looking?"

"Suppose," responded Ernie grumpily.

"Can't you smarten yourself up a bit?"

Ernie bridled. "What d'you mean? I always dress nice."

"Aftershave?"

Ernie was becoming more touchy with each question and snapped back at Jack.

"You saying I smell?"

"Nah, nah, keep your hair on."

With slow emphasis, Ernie said "Jack, there's nothing wrong with my barnet, neither."

"If you're going to be like that, I'll shut up," replied Jack. Secretly though he couldn't help thinking that Don was serious competition and maybe his friend was in need of an image makeover.

The work continued in strained silence, and Celia lost interest, eventually returning her attention to the knitting lying forgotten on her lap.

Chapter 2

If you go into a graveyard, there is a fair possibility, if you are local, that you may find an ancestor of two or even three hundred years ago, and perhaps even stand on that grave. The chances of someone standing on a pavement exactly over the burial of a five hundred-year-old corpse of their own bloodline must be astronomical, but, astoundingly, this is exactly what happened to Ernie, as he pounded tar vehemently to vent his anger. Far under the surface, the vibration reached the crumbling bones, and a frisson of some unseen supernatural force surfaced to connect with the man above. Ernie, who indeed had a good head of hair, felt it rise perceptibly, as a chill ran up his spine and he stopped, eyes wide, shivering,

"Ohmygawd! There must be electrics under here," he yelped.

"Nah, they checked all that out," said Jack, who was about to make a derisive remark when he saw how pale Ernie looked, and realised his scare was genuine.

"What's up, then?" Jack said, thinking that Ernie looked like a cartoon cat, with its fur standing on end.

"Look!" said a terrified Ernie, pointing behind Jack, who swung round and saw – nothing.

His jaw slack, Ernie watched in horror as what looked like a cowled monk walked away from him, a huge dagger protruding from his back.

"It's horrible. Whatever did he do to have that done to him? Can't you see him?" said the astonished Ernie. He looked into Jack's face, which was blank with incomprehension.

Jack was beginning to think the pressure of Ernies' love life was stressing him out and said. "See who? You been drinking? Hallucinat'ry drugs or something?"

Ernie tried to pull himself together, rubbing his eyes and shaking his head in an effort to clear his mind.

"Must be like that," he muttered. "Don't know how."

But it made no difference; he didn't mention to Jack that he could still see the 'hallucination', who by this time had turned to face him.

There was real agony on its face; a look of pleading that caused Ernie to start forward as if to catch the apparition before it fell.

He raised his arms high and wide helplessly and addressed the monk.

"For heaven's sake, get out of here."

"Come here, mate," said the practical Jack. "You better take a break. I'll knock on the door here and see if someone can give you a cuppa." He had been using a rake to smooth the tar, and he leaned this against the garden wall, then he stripped off his work gloves before moving to enter Celia's gate, watched by an appalled Ernie who could see the monk staggering through ahead of Jack and disappearing round the side of the house.

When Jack had explained to Celia that his mate had had 'a bit of a turn', she brought out a kitchen chair for him, then set to with kettle and teapot, privately thinking as Jack had, that Ernie had become too worked up about his lady friend. She glanced out of her kitchen window, and was startled to see she had an intruder in the garden. Bearing in mind the tales she had heard of con-men who tricked their way in to rob old ladies, she scurried back to the front door, to find both men still outside.

"Who is that man in my garden?" she demanded breathlessly, her heart still pounding from the shock and exertion.

"Dunno, ma'am. What man do you mean, there's only us two here. Can anyone get in from the back?" asked Jack.

Celia shook her head and thought Ernie looked guilty.

"Is he a friend of yours?" she persisted, targeting Ernie with the question.

"Don't know him," said a frightened Ernie.

"So there is someone," she said almost triumphantly.

At that moment, the monk reappeared round the house, and Celia and Ernie both shrieked. Jack just stared at them in amazement.

"You can see him, too, can't you?" Ernie appealed to Celia.

Celia, who had no idea she was psychic, said prosaically, "Of course I can see him. What sort of a fool do you take me for? Whoever he is, get him out of here. Now."

Jack realised something very strange was going on; even he could not believe Celia had been taking drugs so he played along and addressed a corner of the front garden, and said sternly, "Move along, there, mate – what you doing there?"

Celia and Ernie looked at each other bewildered, and declared in unison, "He's over there, not here."

By this time the monk had reeled out of the gate, and stood staring at Ernie. The poor workman felt his strength draining from him, and almost fell off the chair.

"He's absorbing me, or something," he surmised. "Didn't know spooks could do that. What's he want with me?"

"Spooks?" yelped Jack. "You two barmy or something?"

"Oh, dear," said Celia, who still believed the monk to be a living man. "Are you two playing a prank on an old lady? I do not find it the slightest bit funny."

At this point the monk moved to face Ernie, clasped his hands together as if in prayer, and bowed. Then he turned away, and glided off down the street.

Celia put both hands over her mouth, and mewed.

"That dagger. Who did that to him? Does he need an ambulance?"

"He's past all that," said Ernie. "Maybe he wants to have revenge on whoever did it. I mean, when have you ever seen a monk like that around here?" In the back of his mind, Ernie was remembering pictures in a text book from a school history lesson. The only monks in the area had been routed by Henry VIII's men, hundreds of years ago.

Bewildered, Celia turned to Jack. "You didn't see him?" she queried. Jack shook his head vigorously.

"But you did?" she asked Ernie.

"More's the pity," he replied. "He has used all my energy. I feel proper worn out."

By this time, the monk was well down the road, and suddenly he branched off at an impossible angle, through a wall, vanishing into a building as though it was not there.

Ernie heaved a sigh of relief. "That's me finished for today," he said flatly, rising wearily from Celia's kitchen chair. "I'm off home."

"Great!" said Jack sarcastically. "And what do I tell the boss?"

"Tell him what you like. Tell him I'm sick, I feel like it at the moment, I've had it," said Ernie, grabbing his coat off the machinery, and walking purposefully in the opposite direction, along the road away from the ancestor, leaving his colleague gaping after him in dismay.

Chapter 3

Father Matthew had commenced as a novice of the Cluniac Order at Prittlewell Priory when he was just a young lad. He was the eldest child of the local farrier, who had more mouths to feed than money to feed them, being a lusty, virile man who had married an attractive fecund wife. Matthew had been a delicate child, not fit to take on his father's work when fully grown, and his parents were glad to have a suitable vocation for their son at the monastery. Over the years, Matthew's diligence and piety had advanced him in the hierarchy of the monastery. His affinity with nature and the medicinal use of plants made him an asset in the Priory and he had risen to become head of the infirmary. So it was that on a balmy spring day in 1536 he began a mission of mercy to a family in the little settlement on the Ness, nearly a ten-mile walk from the Priory. As a devout Catholic, he knew of the devastation which was occurring throughout the realm, due to the heretic King of England, who had renounced his allegiance to the Pope and was destroying many religious establishments, appropriating their wealth and lands for his own use. So far, Father Matthew had been unaware of any activity in the neighbourhood likely to be of a threatening nature, so he went blithely on his way across fields and farmsteads, with a scrip full of herbs and salves for ministering to the sick he was visiting. As he walked along a narrow winding lane between sparse hedges, their leaves brittle and autumnal, he heard feet pounding towards him from round a corner. A youth came into view, panting with exertion, his breath hanging like mist in the air. It was the son of the family on the Ness he was due to visit. Perspiration was pouring from his face, his shabby clothing more rag than garment hanging limp with sweat on his spare frame. "Father Matthew, get back to the Priory immediately. The King's men are on their way to ravage the monastery. You need to warn the Prior."

Father Matthew was more concerned for the boy and his sick mother than himself and said "Here, Joseph, take these herbs to your family, and Godspeed, boy. My thanks to you for the warning."

Father Matthew thrust the well-worn wallet into the boy's hands. "Boil the herbs awhile on the fire in enough water to give your mother a brew when you have strained out the leaves. Pray God it will reduce her fever. If I can, I will return later." He turned, and headed back towards the Priory. He knew he was too old to run the distance, and the King's men would most likely be mounted, so he made for a small farm where they were wealthy enough to keep a horse. Perhaps one of the men there could be persuaded to ride to the Priory and raise the alarm.

He took a short cut through a small orchard on his way, and weaved his way between the trees, dodging the farmer's swine rooting for food in the undergrowth. As he approached the buildings, he saw that he was too late. Several men, some mounted, some on foot, surrounded the farmer, who was gesticulating and pointing in the direction of the Priory, his frightened face evidence to Father Matthew that the soldiers would have no hesitation in killing the man, should he refuse to tell them where to find the monastery.

One of the foot soldiers caught sight of some movement of the black habit among the trees, and moved stealthily towards the defenceless monk, who turned and fled, praying as he ran. The soldier rapidly gained on the ill-shod and ageing cleric, and once he came within reach, he hurled a dagger at Father Matthew's back, slaying him instantly. The murderer ran forward, intending to retrieve his weapon, but was recalled imperiously by the officer in charge, who was anxious to be on his way. The soldier hesitated, to be sure his victim was truly slain, and then muttering under his breath, reluctantly returned to his companions.

The farmer had not seen what had occurred, being surrounded by soldiers and full of fear for himself and his family. The soldiery assembled ready to march towards Prittlewell and the Priory, intent on destroying the monastic order. Their commanding officer was impatient to be gathering the spoils of the Priory's wealth and lead the way on a lively black mount, shouting at his men to keep up.

It was a few days before the farmer found the body among the trees. He was a nervous man, and his experiences with the King's men had rendered him furtive, afraid to be connected in any way with the doomed Priory. Added to this was the fear of eternal damnation should he be found guilty in some way by the priesthood of complicity in the monk's death. His fear led him to dig a deep hole beside the body to conceal it. He found himself quite unable to touch the poor cleric's corpse, nor to remove the weapon from his back, simply tipping him in with his spade, unshriven and anonymous, never to be traced. He hid the newly turned earth beneath the fallen leaves from the orchard, crossing himself as he left, praying silently to God for forgiveness for his actions. And so it was that Father Matthew was unceremoniously buried where he had fallen. And there he remained, lying among the trees, under increasing layers of debris for almost five hundred years.

Chapter 4

As a bemused Ernie made his way homeward along the newly tarred pathway, he realised he would not have the benefit of travelling in the company van, having abandoned Jack. He wondered whether to take the bus straight home, but in his agitated mental state, he reverted as many of us do, to a longing to see his mum for some comfort, just like a child with a grazed knee. Her residential home was only a few streets away, so he headed off in that direction, mentally rerunning the events of the last half an hour through his mind. He was too muddled to remember the entrance security code and eventually a cheerful-faced helper heard him buzzing the intercom, recognised him and let him in. He headed off down the corridor to his mother's room. Fortunately, she was not in the common room, but watching her favourite 'soap' in what she had hoped was the privacy and peace of her room. At heart, she wished Ernie had called at any other time, as she had little else to do except watch TV, and was not overjoyed to be missing her drama. She turned the volume down reluctantly, unwilling to switch it off altogether, and turned her attention to her son.

"Hallo, Ernie. Lovely to see you, boy, but shouldn't you be at work?"

"Yeah, well, that's why I'm here. Had a nasty experience."

"I thought you looked a bit flustered, dear, what sort of nasty experience are you talking about? You didn't get into a fight with someone, did you?"

"No Mum, you're getting confused; it's Alfie that's got the temper in our family, not me. What happened was we disturbed something, repairing the pavement and I think I saw a spook."

"Oh, just like your Dad. He was always seeing them. It's why he went to them spiritualist people such a lot."

"Dad did? He never told me that."

"He used to get embarrassed about it, said most people would think he was mad if he told them. But they seemed to help him understand what was going on."

"It would take some explaining, what I saw."

He went on to tell his mother about the monk, the dagger, the fact that Celia saw it all too, and how weak he was feeling, as if part of him had been taken over by the ghost. His mother listened attentively, then said wisely, "The monk must mean something special to you, son, and maybe to the lady of the house, too. Why don't you do the same as your Dad used to?"

"Won't they think I'm barmy turning up out of the blue with a story like that?"

"They reckon they see dead people all the time! Tell them whose son you are; they'll remember your Dad."

"Yeah, well, I might do that then."

For once, Ernie's mother had found something more exciting than a soap episode, and she watched with interest as Ernie left and took the bus home. He purchased a local paper on his way. He guessed, rightly, that spiritualists might advertise their meetings, so he sat down to check that out, once he had popped a ready-meal into the microwave. One was advertised for the following evening. As it would be a Saturday event, he thought he would ask Maisie to go with him. She lived with her parents a couple of streets away, so after clearing his meal, he showered, shaved, put on a clean shirt and newly pressed trousers, and slicked his hair smoothly back from his face. Taking Jack's comment earlier to heart, he even dabbed on a bit of the aftershave his aunt had given him for Christmas. Satisfied that he had done all he could to appear his best, he put on gleaming black shoes and went out to call on his lady-love. He turned the corner into the street where she lived and stopped in his tracks. She was leaving her house and loading cases into the tiny boot of his rival Don's Ferrari. Despondently, he turned around and headed back home, his dreams shattered, and taking out his disappointment on a discarded drinks can, he kicked it angrily along the road as he went, vaguely wishing it was Don.

Chapter 5

When Father Matthew had risen to face Ernie, he had no idea he was dead. He saw the man in strange clothes with shining yellow bands, and believed he was seeing an angel giving him strength to go towards the Priory. In his strange spiritual limbo, the orchard and farmyard surrounded him; he was never aware of the twenty-first century road and houses, nor of the existence of Jack, and only vaguely of Celia. He was puzzled, because the farm seemed deserted. He could not know that the soldiery had moved on, and that in the intervening centuries, the farmer and his descendants had all died and departed to either celestial or demonic worlds, according to how they had lived. There was only one exception, and that was the foot soldier who had killed him. His spirit had been condemned to roam the earth for the merciless slaughter of the good Father Matthew. He had also been so enraged at being obliged to leave his dagger in the monk's corpse that, when he was later killed in battle and joined the spiritual limbo, he vowed to roam the spirit realms searching for his weapon. He had many miles of foot-slogging to do, as he had died near Colchester. For the moment, Father Matthew now believed he must retrace his steps as fast as he could to the Priory. On his way he caught shadowy glimpses of strange beings intent on their own affairs. These were other lost souls from different eras, unable to escape the limbo, and if they saw Father Matthew, they gave no sign. He trudged on, surprised not to be weary, and gave thanks to God for sending his angel. It cheered him to think he might succeed in his mission. But when he got there, the Priory, like the farm, was deserted; worse, it was desecrated. Father Matthew sank to his knees at the shattered altar in despair, and prayed for guidance.

Chapter 6

The spiritualist meeting was on the Saturday evening, so Ernie had all day to think about what to say, if he decided to go. It was his opinion that such a quest was dubious, in spite of his father's former association, and he felt he was likely to make a fool of himself. He rather wished it had all been a bad dream, it sounded so weird and unlikely when looked at in the cold light of day. He was feeling very sensitive to ridicule after realising Maisie had been stringing him along, all the time meaning to go off with Don. The spiritualists were offering private readings – at a price. He felt sure it would be a waste of money, in spite of his mother's recommendation. He went to bed miserable, a confused and disappointed man, and propped himself up against his pillow with his arms crossed, hugging his chest, as if to defend himself from any further horror. He eventually drifted off into a restless sleep.

He awoke in the morning feeling almost as tired as when he had gone to bed. He had tossed and turned all night, or so it seemed, and he had the disturbing feeling that there was something important he should remember from the weird dreams he had experienced. He took another shower to clear his head and decided to ring Jack, as he felt he owed him an apology for running off and leaving him the previous day.

"Hello?" said a cheerful female voice.

Ernie was thrown off balance for a second, he had no idea Jack had a woman in his life. He recovered quickly and blurted out, "Er – is Jack there, please? It's his mate Ernie."

"Hold on, I'll get him."

After a short pause, Jack came on the line.

"Wotcher, Ernie. Feeling better?"

"Yes, sorry about hopping it yesterday – I was scared stiff and I just felt like I'd got the flu coming I was so drained."

"Weird do, I must say – both you and the old lady seeing things."

"I think I had a bit of a dream about it last night, but I can't remember it. Don't know what to do to stop the spook coming back, though."

As he said that, Ernie's mind seemed to recall a misty image of his father from the night before. He remembered being astonished at finding himself floating up and away with his father — at least, he thought he must have been, but looking at his bed as he departed, he saw that his body still sat there, silent and unmoving.

As they floated, his father had said something about being in some other dimension.

"It is a place you do not know about in your day-to-day life, but where spirit beings like me can come if necessary to help people we love," his father had told him.

While Ernie digested this new idea, he was aware that he was no longer in his bedroom, but had landed on uncultivated ground outside what appeared to be a ramshackle shed. There was a clanging sound from within, and father and son glided through the door to where a man in a leather apron was hammering with precision on a glowing metal bar, gradually shaping it into a horseshoe. Standing by him was a slight, teenage boy with delicate features, a complete contrast to the burly farrier.

He remembered thinking it was like one of those TV costume dramas.

His father read his thoughts and said, "Yes, well, maybe, but that boy is the person you saw with the dagger in his back, only of course, he was an old man by then, the victim of one of the King's purges. He was left to rot just where you were thumping the other day, and it disturbed his spirit, which had never made it home."

"What's that got to do with me?" demanded Ernie.

The dream image vanished as quickly as it had arrived and suddenly Ernie was aware of his colleague calling down the phone to him.

"Ernie, are you still there mate? I said why don't you come over this evening and chat to us about it?"

Ernie recovered his composure and said hastily "What, oh sorry about that Jack. Who's 'us'? I didn't know you was hitched."

"I thought I'd told you – I live with my sister since the old folk died. She's a good cook – why don't you come to supper? Or are you going out with Maisie? Bring her too!"

Ernie grunted, and told Jack how he had seen the end of his hopes dashed the night before, as Maisie got into Don's car.

"Thanks," he said at the end of his tale. "Coming to supper sounds better than going to a séance, like Mum suggested." At the back of his mind he felt he was somehow getting closer to a solution without the need for help from the spiritualists.

He rang off, and sat thinking about the dreamlike image of his father again. Without realising it, he slipped back into his memory of his father at the point where Jack had broken into his reverie.

"Perhaps you have already done your bit, rousing him. His father was your grandfather, umpteen times removed."

"Oh, right!" said Ernie grumpily. *"And I'm going to be the end of the line, now Maisie's gone off with Don. No wedding bells for me."*

"Wait and see," said his father. *"You will soon find your soul mate, and the Farriers will go on for generations yet."*

"Yeah?" Ernie looked at his father in disbelief.

As he gave this some thought, he remembered how he had found himself in the night propped up against his pillow, staring sleepily at the wall beyond his bed, as a misty shape seemed to disintegrate before his gaze.

Ernie's focus returned to earth as his growling stomach reminded him he had not yet eaten. He briefly wondered what Jack's sister looked like, then dismissed it from his mind as he thought about how Maisie had cheated on him. He mulled over the dream conversations again as he ate breakfast, and decided, almost against his better judgement, to return on the bus to the road where everything had happened. Just before he got off the bus, he realised he was passing a Catholic church. Of course! The monk would have been a Catholic. Surely the priest would tell him what to do? He walked purposefully towards the church, only to see a portly clerical figure crossing the road away from him, clearly the very man he had hoped to approach. On reflection, he thought maybe his reception would not have been favourable, as he was dressed casually in baseball cap, leather jacket, denims and trainers, which might have given the priest the impression he was not to be taken seriously. So he walked on, wending his way through the streets towards Celia's house. As he drew near, he saw that Celia was pruning some roses in the front garden. She noticed him coming along and moved into the road to speak to him.

"Good morning, Mr, – er…"

"Farrier, madam. Ernest Farrier."

"Ah, yes. You look a bit better than when you left yesterday, have you heard any more of that strange man we saw yesterday?"

Celia still could not bring herself to believe she had seen a ghost, and hoped Ernie would debunk that. Instead, he told her of his visit to his mother, and his thoughts on going to have a reading. For some reason he held back and didn't mention the flash backs of dream images he had been having.

"Oh, I don't think that will do any good," said Celia primly, trying to disguise her feeling that mediums were all con men that preyed on bereft people's emotions. "Lot of nonsense, what's more, I cannot see that talking to the priest will help. He can hardly come here with bell, book and candle if no-one knows where the ghost got to."

"Why would the priest want to bring those things, anyway?" asked Ernie.

"To exorcise him, of course." Celia was scornful of Ernie's ignorance of the rites involved in sending a wandering spirit on its way, even if she did not really believe in ghosts anyway.

"Yeah, well, like you say, we don't know where he is. He might never come back this way. But I wonder why we can see him, in any case. Jack couldn't. Could he?"

"You're right," admitted Celia. "Is Jack a local man? Are you? My family goes back several generations hereabouts – my niece has researched it – and it is a military background. Perhaps she would know to what period that dreadful dagger belongs."

"Jack's from Dagenham. I have heard that my lot came from somewhere near Prittlewell, way back." He thought for a moment about the dream and what his father had said about the monk. He was still keeping the dream to himself, but steered the conversation by asking "Do you reckon the..." Ernie struggled to give a name to the apparition, "–the monk, came from the Priory?"

"It seems the most logical answer, but why he should be so far from it, and why someone would want to kill him......?" Celia ran out of theories and stood pensively, absentmindedly snipping bits off a rosebush with secateurs.

Ernie bit his tongue as he nearly joked 'Perhaps one of your military ancestors did it?' He instantly regretted it and thought Celia might not be amused; he did not want to antagonise the one person he could talk to about the ghost.

Nevertheless, unwittingly, Ernie had hit the nail on the head. The foot soldier was indeed a forebear of hers, and at that very moment, if time counted for anything in his half-world, he was marching boldly towards the Southend area in search of the corpse he had left in the orchard. It was the presence of his dagger that had made the mystical connection with Celia, enabling her to become party to the curious drama outside her house.

Chapter 7

Father Matthew rose from his prayers at the altar, dispirited, but decisive in his determination to follow his calling to the best of his ability, so he began to retrace his steps back to the Ness, where he hoped to find Joseph and his family. He was unaware that he had not tired unduly, nor that he had no need of food or sleep, so he went steadily on his way back to the orchard of his demise. Thus the spiritual limbo began to draw the monk and his killer to a rendezvous at the very spot where Ernie and Celia were talking by the gate of her twenty-first century home.

Father Matthew turned from the farm lane on to the path to the orchard, which lay on the same route as the newly-tarred footpath on which Ernie and Celia stood. The monk paused, as Ernie was visible to him, also a strangely clad woman beside him. Ernie now looked more like a robber or a thief than an angel. As his mission to the Priory had failed, Father Matthew wondered if he had been deceived by the Devil. The fact that he could see Celia clearly now was due to the proximity of the foot soldier who was creeping towards him, having trudged the many miles across country to the same spot.

At this moment, Celia looked up from her pruning and gasped. "There he is!" she cried. "And look at that soldier behind him. Whatever is he doing?"

"Soldier?" asked Ernie, swinging round to look. "Dunno what the sergeant-major would have made of that one at the barracks."

As they spoke, it began to rain, lightly at first, then in a torrent.

"Oh, my!" said Celia. "You must come under cover in the porch."

They quickly took shelter, and through the curtain of rain, they watched spellbound as the foot soldier caught up with Father Matthew outside the gate. He did not stop to reason why the monk was not a corpse on the ground as expected. He leapt forward with an angry roar.

"You ranting Papist! I'll have my weapon back at last."

Father Matthew stood very upright and raised the cross from round his neck, holding it out in front of his face.

"Cease your impiety and depart in peace," he cried.

The soldier snorted in disdain and grappled with the monk, dislodging the dagger and pulling it out in triumph from the old man's back.

Three things happened simultaneously.

Father Matthew realised that he was facing a beam of white light beckoning him forward, that he had departed his mortal life, and that his time had come to leave the earthly domain.

The foot soldier gave a sudden yelp of pain and dropped the dagger as demons erupted in flames at his feet to drag him down into the inferno.

And in Ernie's world, there was an almighty *flash/bang* as lightning struck the pavement where he had been standing only moments before.

In the limbo, Father Matthew whispered to the Light, "Please wait a moment, Lord." He turned to the foot soldier, making the sign of the cross on his forehead and saying, "I forgive you. Come with me, brother, and ask forgiveness of your Maker." He grasped his murderer by the hand, and both faded and disappeared into the ethereal light.

Ernie, for once, had been struck dumb by events, but Celia burst into tears and gabbled nonsense in hysteria, until Ernie patted her on the shoulder and said in a subdued voice "It's all over now, and the rain has stopped." He had sensed that the sudden storm was connected with the ghosts.

Slightly calmer, Celia said, "I suppose you and your colleague will have to come back and fill the hole in on Monday."

Ernie walked out of the gate to survey the damage.

"Nah, missus. We will have to let the authorities see what's in there. I think it's an archaeology job now."

Celia came to stand beside him, and together they looked down upon a jumble of bones, a small metal cross and a 16th century dagger.

"They have gone, then?" queried Celia.

"Yeah," said Ernie with an irreverent grin. "I wonder if they went upstairs or downstairs."

Printed in the United Kingdom by
Lightning Source UK Ltd., Milton Keynes
139672UK00001B/2/P